BELLS

By: Kristine Meier-Skiff

Gift an Author Publishing, LLC

This book is dedicated to my parents, Kevin and Katherine Meier.

Dad and Mom, you gave me a great gift when you didn't allow a television in our house for the first fourteen years of my life. I got a crash course on writing from the greats like Bronte, C.S. Lewis, Austen, and Dickens. I learned how to tell a fantastic story by listening to old-time radio shows together every Sunday night. You can't pay for that kind of education. It is priceless!

So thank you for giving me a love of stories and writing, which have turned into a career I love.

Table of Contents

ISBN: 979-8-9883573-1-5 (Paperback)

ISBN: 979-8-9883573-2-2 (Hardcover)

Library of Congress Control Number: 00000000000

Any references to historical events, real people, or places are fictitious. Names, characters, and places are products of the author's imagination.

Front cover image by Michelle Hartfield

Second Edition 2023.

Gift an Author Publishing, LLC

5405 Zara Drive

Denton, Texas, 76207

www.giftanauthor.com

Chapter One

Windshield wipers beat a sharp staccato as she drove through the night. The rain, which had begun as a soft drizzle, was now a torrential downpour. The defroster had stopped working 30 miles back, and she was forced to lean out the rolled-down window every few feet to see the road ahead. After another 50 miles, she would find a rest stop and, finally, stop for the night. Sleeping at a rest stop was dangerous for a woman traveling alone, but she had no choice. She had spent a good portion of her cash on the clunker she currently drove. Besides, the truck stop could hold no monster more terrifying than the one from whom she now ran. She laughed at the irony her life had become. Once a power player, strong and independent, she was now weak, scared, and disillusioned. A mere whisper of the woman she once was. She shivered at the mixture of cold and memories, threatening to rise again to the surface of her consciousness. She reached into the console and ran her fingers over the knife she had secreted there. She was not defenseless, she reminded herself. Not now, at least......never again. She pushed the memories down, swallowed the lump of fear in her throat, and forced her hand to release the knife.

Her eyes were growing heavy from lack of sleep. Because she was determined to put as much distance as possible between herself and the monster of her nightmares, she had not slept in forty-eight hours. She had driven across much of the country. It was almost comical. She was checking off one of her bucket list items and could not even appreciate it. Could a nameless woman even have a bucket list or dreams, or were all her hopes, thoughts, and ambitions gone along with her name? Another of life's ironies, she, who had once been so proud of her name, her lineage, and now it was gone; forever, gone.

Elizabeth, Lisa, Sue, Anne, Catherine, Becky, Marianne, Emily, Hannah....she said each name aloud, trying to settle on one that felt right. It had to be simple, something she would remember to respond to if called out: Erin, Melissa, Rachel, Kate.....Kate.....Kate. Yes, Kate was simple and easy. Something she could remember. She cleaned her rear-view mirror with her sleeve and tried to glimpse herself in the smeared darkness. Could she pass for a Kate? Nope, she couldn't tell right now. She would have to wait until morning to decide.

Finally, she caught sight of the rest stop ahead. Bone weary, she pulled into a brightly lit spot. She shoved her drenched hair into a ball cap; she would have to cut it soon. It was the one vanity of her former life she had yet to give up. After drying the vinyl interior, she put the sun reflector in the windshield. She hung towels on her side windows to shield herself from the view of curious onlookers. She dared not change out of her sodden clothes completely, but she had to put on a dry sweatshirt at least. She slipped out of her soaking sweatshirt and replaced it with a dry one. Her teeth still chattered, her soaked jeans clinging to her legs. To hell with modesty; she had to get dry. She wiggled her way out of the wet jeans, wiggled back into a dry pair, and cranked the heat in the car, not that it worked all that well. Somewhat dry, she reached into the back seat for a blanket and a granola bar. She hadn't eaten anything since lunch and was suddenly famished and thirsty. She grabbed a bottle of water while she rummaged around. Though her stomach rumbled, she still had to force herself to eat. Her grief made eating anything a chore.

Now that she was warming up and her stomach had something in it, her eyes grew heavy. Just as she was about to doze off, she began hyperventilating because she felt trapped and claustrophobic. Frantically, she tore down the towels and the sun reflector and looked around, looking hard into the darkness to see if any shadow was out of place. Everything seemed alright, but once you've met a monster, you know better than ever to feel truly safe. She double-checked to ensure her doors were locked tight and her windows rolled up as far as they would go. She took the knife from the console and placed it in her lap under the blanket. She would feel safer if it was a gun, but you cannot buy one when you are nameless. Well, she was sure you could, but she didn't know how to do it. She would learn, she promised herself, oh she would learn. She took a long drink of water, closed her eyes, and tried to grab a few minutes of restless sleep.

The sun peaked over the horizon, turning the sky into a masterpiece of reds, pinks, and purples. She looked at the beauty of the morning and smiled a sad smile. Memories began to flood over her again, faces, places, smells, and sounds that no longer belonged to her; pictures and memories of another life, another love, another time. Sometimes she wished she could erase her memories like she erased her name. It would be so much easier to walk away if you did not know what you were walking away from. But now, other memories began to encroach, memories of darkness and needles and screams. Memories of endless corridors and insanity and bells and blood...so much blood.

Now it was easy to remember why she had run away, not walked away, but run like the devil himself chased her because he did. The panic began to rise. Her heart began to race, and her breathing came hard and fast. She reached into her purse and grabbed a prescription bottle. She desperately fought with the child safety lid and finally poured one pill into her shaking hand. She looked at it, sitting in her palm. She could swallow it, and her world would right itself again in fifteen minutes. The terror would fade; the memories would become hazy and painless. Yes, she could swallow this oblong slice of oblivion, and everything she had fought so hard to accomplish would be for nothing. Slowly, she opened the prescription bottle once again. She forced herself to place the pill back inside the bottle, close the lid and place it back into her purse. She willed herself to take slow, deep breaths and counted backward from one hundred silently. By the time she reached thirty-five, she was calm again, in control of her thoughts and fear. She glanced at the purse and thought about dumping the pills for good. But no, she needed the reminder. Yes, some memories one should never forget.

She cautiously looked around the parking lot. It was empty. First, placing the knife in her purse, she unlocked her door, put her sneaker-clad feet on the pavement, and stretched. She locked the driver's side door again and made her way to the restrooms, her sneakers making a slight squishing sound as she went. They still had not dried from last night's monsoon.

The smell of stale urine assaulted her senses the moment she stepped through the door, causing her to wrinkle her nose in disgust. She glimpsed herself in the grime-streaked mirror. She looked like a street urchin, her hair still piled in the baseball cap, clothes loose and ill-fitting, and her eyes over large and haunted. She looked more closely. Yes, she could be a Kate. It suited her almost as well as her old name, maybe even better. Kate, Kate, what? Why Smith, of course!! She laughed aloud, the sound of her own voice startling in the empty bathroom. Listening to the sound of her laughter Kate realized it had been forty-eight hours since she had heard another human voice. She cleared her throat and held her hand to the mirror as if to shake hands. "Hello.

It's nice to meet you, Kate Smith. You and I are going to be great friends."

Kate smiled at herself as she glanced in the mirror on her way out. It felt good to have an identity again, even if it was one she had created for herself. She quickly jogged back to her car. She wanted to be long gone before anyone happened to stop at this deserted rest stop. Though the chances were slim, she might still be recognized, which was not a chance she was willing to take. She turned on the radio and started to sing along to Miley Cyrus' song *Flowers* as she drove onto the lonely, early morning highway. She smiled again; she was out of practice, so it felt strange. This was going to be a fantastic day! It was a turning point, a brand-new start. If she didn't need a fresh start, she didn't know who did.

The day progressed without much excitement. She continued driving, never in a straight line. If anyone were to view her zig-zaggy, loopy path on a map, they would think her directionally challenged. In truth, she wanted a confusing trail that would make it very hard for the men who were sure to come looking for her. And come they would, he would hire the best as soon as he figured out she had escaped. She could only hope she still had a few days to disappear before he found out. Hope was all she could do; she dared not contact anyone who once knew her. Phone calls could be traced. It was a sure bet he would comb through the phone records of anyone with whom she was even remotely connected.

Maybe it was having a new name, the culmination of her complete exhaustion after nearly 72 hours in a car, or perhaps just her overwhelming need for a real shower; whatever the reason, Kate decided tonight she would stop at a motel. She was in a small town in west Texas but might as well have been in a different universe than her life in New York. There wasn't much but a rundown motel off Main Street. If they took cash, had running water, and a bed, she didn't care about anything else. She pulled into the parking lot, pulled five twenties off her dwindling pile of cash, and shoved it in the pocket of her jeans. She put the rest back into her purse, along with the knife, and quickly looked around the parking lot. When she saw nothing suspicious, she approached the main office.

Chapter Two

The bell above the door jingled loudly as Kate pushed open the door, causing her to jump. Damn, she hated bells. A plump lady with what could only be described as purple hair sat behind a battered counter. She was watching an old television mounted high in the corner of the room. She never even glanced in Kate's direction; instead just said, "It's 50 bucks a night for a single room and 75 for a double." She then picked up a burning cigarette in an ashtray to her left and took a long, deep drag. Kate purposely walked up to the counter, trying to avoid as much smoke as possible. Smoke and asthma didn't mix well. "I'll take the single for one night," she said and cleared her throat. She pulled three twenties out of her pocket and laid them on the counter. Without glancing in her direction, the woman pulled a key out of the drawer behind the counter and slid it to Kate. She then put the cash in the cash drawer, pulling out a ten as change. Still only looking above Kate's head at the screen, she slid the ten to Kate. "It's room 19, honey. Be sure to check out by 11 o'clock. We have donuts and coffee here in the office in the morning if you get a hankering for something. There are ice, soda, and snack machines at the end of the hall." Kate picked up the key and money and shoved them in her pocket. "Thank you. I'll be checking out early in the morning." With that, she walked outside to find her room.

The room was nothing to brag about, but after 72 hours in a car, it felt like a slice of heaven to Kate, if heaven was decorated in the 1980s by an angel with a thing for mauve and peach. Still, it was surprisingly clean. Kate brought in her suitcase and locked the door with the door lock and the deadbolt. She shoved a chair under the doorknob for good measure, she didn't know if it would do any good, but they always did it in the movies. Then she went to take her first shower in three days. Yup, this was definitely a little slice of heaven, the shower had high pressure, and the water was scalding hot, just how she liked it. She stood under the pounding, hot stream for what seemed like an eternity, letting the water wash away the miles and grime from the last three days. Her legs turned to jelly under the divine assault. She grudgingly turned off the water, toweled herself dry, and slipped into her oldest, most comfortable pair of sweats.

She went to the bed in the middle of the room and flopped into it. It was surprisingly comfortable. Eric would have laughed uncontrollably if he saw her now. Miss Madison Avenue in a 1.5-star motel in the middle of nowhere and loving it. Eric, she should not have thought about him. Her sorrow and grief overwhelmed her almost as much as her guilt. "Eric, I miss you so much. God, I'm so sorry. I was stupid; I thought I could protect you from him. I thought our love made us invincible, but I was so wrong. "Kate hugged the extra pillow as hard as she could, curled herself into a ball, and sobbed. She sobbed for what seemed like hours until she sobbed herself dry. She finally fell into a deep, healing sleep.

Miss Annetta shook her head as the little slip of a girl walked out of the motel office. She had seen her jump like a gun had gone off when that bell had rung. She knew that look. She knew it in a way that only another survivor could. That girl had tangled with monsters and survived. If she was a betting woman, she would lay odds that this little girl was still running from one of those monsters. Oh yeah, another survivor always knows. Well, tonight, that girl was gonna be safe. Indeed, she would because anything that came after her would have to get through Miss Annetta first. Well, Miss Annetta and her 12-gauge shotgun.

Kate sat up in bed and stretched. It was so nice to wake up in a real bed. She glanced at the bedside clock....10:30!! In the morning? No, it couldn't be. She had planned to be gone before sunrise so that no one could get a good look at her or her car. She changed out of her sleep-rumpled sweats and threw on a pair of clean jeans, a tee shirt, and her sneakers. She quickly shoved her old clothes back into her overnight pack. She brushed her teeth and ran a brush quickly through her hair. She smiled sadly, thinking this was the last time she would brush the waist-length tresses. Eric had loved her hair. She would wake many mornings to find his hands tangled up in it. She would try to quietly untangle herself so she could slip out of bed undetected, but he would always awaken, and she would always end up being pulled back into bed, more than once making her late for work; one of those little annoyances between lovers. Now she would give everything she had to feel the tug of Eric's hands in her hair again. Silent tears spilled down her cheeks as she counted the brush strokes. 98, 99, 100. Such a silly ritual and yet one she had never been able to break. She pulled a pair of scissors out of her overnight bag, her hands shaky. It was silly, really. After all, she had been through, she was shaking at the thought of cutting her hair. The ridiculousness of it all made Kate smile a sad smile. She took one last look in the mirror, took a deep breath, and started to cut. When it was all done, she wanted to cry.

Most of her hair was in piles on the floor. What was left on her head was an uneven, jagged, shoulder-length mess. If she was going for inconspicuous, this was not it. She would have to get it trimmed by a professional. She hopped into the shower and let her tears of loss mingle with the streams of hot water flowing down her face. Her hair was no big thing, but it represented the last piece of her old self. Now she was truly gone.

Kate glanced at her watch.... shoot 11:25. Check out was at 11, and she still had to clean up her hair mess and wipe down the room. She couldn't risk leaving her fingerprints here. Most would think her ridiculous, but they had never been hunted. She had learned her lessons from the last time; she would never be caught again. This time she would run until she was free or die trying. Sometimes she wondered why he didn't just kill her himself after they caught her. He had enough money to squelch any suspicions or inconveniences her death may raise. If she could answer that question, she would be one step closer to understanding this whole mad situation.

Kate picked up the phone and called the desk. The same lady who checked her in last night picked up. Her raspy voice was one of a kind. "I've decided to stay an extra night. Would it be possible for me to keep this room?" The voice on the other end laughed and assured her it wouldn't be a problem. "Thank you. I'll stop in the office in about ten minutes to pay for the night."

Kate shoved the ten from last night's change and two more twenties in the pocket of her jeans, put on her ball cap, ensured she could get at the knife quickly, and started out for the day. This time when the bell on the office door jingled, she was ready for it, but it still grated on her nerves. She plastered on a friendly smile and went to speak to the purple-haired lady at the desk.

"Hey honey, did you sleep well last night?" The desk keeper smiled, showing nicotine-stained teeth.

"Actually, I did." Kate placed the money on the counter and made a move to leave. She had no desire to make small talk, but the purple-haired lady seemed to be in a chatty mood.

"Well, you missed our continental breakfast, not that it's much to brag about, just a few donuts and some passable coffee. If you're hungry, Uncle Joe's will fix you a decent meal at a reasonable price. It's right here on Main Street, only a little way down. Young thing like you could walk there with no problem at all."

"Thank you. I guess maybe I'll head that way then" Kate lowered her eyes, ready for this conversation to be over.

"No problem at all. My name is Ms. Annetta if you need anything."

"I appreciate that. I'll be checking out tomorrow morning... Actually, could you tell me if there is a hair salon here in town?" Kate tried to make the question as nonchalant as possible. She could not afford to be memorable.

Ms. Annetta started laughing. "Well honey, I don't know about any salon, but Ms. Betty owns From Hair to

Eternity a little ways past Uncle Joe's on Main Street. Her daughter Brenda runs the place now that Ms. Betty can't stand on her feet all day. If you're looking for a perm or haircut, she can help you. But if you're looking for the stuff they do in them fancy city salons like waxing (she spat the word waxing like it left a dirty taste in her mouth) or whatnot, you won't be finding any of that at Ms. Betty's."

Kate felt her old self shudder on the inside. In her former life, it was normal for Kate to spend a day at a spa pampered by the world's leading beauty experts. In this new life, Kate was going to get her hair cut at a place called From Hair to Eternity by someone named Brenda. If she still believed in God, she would have had to say He had a really ironic sense of humor. Kate quickly put a smile back on her face. "Thanks. Maybe I'll have a chance to check it out later today." Kate left the office and started down Main Street. Her stomach rumbled loudly. Well, it seems I'm getting my appetite back, she thought to herself; now to find Uncle Joe's....whatever that was.

Uncle Joe's Diner was a rundown brick building almost at the end of Main Street. Kate couldn't decide if the heavenly smells wafting from inside were real or inhaled mirages brought on by extreme hunger. Either way, she was too hungry to care. She managed to hide her startled jump as an overhead bell rang as she walked in. What was it about this town and its infernal bells? In stark contrast to its dilapidated exterior, the inside was bright and cheery with yellow checked curtains, matching yellow tablecloths, and white lace doilies on the center of each table. It wasn't very crowded, which suited Kate just fine. Coming between the breakfast and lunch rush had its advantages.

Kate waited a moment to be seated, but when no one appeared to show her to her seat, she sat at a corner table, her back against the wall and a clear line of sight to the door. Running was exhausting her both emotionally and mentally. She muffled a sigh as a cute waitress, in her mid to late twenties, if Kate were to hazard a guess, made her way toward Kate's table. "Hi there, you must be new around here. I'm Lucy. What brings you to our little town?" Lucy was a pretty girl with curly, short blond hair, green eyes, and a spattering of freckles over her nose. Her voice was sweet, almost melodic, with a slight southern twang. Kate would have instantly liked her if she had the luxury of friendships or even acquaintances. "I'm just passing through" Kate looked down at the menu that Lucy had slid across the table, hoping to end any further discussion. Unfortunately, Lucy didn't seem to be able to see the big ' Stay Away" vibe Kate had cloaked herself in that morning. "Well, it's a nice town. You should stay for a few days if you can. We're small, but the people here are friendly, and Miss Doris makes the absolute best pies anywhere. You should definitely get a slice before you leave." Kate nodded and continued to stare blankly at the menu. "You should try our pancakes. They are the best.

Uncle Joe came up with a secret recipe fifty years ago, and Miss Doris still makes them the same way. Or you could try our omelets. Sheriff Tom swears we have the best western omelet he's ever eaten. He would know since he's from Colorado!" Kate had no idea who Sheriff Tom was and was in no hurry to meet him. "I'll take the pancakes." She smiled and handed the menu back to Lucy. "And a cup of coffee, if you've got it." Lucy laughed a musical sound that reminded Kate of a fairy. "Of course, we have coffee. What kind of diner would we be if we didn't serve coffee?" Lucy shook her head, still laughing as she started back toward the kitchen.

The pancakes were ambrosia as far as Kate was concerned. They were light, fluffy, and piled high. Sitting beside them on the plate were a pile of fried potatoes, peppers, and two slices of bacon. Kate dug into the plate like she hadn't had a meal in a week. Come to think of it, besides granola bars and quick sandwiches, she hadn't. She ate with little thought of anything else, enjoying each taste of heaven as it hit her taste buds. Finally, she was having a moment of peace.

Suddenly the bell above the door began to tinkle, making Kate instantly come alert. The sun streaming through the door silhouetted a tall man with a cowboy hat pulled low. Kate shifted further back into the corner and pulled her baseball cap down over her eyes. She slowly lowered her hand to her purse, feeling around for the knife, trying not to make any movement that would draw attention to her. The silhouetted figure turned his head toward her. She tightened her grip on the knife, though she doubted it would do much against the giant in the doorway. She wished she still believed in a god to pray to. But God was no more real than mermaids or Big Foot. She had to believe he was a myth because if he wasn't, if he were real, he was a sadistic bastard. Lucy came bustling out from the kitchen and caught a glimpse of the shadowed man her face broke out in a huge smile, and a blush spread to the roots of her hair. "Why Sheriff Tom, it is good to see you. We missed you at breakfast today."

It had been a day from hell for Tom, and it was only 11:45 in the morning. Already he had been called out to the Benet farm. Charlie Benet and Doug Jenkins were at it again. Every few weeks, one or the other of them called Tom to arrest the other over some slight. It took all his patience and self-control not to just throw them both in a jail cell and let them duke it out. It sure would make his job easier. According to local lore, Charlie and Doug had both been in love with Ella McClarin almost sixty years ago. Ella had been engaged to Doug, but Charlie was not to be dissuaded. He spent every cent he had wooing Ella. Ella was found to be pregnant. Since Ella had insisted they wait until their wedding night to make love, Doug knew the baby couldn't be his. Enraged, he went searching for Charlie. He and Charlie had come to blows outside the old movie theater. Charlie had tried to make peace, swearing that he had never touched Ella. Doug, being the reasonable man, he was, beat Charlie senseless. Despite her fallen state, Doug still married Ella, making her life a living hell for the next forty-three years. When the baby was stillborn, Doug couldn't have been more relieved. Charlie knew Doug was abusing Ella and suspected the baby had died because of something Doug had done.

Charlie bought the farm next to Jenkins's farm, partly to antagonize Doug but mostly to protect Ella. Charlie never married, hoping Ella would one day come to her senses and leave Doug. Ella always gave him a sad smile and shook her head no every time he tried to persuade her to leave. She died a sad and broken woman. The two men had been bitter enemies for going on sixty years now. Today when he arrived at Charlie's farm, both men were in a standoff, complete with shotguns, over a pig. It took him two hours to get them to put down their guns and another hour to sort out the convoluted story. Apparently, Doug's prize pig had escaped from his pen and started tearing up Charlie's fields. Charlie didn't hesitate a second to shoot the pig and stock his freezer with pork for the year. When Doug had gone to Charlie's farm, loaded for bear, to collect his pig, Charlie had enjoyed telling him exactly where his pig had ended up. In the end, Tom told Charlie to pay Doug for the pig. He then told Doug to keep his animals on his land. Crisis averted, and everyone lived for today. Now he could finally have some coffee and a bite to eat.

When he entered Joe's diner, he noticed the woman in the corner; any man would. Despite her obvious attempt to hide it, the woman was hot, as his nephew would say. A man should take a moment to appreciate a new, good-looking woman in town, but that wasn't what really caught his attention. The way she backed up and started to feel around in her purse really got his attention. Now his cop senses were tingling. He tensed, slowly turned and was about to put his hand on his gun when Lucy came bustling out of the kitchen. The woman immediately relaxed and went back to her pancakes. Whatever she was afraid of, it wasn't him. Tom smiled at Lucy and sat at his regular table.

"How's it going, Lucy? Do you think Miss Doris would mind whipping me up my regular? I'm running a bit late today." Tom made small talk with Lucy, but his mind was on the woman in the corner. His natural state was to be pretty laid back, but something about the woman didn't sit right with him. He determined to find out exactly who she was because one thing was for sure, that woman looked like trouble.

Kate breathed a sigh of relief. It was just the town sheriff. She hoped he hadn't been able to get a good enough look at her to recognize her. But she was leaving first thing in the morning anyway. While Lucy was chatting with the sheriff, she took a minute to wipe her fingerprints off the silverware and coffee mug as inconspicuously as possible. She had no idea how much the bill came to, but she figured a twenty should cover

the meal and a tip. She dropped the money on the table
and slipped out the door, the bell jingling as she left.

Chapter Three

From Hair to Eternity turned out to be a small addition on the back of the owner's house. Kate didn't know if she should knock or walk right in. Finishing school had not taught her the proper etiquette for entering a beauty parlor at the back of an old lady's house. She decided she would simply walk in and hope for the best. She braced herself for the damned bell that was sure to be on the door and walked in.

To her surprise, the salon was busy. It seemed Ms. Annetta's purple hair was the must-have style among the town's older women. There were three more purple heads of hair in various stages of the styling process. Kate made a mental note not to get her hair dyed today. At 33 years old, she was simultaneously too old and not old enough to be able to pull off the purple hair look. She found a cracked vinyl chair and sat down. All the conversation in the salon had stopped when she stepped through the door. This was the worst place she could have chosen for someone needing to keep a low profile. Every eye in the room was on her. She smiled at everyone, picked up an outdated issue of People Magazine, and began to flip through the pages.

A middle-aged woman wearing the typical hairdresser's smock started toward Kate. "Hi, I'm Brenda. Welcome to From Hair to Eternity. I don't think we've met. What can I do for you today?"

"I'm just looking for a wash and trim," Kate said, trying to balance rudeness and being too friendly. Both would make her too memorable.

Brenda walked over to the front counter and looked at her appointment book. "That would be our pleasure. We're a little busy right now, so it will be around forty minutes. I hope that works for you." The timer on one of the hair driers sounded, and Brenda made her way over to the older woman sleeping under it. Brenda gently tapped her on the shoulder. "Hazel, honey, your perm is set. Let's go on over and finish you up." All around the room, ladies started chatting back and forth again. It seemed that these women knew about everything and everyone in town. If some sly soul managed to keep something a secret, Kate had no doubt that one of the purple hairs would have it snooped out and reported to everyone at From Hair to Eternity in no time. Kate half listened to the conversation that swirled around her. In a few minutes, she had learned Lloyd Kramer's cat, Sybil, had a litter of kittens. Sheriff Tom was reportedly dating Lucy at Uncle Joe's diner, and Mayor Gibson had again taken up the demon whiskey. Kate didn't know anything about kittens or drunken mayors. But if the blush on Lucy's face was anything to judge by, the purple hairs were right about the sheriff and Lucy. It was nice to sit here and listen to the loves and lives of small-town America. It was so mundane, so normal, so not her life.

Forty minutes passed by quickly. Brenda motioned Kate over to her styling chair. Kate sat down, shifted uncomfortably, and finally removed her baseball cap. Brenda looked at the hatchet job Kate had done on her hair questioningly. Kate smiled apologetically. "I got tired of my hair and took a pair of scissors to it. As it turns out, I make a terrible stylist." Brenda laughed. "Honey, you wouldn't believe some of the things I've had to fix. Once when Lucy was a teenager, she decided that she hated her curly hair. She took her mamma's clothes iron, turned it on high, and tried to iron the curls out. She singed her hair to only about three inches long. I evened it up as best I could but couldn't do much. Now you are in a far better situation. I think you would look fabulous with a chin-length bob."

Kate instinctively liked Brenda. She nodded and smiled. "I think that would be great."

Brenda ran her hands through Kate's hair. "Your hair is so beautiful and thick. I think some caramel highlights would look fantastic!"

Kate remembered all the purple-haired ladies in the beauty parlor earlier and barely suppressed a shudder. "No, I'll just go for a cut right now."

Brenda was a good stylist. She had Kate's hair washed, cut, and styled in no time. Kate looked at herself in the mirror. She really liked the woman she saw staring back.

The shorter hair made her look fun and a little bit flirty. She smiled her first genuine smile in a long time and thanked Brenda. "How much do I owe you?" "A wash and cut are $15.00" Kate couldn't believe she had heard the price correctly. The least she had ever paid for a haircut was $75.00. "I'm sorry, did you say $15.00?" she asked in amazement. "Yes, ma'am. That's what it is for a wash and a cut. We aren't fancy around here." Kate pulled out enough cash to cover the haircut, plus a generous tip. She once again thanked Brenda, gave a toss to her newly styled hair, and left.

It was only 1:30, and Kate had no idea what to do with the rest of her day. She started walking back toward the motel; maybe she would catch a television show or two. Better yet, she would take a nap. She could use one.

Kate was almost to the motel when behind her, there was the loud roar of a truck's engine. Kate jumped, reached in her purse for the knife, and picked up her pace. The truck whizzed by, a bunch of rowdy teenage boys whistling and laying on their horn. She relaxed and cursed the idiot man that had first decided whistling at a woman like she was a dog was in some way flattering. She hoped the man had been flogged.

Tom was walking out of Uncle Joe's when he heard the horn and whistling. He knew it had to be Beau Jenkins and his pack of miscreants. He squinted in the sunlight and saw the object of their affection. She hurriedly walked down the street, a look of irritation on her face. It was the woman from the diner. He had thought she was pretty before when she was wearing that ridiculous ball cap. But she was beautiful without it, with her short brown hair blowing gently away from her face in the breeze. She looked like she belonged on the pages of a fashion magazine, even in faded jeans and a tee shirt. Tom had a strange feeling he had seen that face somewhere before. He tried to place where but came up blank. Hopefully, whoever she was, she would be gone by the next day. His instincts still screamed that woman would cause him a lot of trouble and not the kind of trouble he would enjoy.

Annetta caught a glimpse of the girl as she walked past the motel's office window. So, she had gone to see Brenda after all. The page boy cut looked good on her, much better than the hatchet job she had tried to hide under the ball cap this morning. Something about this little girl reminded Annetta of herself years ago when she first arrived at Cutler's Gap. She had come to Cutler's Gap twenty years ago, scared, beaten, bruised, and broke. She had been on the run from her husband, a real bastard from the backwoods of Louisiana. His favorite pastimes had been drinking and beating her. His last attack had nearly killed her. He had left her lying naked in a pool of her own blood, unconscious for hours. When she finally came to, cold and blessedly alone, she knew the next time he would succeed in killing her. She had run; as fast and far as she could. Her money and gas had run out here in Cutler's Gap. Thank God they had. Here she had been able to start a new life; the people of the small town took her in, protected her, and helped her back onto her feet. That little girl needed the same thing. Now, she had to convince the girl in room nineteen to stay.

Kate awoke from her nap to a rumbling stomach and the sunlight fading. It seemed she had slept most of the day, and now her body was demanding food again. She was surprised her appetite was coming back with such vigor. She hopped out of bed and did a quick look in the mirror. She brushed her hair and applied a little mascara and lip gloss on a whim, and headed out to see what she could find for dinner. She walked to the motel's office to ask about the restaurant options in town. The door was locked, and a sign proclaimed, "Back in 60 minutes," handwritten under that was "or whenever I get here." Uncle Joe's it is, Kate said to herself.

Uncle Joe's diner was the nighttime place to be, it seemed. The place was packed; there wasn't a single empty table. Kate was about to turn around when she noticed Ms. Annetta waving at her. She didn't want to be rude, so she went through the packed restaurant to the table where Ms. Annetta sat.

"Hey there, honey. Pull up a chair with Sheriff Tom and me. Friday night is Miss Doris' famous chicken fried steak night. Everyone in town is usually here." Kate smiled and looked around. How had she missed the tall sheriff sitting diagonally across the table from Ms. Annetta? Now she really wanted to get out of there as quickly as possible.

She got ahold of her rattled nerves. "Thank you, Ms. Annetta, but I don't want to intrude on your dinner. I was going to grab something and bring it back to my room."

"Nonsense, girl! I wouldn't dream of having you sitting all alone in your room, eating by yourself. Here, sit down." Ms. Annetta patted the chair next to hers, directly across the table from the sheriff, who was studying her suspiciously. Kate decided she had no choice; leaving now would only raise his suspicions further.

"Thank you. I appreciate your hospitality." She sat down and tried to smile.

The sheriff was tall with sandy hair and stormy grey eyes. She wanted to squirm under the intensity of the look he was giving her.

"I've already introduced myself, and this is Sheriff Tom Fletcher." Ms. Annetta smiled as she made the introduction.

"It's good to meet you. I'm Kate." Kate shook hands with the sheriff. They both stared uncomfortably at each other.

"Kate has been staying at my motel," Ms. Annetta seemed to try to fill the uncomfortable silence.

"So, how do you like our little town, Kate?" Tom tried to sound casual as he looked at the woman across from him. The glance he had of her walking down the street earlier had not done her justice. She was even more beautiful up close. It was obvious he made her uncomfortable; truth be told, she had the same effect on him. His gut was still screaming a red alert where this woman was concerned.

Kate did her best to sound cheerful and nonchalant. "It has been quite lovely, and the people are very friendly. I'll be sad to leave in the morning." Kate was surprised that she was a bit sad to leave this place. Something about this little town appealed to her.

"It's too bad you can't hang around a few more days. There is a lot of beautiful country here. Those mesas have an incredible view if you hike to the top." Ms. Annetta interjected.

To Kate's relief, the waitress had made her way to their table before she had to respond. The waitress tonight was a young girl, about 16, with long brown hair and braces. "Hi Sheriff, Hi Ms. Annetta, I'm sorry I kept y'all waiting. It's been crazy tonight."

"It's no problem CherylAnne. We know how busy y'all are on Friday nights. We've just been getting to know my guest, Kate. I told her all about Miss Doris' amazing chicken fried steak. That's what I'll be having, along with a sweet tea." Ms. Annetta gave the flustered girl a pat on the hand.

"I'll have the same CherylAnne, and make sure you save me a piece of that coconut cream pie." Sheriff Tom gave the girl a teasing smile. Kate resisted the urge to roll her eyes when CherylAnne blushed to the roots of her hair at that smile. It seemed Lucy wasn't the only one with a crush on Sheriff Tom.

"I'll take the same thing, except I would like unsweetened tea," Kate ordered

The girl looked at Kate like she'd grown horns but wrote down her order without comment.

"I'll have it right out to y'all." CherylAnne gave the sheriff a tentative smile and returned to the kitchen.

"Poor CherylAnne has such a crush on you, Tom." Annetta teased.

"She's a good girl," Tom said a bit uncomfortably.

"Yes, she is, and she lo-oves you." Ms. Annetta batted her eyelashes in jest.

Tom chuckled and rolled his eyes. "You know the only woman for me is you, Ms. Annetta." It was an old, familiar banter.

As Kate watched the interaction between the sheriff and Ms. Annetta, it was obvious there was a lot of affection between the two. It was almost as if they were mother and son. Their connection made Kate feel just a bit jealous. It reminded her just how alone in the world she really was.

"Kate visited Ms. Betty's today. What did you think of From Hair Until Eternity? It looks like Brenda did a good job." Ms. Annetta tried to draw Kate into the conversation.

"It was an interesting experience. I feel like I already know everything about everyone in town after sitting in there for an hour or so." Kate laughed. "Brenda is really great, though. She did a good job on my cut."

"She is a good woman. She went off to Dallas and worked in one of them hoity-toity, uppity salons. But as soon as Miss Betty needed her to take over, she came right home and took over the shop and the taking care of her mamma without a single complaint." Kate was a little surprised to hear Brenda's qualifications. Maybe she should have let her highlight her hair after all.

"She seemed nice and very competent when I met her today." Kate couldn't think of any other response. This whole dinner conversation thing was exhausting when you had to think about every single word you said. It didn't help that the sheriff was still studying her like a speck on a microscope slide.

Tom couldn't decide what to think about Kate. She was so guarded and reserved with everything she said. But when she relaxed and laughed, she seemed like a different person. It didn't escape his notice that she hadn't offered her last name when she introduced herself.

CherylAnne arrived with their drinks. Kate looked slightly confused by the cup of hot water and tea bag she had received. She started to say something but then must have changed her mind. Instead, she opened the tea bag and began to steep her tea. Tom made a mental note; Kate was most definitely not from the South. Her confusion at getting hot tea when she ordered unsweet tea was a dead giveaway.

Kate still couldn't figure out why the waitress had brought her a cup of hot tea instead of iced tea, but she wasn't going to make a fuss over it. Tea was tea, hot or cold. Either way suited her just fine.

"Kate, are you traveling for business or pleasure?" Ms. Annetta sent Tom a sharp look as he broached the question.

Kate visibly tensed for a second before forcing herself to relax. "Pleasure," Kate said with no explanation. Tom obviously wanted to press further, but the silencing look Ms. Annetta shot him over the table, and the solid kick to the shins she delivered under the table seemed to quell his curiosity for the moment.

"I've always wanted to take a road trip just for fun. Good for you, Kate." Ms. Annetta cut in.

Kate gave a faint smile in response. She wanted to get up and run away fast. Only the thought that the nosey sheriff, with the stormy eyes, would follow her kept her glued to her seat. She had spent most of her life smiling through gritted teeth and entertaining the enemy. Surely, she could make it through a diner dinner with a two-bit, small-town sheriff and an old lady with purple hair.

The food arrived just then, saving Kate the need for comment. Kate was quite skeptical of this whole chicken-fried steak thing. She had only ordered it because it was obvious she was expected to. Honestly, the idea of chicken and steak fried together was less than appealing. When her plate came, Kate couldn't help but poke with her fork at the golden fried piece of meat smothered in a cream gravy.

"Would you ladies mind if I said grace?" the Sheriff asked.

"You go right on ahead, Tom," Annetta spoke around the food already in her mouth.

Kate shook her head and stared blankly at the floor as the sheriff offered a simple prayer of thanksgiving.

"Dear God, thank you for this food and the good company I share it with. Please bless the food and our conversation. Amen"

Kate began to slice at her chicken fried steak thingy; she might as well take a bite and get it over with. Kate took her first bite, her widening in surprise. It was the most amazing comfort food she'd ever had!

"This is amazing, but where's the chicken?" Kate burst out.

Both the sheriff and Ms. Annetta broke into fits of laughter. Kate couldn't figure out what they found so hilarious, but she had obviously made some major faux pas. Her cheeks reddened in embarrassment.

"Oh honey, I'm sorry. It's called chicken fried steak because the steak is breaded and served with gravy, the way you do with fried chicken. It isn't made with chicken. You obviously aren't from the South." Annetta managed to explain through her laughter.

Kate smiled ruefully and shook her head. Everyone tucked back into their food, with only the briefest comments interrupting their eating. This suited Kate just fine. The last comment about where she came from was venturing into dangerous territory.

Dinner continued without incident. Sheriff Tom seemed to relax and grow less suspicious of her as the meal progressed. Kate laughed as Ms. Annetta regaled them with stories from her time as a motel owner.

"The strangest request I have ever had was from a little old lady, probably in her eighties. She called, asking for our honeymoon suite and a single room. I told her we were a motel; we didn't have a honeymoon suite. She became quite distraught. She kept saying that "Sonny must have a honeymoon suite." Trying to appease her, I said I would figure something out. The next day I decorated one of our double rooms with heart pillows, rose petals, and balloons. I even put chocolates on the bed. I was feeling really good about going above and beyond for my guests. Later that day, the old lady arrived with two pugs. She introduced one as Sonny and the other as Cher. They were the newlyweds in need of the honeymoon suite! She would take the single room next door. Now I was jumping mad. There was no way I was letting two pugs stay alone in what was now my honeymoon suite! I showed her around back to the old doghouse and run I had put up years ago for my dog Daisy. I stuck a Do Not Disturb sign over the door, tied a few balloons to the run, and told her this was our canine honeymoon suite. That was that. The pugs were happy, and I still charged her for the double room! She called me a few months later to say that the union had been blessed and they were expecting puppies." Kate laughed so hard that she was almost in tears when Ms. Annetta finished her story. It was nice to sit here and talk and laugh. It was almost normal.

CherylAnne finally came back to the table with Sheriff's pie.

"Can I get you, ladies, any dessert?" she asked as she cleared away their plates.

"No. I can't eat another bite; I'm so full. Could I have my check, please?" Kate was in a hurry to leave. She was getting too comfortable sitting here laughing. She had almost forgotten that she wasn't Kate and couldn't afford to have friends.

"Don't worry about the check. It would be my pleasure to buy two beautiful ladies' dinners." The Sheriff was taking his wallet out of his pocket.

"That really isn't necessary, Sheriff. I do appreciate the offer."

"Hush now, girl, let the man buy our dinner. When you get to be my age, you learn to never take such male attention for granted!"

"Well, then, I thank you for dinner, Sheriff."

"I think if a man buys you dinner, you get to be on a first-name basis with him. Just call me Tom."

Kate smiled. "Okay, thank you, Tom. I'll say goodnight" Kate got up to leave and was surprised when Ms. Annetta and the sheriff got up from the table with her.

"If you don't mind, I'll walk back to the motel with you, Kate. Thanks for dinner, Tom."

"I'll walk you both back to the motel. It's on my way to the station anyway."

"Really, this isn't necessary. I'm fine walking by myself. You haven't even finished your pie." Kate objected. She really needed to get away from these people. They were too nice, too funny, too interested in her.

"What kind of officer of the law would I be if I let two lovely ladies go out alone onto the dangerous streets of Cutler's Gap? I always get my pie to go anyway." He nodded at CherylAnne, who brought him a Styrofoam to-go box.

Kate could see this was an argument she would not win. She put on her best smile and waited for the Sheriff to finish paying and box his pie.

The bell jingled on their way out, making Kate grit her teeth. She wanted to tear every stupid bell down in this town. It was a very good thing she was leaving in the morning. They walked in silence, each lost in their own thoughts.

The walk to the motel was a short one. The sheriff tipped his hat and wished them both a good night. Kate was about to go to her room when Ms. Annetta stopped her. "Kate, I wonder if you have a minute. There is something I want to talk to you about."

"I was just heading back to my room to sleep." Kate really needed some space to breathe and rebuild her defenses.

"It will only take a minute. It's important."

Kate had no idea what could be so important. Then terror washed over her. They had found her. That was the only thing that made any sense. She had to get out of here NOW!! Ms. Annetta clearly saw the look of complete fear on her face.

"Now honey, it's nothing to be worried about. I have a business proposition I want to discuss with you."

Kate felt the oxygen rush back into her lungs. She hadn't even realized she was holding her breath. She pushed down the fear, forced herself to smile, and followed Ms. Annetta into her office.

Annetta sat down in her old wooden office chair and stroked the arm absentmindedly. She loved this chair with its cracked green leather upholstery and squeaky wheels. Those things only made it more precious besides, she had her own cracks, wrinkles, and creaks.

She and this chair had been through a lot of life together. It was one of the first pieces of furniture she had purchased when she started her new life here in Cutler's Gap. She had bought it at a thrift store for $10.00. This chair, an old card table, and a lumpy secondhand mattress had been her only furniture for the first year she had lived here. Starting over had its fair share of hardships, but they made her into the woman she was today.

Annetta looked at the girl sitting in the chair across her desk. She looked like a China doll; porcelain skin, dark hair, and blue eyes; beautiful in a reserved, almost cold way. It was her eyes that defied the cool, reserved image. Her eyes held sadness, grief, and terror. Annetta sighed, still trying to find the right words to keep this little, scared bird from flying away.

"I know you are enjoying a bit of a road trip, but I wanted to see if you are interested in a position at the motel. I need another person to watch the desk and help clean the rooms. It would only be part-time, and I couldn't pay much, but I would give you a room as part of your pay. I know that Brenda needs someone to help her with her books a few hours a week, and Miss Doris has been looking for another part-time waitress too."

"I appreciate the offer, but I'm not looking to stay. I have to say, although I'm flattered, I'm not really sure why you're asking me."

"Kate, I'm gonna be honest with you. It's obvious you are running from some kind of trouble. I saw it all over you from the minute you stepped into the motel office. I'm not gonna ask a bunch of questions or pry. Your business is your business. But I know what it's like to be scared, alone, and running from something. That's how I ended up here in Cutler's Gap. The people here are good, and they protect their own. It wouldn't take much for you to become one of us. Sometimes being alone is the absolute worst way to escape trouble."

Kate swallowed hard. The fear she had been pushing down was fighting its way up her throat. She had to get out of here, now. Ms. Annetta had guessed too much. This was dangerous for everyone.

"Thank you so much for trying to help me. I think you have the wrong impression of me, though. I'm not in any trouble. I just wanted to escape the daily grind for a few weeks." Kate made herself smile and laugh. Her laugh sounded hollow, even to her own ears.

She could tell Ms. Annetta wasn't buying a word of what she was saying, but she could not put another innocent at risk with the truth.

"Just know, Kate, the offer stands. Here is my number." Ms. Annetta pushed a business card across the desk to her. "Call me anytime, from anywhere, and I will help if I can."

Kate swallowed the lump of emotion forming in her throat. Only one other person had ever shown her this much kindness. She longed to stay, belong, be a part of a community, and have a family again. It had been so long. Eric had been all those things to her and more. Eric had loved her, Eric had helped her, Eric had protected her; Eric was dead.

Kate took the business card, shoved it into her jeans pocket, and stood up. Ms. Annetta walked her to the office door with a look of sad compassion on her face. On impulse, Kate hugged her and left the office without looking back. Tears were in her eyes as she returned to room nineteen. She knew this would be the last time she would ever see the gruff lady with purple hair and a heart of gold.

Chapter Four

Kate slowly drove out of town just as the first rays of the sun were stroking the morning sky. Sadness was heavy in her heart as she drove past the sign welcoming visitors to the town and turned onto the highway. The little rundown town had been a safe haven for her these past two days. She had let herself start to feel like a person again, to start to want friendships and a place. She couldn't risk opening herself up like that again. She wasn't a person; she was prey and could never stop running.

She made good time that morning, but every mile she put between her and Cutler's Gap made her heart heavier. Around eleven am, she stopped at a rest stop, grabbed a granola bar, and looked at the map. It was weird using a real paper map after years of using the GPS navigation system in her car. She studied the map, trying to decide which direction to go. She had no final destination in mind. She was going to run until she couldn't run anymore. She counted the money she had hidden in her purse. She was down to $5,000. That wasn't much money to live on for the rest of her life. Eventually, she would have to stop running and find a way to make money. The car's engine had been making a thumping sound since she had bought it. The sound was getting louder with every mile she drove. The car may not outlast her money at this point. Kate fingered the business card in her jeans pocket. She crumpled up the wrapper from the granola bar and tossed it in the trash can beside her car. Impulsively, she started the car and headed back in the direction she had just left. Cutler's Gap may not be much to look at, but it felt like as good a place as any to start over. Besides, she already had a job and a place to stay waiting for her.

The sun was setting as Kate pulled back into Cutler's Gap. She was exhausted, hungry, and strangely at peace. She pulled up to the motel and felt a sense of homecoming. She parked the car and made her way to the office. She almost smiled when the damn bell rang as she entered. Ms. Annetta, sitting behind the counter, looked up as Kate walked in.

"Someone told me you were in the market for an assistant."

Ms. Annetta smiled, showing off her nicotine-stained teeth. "It so happens I am. Are you applying for the job?"

"It looks like I am." Kate gave her a sheepish grin.

"Well, good. The job's yours. Out of curiosity, what changed your mind?"

"To be honest, I'm not really sure. I stopped to grab a bite to eat, and the next thing I knew, I was on my way back here. I guess it just felt like a good place to stop for a while."

"I'm glad you're back. I'm going to keep my word. I won't pry. But if you ever are in trouble or want to talk, I want you to know you can always come to me. Now how do you feel about your old having your old room back?"

Kate smiled; she'd become quite fond of room nineteen, "That would be great."

"Good. Tomorrow we will talk about your duties; for tonight, I expect you're tired. Why don't you grab something to eat and rest."

Kate picked up the key that Ms. Annetta slid across the counter to her, slid it into her pocket, and headed back to her car. Tonight, she would actually unpack the two suitcases and one overnight bag she had brought. Her meager wardrobe would be hung up in a closet or put in dresser drawers. It's funny how something so normal and mundane could feel so exciting, Kate thought.

Annetta was relieved to see her little injured bird return to the nest. She wasn't someone who nosed around other people's affairs. She left that to all the other old biddies in the town. But this little girl needed her; Annetta had known that from the moment she set eyes on her. Besides, she'd never had any children. Tom was like a son to her, but it would be nice to have a surrogate daughter too.

Tom was walking toward Uncle Joe's when he saw Kate as she pulled into the motel parking lot. He had very mixed emotions at the sight of her. When he stopped by the motel this morning, he felt strangely bereft, and Ms. Annetta told him Kate was gone. She was worried for the girl, she'd said. She was convinced Kate was in danger. Tom had done his best to ease her mind. All the while, he had a suspicion she was right. Now Kate was back. Whatever trouble or danger she was running from was now headed straight his way. He had better get prepared.

The crystal decanter flew through the air and hit the wall with a loud crash, the pieces showering a middle-aged woman cowering in the corner. She had a bright red handprint across the side of her face and a line of blood trickling from the corner of her mouth. She used her hands to shield her head from the shards of glass raining down around her like ice.

"Damn the bitch; how dare she run away from me!!?" He paced the room, paying no mind to shattered glass or the terrified woman in the corner. How had she done it? He'd been so bloody careful. He'd paid someone to watch her. She was so drugged the last time he saw her she could barely stand. This thought brought his attention back to the woman in the corner. She shrank further into its dark recesses, shaking as his fury was once again pointed at her.

"You stupid, worthless cow of a woman; you had one and only one job; make sure that bitch didn't leave my house. That was it. Keep one drugged girl from escaping, and you managed to screw even that up." He grabbed the woman's shoulders and shook her so hard her teeth rattled in her head. He pushed her back down and smacked her across the face once again. The trickle of blood became a stream. He kicked her in the ribs and shouted, "Get out of my house. I don't ever want to see your cow face again." The shaking and battered woman scrambled to her feet and ran out of the house's front door.

The man began pacing again; he could not afford this right now, not when everything was finally coming together. He had to find her. It shouldn't be that difficult. She had run away once before, and he had found her in a few days. Despite what everyone thought, she wasn't exactly the brightest bulb in the pack. She certainly had never been able to outwit him. No, this was a minor setback in the grand scheme of things. He went to his desk, unlocked the top drawer, and picked up the false bottom. Underneath was a small black diary; inside was a list of names and phone numbers. These were the people he relied on to do the things he couldn't do, things that were best done under cover of darkness. Never would he admit to knowing them, but ironically, they knew him better than anyone else. He found the name he needed, picked up the emergency burner phone in the drawer, and placed the call.

"I need your expertise. She's gone again. Find her" The voice on the other end of the call grumbled a question.

"No, I don't know how she escaped! Find her and bring her back alive." There was grumbling on the other end of the line again.

"No, she must be alive. That is the only requirement. Find her and bring her back alive. What you do, how you do it, and the cost is of no consequence. Just get her back here before she makes a mess of everything." The voice on the other end of the call was clearly unhappy with the job. "Oh, speaking of messes, I need you to take care of that cow of a woman, Maria. This one is on you. You brought her to me and assured me of her reliability. Now we have this mess to clean up." The voice was obviously irritated with this new development.

"Do what you want. I just want her to disappear for good. Call me at this number if you have any information. It is a safe line and can't be traced to either of us." With that, he hit end call, turned the phone off, and put it back in the drawer with the black diary. He then replaced the false bottom of the drawer and locked it. He'd been too soft on her the last time she had run away. He'd allowed himself to listen to her pleas and promises and caved to sentiment. He wouldn't make the same mistake again. This time she wouldn't be so lucky; she would pay for her defiance, lies, and abandonment of him. She would be punished so that she never dared run again. It really was for her good; she needed to learn her place. With that mood-improving thought, he straightened his tie and headed for the door. He had a board meeting to lead in fifteen minutes.

Griffin threw the phone down on the coffee table. Damn it all; he had never wanted to hear that voice again. That man would get him killed or, worse yet, caught. Griffin was very selective in who he took on as clients and what jobs he would do for them. When that jackass had been referred to him, he had thought him just another rich pansy that needed someone else to do the more unpleasant things for him. He'd been wrong, and now he, a pretty scary spider in his own right, was caught in the web of an even bigger, scarier spider. This was the last job he would take. One way or another, he would free himself.

Now onto the most pressing thing, he had to find Maria and take care of her. The poor woman was nothing more than a pawn in this chess game, but her usefulness had come to an end, and she was expendable. The information she had passed on to him during her time as the jackass' employee had been helpful but not nearly as game-changing as he'd hoped. In the end, he had been forced to speed the game along. The girl had thought she had escaped on her own. But Maria had been the head nurse at a psychiatric hospital in Mexico City. She knew the girl was only pretending to take the pills and slipping them under her mattress. She knew all the tricks. She had allowed the girl to escape on his orders. It was too bad that he had to kill her now; he had developed a fondness for the old battle ax. He would send the rest of her pay to her family back in Mexico; that should even things up.

Griffin went to his garage and pulled out his tool chest. Every artisan was only as good as the tools he relied on. Therefore, he took meticulous care of his tools. He began putting together the kit he would need tonight. He stopped to stroke his first knife, a military-issued K-BAR from his days in the Marines. He smiled fondly and added it to his pack, along with yards of plastic sheeting, an electric bone saw, and several butcher knives. He stuck a thin, coiled, stainless steel wire in his pocket. He loaded the kit, a disposable clean suit, and ten Styrofoam coolers into his SUV. Before heading to Maria's house, he would have to stop at several stores to pick up dry ice. Tonight promised to be long with a lot of hard work. No one ever warned you how much physical labor it was to properly dispose of a body. The killing was easy; it was the disposal and clean-up that was the real bitch. Oh well, whining about it wouldn't get the job done.

Maria held a bag of ice to her lip, the side of her face black and blue when she answered her door to him. She was furious, cursing him to hell and back in Spanish. She demanded more money and to be sent home far from the monster in the big house he had sent her to work for.

"I'm so sorry, Maria. I had no idea he would treat you so badly." He patted her hand and smiled an apologetic smile. "Of course, you deserve more money after all you suffered. I'll book you a ticket back to Mexico City tonight. I feel terrible that you were abused like that." Griffin spent a few minutes sitting next to her, comforting her.

Her fury appeased; she offered him a drink. When she had her back to him, he pulled the thin wire from his pocket and soundlessly slipped it around her neck and pulled tight.

"No worries, Maria, I will send your money to your family." He whispered in her ear as she tried to claw at him for a few seconds and then went limp. Now came the bigger part of the job, he thought with distaste. He pulled her heavy, limp, lifeless body down the hallway to the bathroom and finagled her into the bathtub. He left her there while he went back to his car for his supplies. It was going to be a very long night.

Chapter Five

Kate made her way to Uncle Joe's Diner. Her stomach growled, reminding her she had only eaten a granola bar all day. She was glad to see that there were still tables available. It seemed Saturday nights weren't quite as busy as Friday nights. She sat down at her favorite table in the corner. "Hey, you're back" Lucy gave her a big smile. Kate would give almost anything to be as happy and open as Lucy. Her smile was almost contagious.

"Yeah, I decided to stay for a while. The town grows on you."

"That's great! There aren't many women around my age here in town; you and I will have to stick together."

Kate couldn't help but laugh. "I'm sure we will." Lucy slid a menu to her and walked to another table where an old man sat. Kate half listened as Lucy chatted with him and took his order while she looked over the menu. She was deciding between meatloaf and a grilled chicken salad when she felt someone standing over her. She looked up straight into a pair of stormy grey eyes.

"Welcome back, Kate."

"Hey, Sheriff, long time no see." Kate tried not to grimace. Why did this man have to show up whenever she tried to eat? It was bad for her digestion.

"I thought we agreed last night that you would call me Tom." Tom had to admit he was enjoying how hard she tried to hide her irritation at seeing him. He decided to see how far he could push her. After all, Cutler's Gap was a small town; one had to find entertainment where one could. He pulled out the chair across from her and sat down. This time she didn't even bother to hide the look of irritation that crossed her face.

"Do you mind if I join you for dinner?" He asked mockingly

"Actually, I'm quite tired. I've had a long day. I think I'm just going to take my dinner back to the motel." She went back to perusing the menu.

"Well, I'll keep you company until your order is done. I wouldn't want you to think we aren't friendly around here." Her blue eyes flashed daggers at him, but she smiled a saccharine smile.

"Hey, Sheriff, I see you've met my new best friend." Kate could have kissed Lucy for her timely interruption.

"Yes, Kate and I are old friends. Aren't we?" He gave Kate one of his devastating smiles, which made all the women in town weak-kneed but seemed to make her want to punch his teeth in.

"If by old friends you mean we met yesterday, then absolutely." Kate ground out.

"Lucy, I'm ready to order. I'll have a grilled chicken salad and an order of French fries. Could I get that order to go? I am suddenly exhausted and have a nagging headache." Kate gave Tom a pointed look.

"Sure, Kate, that won't be a problem at all. I hope you feel better."

"Lucy, I'll go ahead and get my order to go to. I need to head back to the station. I'll get my usual."

"Alright, Sheriff, I'll have those up in a jiffy." As Lucy returned to the kitchen, she couldn't help but feel a bit jealous of Kate. She had been flirting with the sheriff for two years, and he'd never once looked at her the way he looked at Kate. Of course, Kate didn't seem to like him at all. Lucy couldn't imagine what was wrong with her. Sheriff Tom was the most handsome man she'd ever met. There was no accounting for some people's tastes.

Kate looked across the table at the infuriating man across from her. He was enjoying making her squirm. It was written all over his overly confident face. Why couldn't he leave her alone?

"I've only been here three times, but every time I've been in here, so have you. Don't you ever cook?" Kate figured she could give as good as she got.

"Sure, I cook. I just don't cook well." Tom laughed.

They settled back into an awkward silence. Minutes ticked by slowly as they waited for Lucy to bring their food. Kate studied the pressed tin ceiling, the curtains, the floor, everything but the disconcerting man before her. Every time she did look at the Sheriff, he had that intense look in his eyes again. It was obvious he had questions for her; she hoped she could come up with some good answers before he started asking them.

Tom was trying to figure out the woman in front of him. She was like a puzzle with pieces missing and pieces from other puzzles mixed in for the hell of it, a definite mystery. There were moments where she was funny and quick-witted, there were other moments where she acted like a whipped puppy, and then there were other times that she acted like she was guilty of some big crime. Tom had been obsessed with puzzles as a kid. He couldn't rest until he had put all the pieces together. It's the same obsession that had made him shoot to the top of his career in Denver PD. At 24 years old, he had been the youngest cop to ever make a detective in the department. It was the same obsession that had eventually ended his career there. This woman was hitting all the same buttons. She was a mystery that needed solving. And why did she look so familiar to him? He couldn't shake the feeling that he had seen her somewhere before.

Lucy finally brought their food to the table. Kate couldn't pay and leave fast enough. Unfortunately, Tom was right behind her. Could the man not take a hint? He matched his long stride with her much shorter one.

After a few moments of silence, he finally brought up what was on his mind.

"So why did you come back, Kate?" Kate heard the seriousness in the Sheriff's voice. Well, here it is, the questions we've been dancing around for two days, she thought to herself.

"Ms. Annetta offered me a job. At first, I told her no, but as I was driving, I changed my mind. It's a woman's prerogative to change her mind, you know." Kate answered playfully

"And that's the story you're sticking with?"

"It's not a story. It's what happened." She knew she was splitting hairs, but she was telling the truth, at least in part. Somehow, she didn't think Tom would accept her partial truth.

"I'm giving you this chance to tell me if you are in trouble or need help. We don't have to be adversaries, Kate. I can help you if you let me. Tell me what you're running from. If you're in trouble, it's better to come clean and turn yourself in. Why are you really here? Tell me the truth." Kate couldn't see the Sheriff's face clearly in the moonlight, but she could hear the determination in his voice. He wasn't going to make this easy for her.

"I'm not wanted or in trouble with the law." That much was true, at least. "I really did come back because of Ms. Annetta's offer. I'm not sure what I did to make you so suspicious of me, but there really isn't anything for me to tell." Okay, that, right there, was a whopper of a lie. Kate was surprised at the flash of guilt she felt at lying to Tom. But it couldn't be helped.

Thankfully they had made it to the motel. She could end this conversation simply by saying goodnight. But before she could speak, Sheriff Tom put his hand on her arm to stop her from walking away.

"I want you to remember that I gave you this chance to come clean, to get help. If I find out you're lying or anyone in this town gets hurt because of trouble you brought, I will not hesitate to lock you up. Are we clear?" Sheriff Tom's voice was as sharp as steel. He clearly knew she was lying, and he was pissed.

"I can assure you that I would never do anything to hurt anyone in your town. I'm just here to work. Goodnight, Sheriff. I'm done being insulted."

"Goodnight, Kate. I'll be seeing you around." Tom watched as Kate turned and walked away without a backward glance. He was more convinced than ever that she was in some serious trouble. He hoped he would be prepared for whatever trouble she brought to town.

Kate paced her motel room. The Sheriff had set her teeth on edge. The peaceful feeling she had when she returned to town was gone, replaced with an edgy anger. How dare he interrogate her like she was some common criminal? She had never done a thing to the man other than not punch his infuriating teeth in when he clearly deserved it. She had already unpacked her meager belongings, had a shower, and even tried to watch a movie on TV, none of which had calmed her nerves. She couldn't sit still; she felt the walls closing in on her. She wanted to run until she couldn't run anymore. She wanted to scream until she had no voice left, she wanted to sleep until the hell she lived in disappeared and time had long since forgotten her. Finally, around midnight, Kate fell into a fitful sleep. The dreams came again. She saw flashes of blood and flames and her parents' lifeless eyes staring at her. She awoke in a cold sweat, tears streaming down her cheeks, screaming silent screams. It's not real. It's just a dream; you know this didn't happen. She chanted this over and over again until she almost believed what she said. God, she couldn't lose it now. She was fine, she was sane, and she was going to make it.

Kate was relieved when the sun finally rose in the morning sky. She was ready to do something productive, some normalcy to keep her mind occupied. She headed over to the office, prepared to do whatever jobs Miss Annetta might have for her. Miss Annetta was sitting in her usual spot, at the counter, her seemingly never-ending cigarette burning in the ashtray, watching the morning news.

"Well, you're up bright and early this morning."

"Yeah, I wanted to get started with my jobs."

"I always appreciate an eager employee but come sit on down for a minute. I want to have a quick chat with you, find out what you have experience in and what not."

Kate nodded and sat in the chair next to Miss Annetta.

"So, I'm gonna need some help cleaning the rooms once in a while. Bernadette does it most days, but sometimes she needs help. I figure just about anyone can handle scrubbing toilets, making beds, and running a vacuum cleaner. I'll also need help at the counter for a couple of shifts a week. What I really need help with is my books, but that's a bit more specialized. You wouldn't happen to know anything about accounting and bookkeeping and all that financial stuff, would you?"

Kate tried not to laugh out loud. Did she have experience? She'd only been reading quarterly financial reports and stock portfolios since she was old enough to know the difference between a letter and a number. Of course, she couldn't tell Miss Annetta that. She smiled and said, "Yeah, I've had some experience with bookkeeping and filing taxes."

"Really; that's fabulous!! If you get bored, I know Brenda is also looking for someone to help with her stuff. Miss Betty has dementia, and none of us realized how bad it had gotten until Brenda came home. Her books are an absolute mess." Most people would find that kind of financial mess a nightmare; to Kate, it was a challenge. Numbers had always made sense to her. No matter how crazy her life had become, numbers were constant; they never changed, unlike people.

Miss Annetta noticed the excited smile that lit Kate's eyes. So, our little bird likes math, does she? This was going to work well for everyone, it would seem. Now to convince Brenda to let Kate take on that mountain of papers in her office.

Once Miss Annetta had learned she could do the books, all other duties were forgotten. She led Kate back to her office and opened a filing cabinet. Inside was an old ledger that looked like something from 1890. A look of horror must have crossed Kate's face because Miss

Annetta quickly said, "Yeah, I don't understand them computers and the internets."

"Would you be too offended if I brought your bookkeeping into at least the 20th century, if not the 21st?"

"You do it however you want, as long as it gets done. There is a laptop over there under that bunch of papers. Tom gave it to me for Christmas last year. He's been trying to teach me to use it. I don't see the appeal. But you're welcome to it if that kind of thing floats your boat." With that, Ms. Annetta walked out of the office, seemingly in a hurry to be as far away as possible from the dreaded books.

Annetta was on a mission when she opened the door to From Hair to Eternity. Brenda needed a bookkeeper. Kate needed another job. It was a match made in heaven as far as she was concerned, but Brenda was an independent, stubborn woman. Getting her to admit she needed help would take some doing.

"Hi Annetta, did you have an appointment today that I forgot? I've been a bit scatterbrained lately." Brenda looked up from her desk, where she sat, surrounded by haphazard stacks of paperwork everywhere; on the desk, on the floor, on the windowsill; literally everywhere.

"Nope, I came to talk with you."

"Oh, what's on your mind?"

"I know you met my guest Kate a couple days ago." Brenda nodded that she remembered Kate. "I offered her a job, and she's staying on. It turns out she is a bookkeeper or accountant or something. Anyway, she's good at what she does. I can't afford to have her on full-time, but maybe you could use her help a few hours a week." Annetta looked pointedly at the stacks of paperwork everywhere.

"I have more than a few hours a week worth of work here, but I don't know how I could possibly hand this mess off to someone else. I can't make heads or tails of it myself!"

"Why don't you have her come over and look at it all. Maybe then you'll have an idea of what she can do."

"I can't promise anything, but I'll meet with her. I hope she can help because this makes me want to pull out my hair. And you know that's not a good look for a stylist."

"Ain't that the truth? So, how's Miss Betty doing?"

"Mom has her good days and her bad days. She needs more supervision lately because she wanders and then forgets where she's at. I have her going to the senior center a couple times a week. They have a bus that picks her up and brings her home. She seems to enjoy it, and I have a few hours to do the things I need to do."

They spent the next hour chatting and catching up. Annetta always enjoyed Brenda's company. By the time she left, it was decided that Kate should come by in a few days to look over Brenda's paperwork disaster.

Chapter Six

Griffin stood in line at the local Fed-Ex store; this was the last package he had to ship. There had been ten when he had finished a few nights before. Each Styrofoam cooler had been packed with dry ice and the frozen merchandise, then packaged and carefully addressed. He then shipped each cooler from a different location around the city over several days. Finally, this was the last one; adios Maria and good riddance. His fondness for her had disappeared in the hours he spent leaning over her bathtub, preparing her for transport. Thank God John would ensure she was properly disposed of in the desert of Arizona. There really was nothing like the brotherhood that war forged. "Finally, I'm next," he thought when the person in front of him approached the counter. He picked up the heavy package, stepped up to have it weighed, and paid the overnight delivery fees. He jotted down the numbers in a small notebook in his shirt pocket. He'd carefully tracked how much it had cost him to dispose of Maria. He was deducting that from the pay he sent her family. It was only fair that they share the financial burden of her disposal.

"It's done; Maria will not be an issue anymore." Griffin walked at a clipped pace down the sidewalk.

"Have you made any progress yet on our bigger issue?"

"I was able to track her driving from New York to Baltimore. She gave her car to a single mom she met at the bus station. I haven't been able to find her trail from there. I know that she didn't take one of the buses and she did not buy an airline ticket. I have a few contacts in Baltimore. Now that the Maria situation is handled, I'm flying there tonight. I'll find her trail."

"She GAVE away her Mercedes? To a single mom she had just met at a bus station?"

"Yes, she signed the title over to her and even gave her money to fill the tank."

"She GAVE away the Mercedes I BOUGHT FOR HER??? She did it to spite me, but we can use this to our advantage. She'll be much easier to find now that she has no transportation." Griffin didn't agree with the jackass. His guess was that the girl was long gone from Baltimore, and he would have a harder time finding her than the last time. She was showing herself surprisingly adept at evading him. The last time, it had been easy to track her and her besotted boyfriend across the country. It had taken him less than three days to find them in Portland, holed up in a small bed and breakfast. The boyfriend had been difficult to handle at first, but he had just blasted him a few times with the Taser, and he'd settled right down for the rest of the trip back to New

York. This time, the girl presented a bit more of a challenge than he had anticipated when he had facilitated her escape, but no matter. However good she got at running, she would never be good enough to outrun him.

"I'm sure you're right." Despite his inward misgivings, he reassured the bastard on the other end of the line. There was no need to get him any more stirred up than he already was, at least not yet. Griffin disconnected the call and immediately started making plans to fly to Baltimore.

Kate smiled as she leaned back in the old desk chair. When she had taken over Ms. Annetta's books three weeks ago, they had been an antiquated mess. Though she was still far from done, she had made good progress at sorting the books. She even started transferring everything into the bookkeeping program she installed on the laptop. Ms. Annetta was still skeptical of the "damned computer and that internets," but slowly, she was coming around. With luck, Kate would even convince her to use the computer to do her bookings and registrations. Kate closed the computer and stretched. It was time for her to head over to Brenda's. If Ms. Annetta's books were challenging, Brenda's were downright daunting. She loved every frustrating minute of figuring it all out.

She remembered the first time she'd seen Brenda's books, three weeks ago. Brenda had brought her to the dining room table and started dumping 30-gallon trash bags of receipts and invoices on it. After she had dumped five or six bags onto the table, she pointed to the stacks of Folgers coffee cans lining the wall. "Those are filled with more. I have no idea what most of these receipts are for, when and where they are from, or anything else. My mom has dementia. I had no idea how bad it had become until Doc Greene called and told me that I needed to consider getting her help. When I came back, I found the business was in ruins. The IRS is sending letters because she didn't file her business taxes for 5 years. I need help, but I need you to understand what you are taking on." Kate's brain refused to comprehend the mountains of chaos before her; she was horrified and yet oddly excited. This would be the Mount Everest of her accounting career.

"Hey, Brenda, it's just me," Kate called out as she entered From Hair Until Eternity. Brenda did not need to stop what she was doing just to greet her.

"Hi Kate, I'm in here doing a cut. I'll be with you in the dining room when I'm done."

"No need to hurry. I've got everything under control."

"Sheriff, I think what she is too polite to say is that I actually get in her way more than I help. You should see Kate once she gets going. I've never seen anyone with a head for numbers like that girl." Oh great, the Sheriff is here, Kate thought. She'd managed to avoid him completely for the last three weeks since their last conversation the night she'd returned to town.

"Hi Kate, long time no see," Tom called back to her.

"Not long enough," Kate mumbled under her breath.

"I heard that, Katie girl. You know you've missed me and my stimulating company." Tom couldn't resist teasing her.

"Don't call me Katie. My name is Kate." Kate ground out through gritted teeth

"You'll always be Katie to me, with our history and all."

"Oh, just shut up." Kate didn't even bother trying to be quiet.

"Tom, what did you do to my girl Kate? Usually, all the girls are melting into puddles at your feet with all your charm. You obviously ticked her off. That girl never has a harsh word to say to anyone."

"It's just our long and twisted history." Tom joked

"You and Kate knew each other before she came to town?" Brenda sensed a juicy bit of gossip coming her way.

"No, we did not. He just likes to irritate me." Kate called back from the office.

"Awe, he's pulling your pigtails. Tom, you ought to know how to flirt with a girl better than that by now." Brenda teased, only slightly disappointed there was not more to the story.

"I guess I'm still a kid at heart." Tom teased right back

Kate tried to ignore the conversation in the other room. She sat at the table and started sorting where she had left off yesterday. Soon, the numbers became all she could see and hear. She was in her zone, her happy place. The minutes ticked by, and Kate was completely unaware.

Tom stood in the doorway of Brenda's dining room. Kate sat surrounded by papers, an adorable pair of glasses perched on her nose, oblivious to everything except the paper she was studying. Yet another side of this mysterious woman, a completely adorable side, he thought. She looked right at home with a laptop computer, calculator, stapler, piles of paperclips, and more colors of post-It notes than he knew existed scattered around her.

"Hey there, Katie-did." The Sheriff's voice startled Kate, making her lose her place on the invoice she was trying to decipher. Miss Betty's handwriting was bad to start with, but once dementia had truly set in, it was pretty much illegible.

"It's Kate, and what can I do for you, Sheriff? Did you forget to ask me something the last time you interrogated me, or are you here to annoy me and interrupt my work?"

"No, I don't have any more questions. I'm still waiting for honest answers to the last ones I asked. I'm just here for my regular haircut. I figured I'd say hi, being the friendly guy I am."

"Well then, 'Hi, Sheriff.'" Kate rolled her eyes and tried to focus on the invoice again.

"Katie, I know I've seen you somewhere before. A man doesn't forget a woman as beautiful as you are. I will remember where." There was a quiet warning in Tom's voice.

"Why, Sheriff, if I didn't know better, I'd think you just complimented me. But I can assure you we've never met. I'm just an ordinary girl trying to make an honest living."

"Katie-did there is not one thing ordinary about you." With that, Tom walked out the door to the street.

"It's Kate; just plain old, ordinary, Kate," Kate called after him.

Brenda came in a few minutes later, rubbing a sweet-smelling lotion onto her dry hands.

"So, what's going on with you and Tom? I've never seen him take a liking to a girl the way he has you."

"Brenda, you are reading him all wrong. He doesn't like me at all; as a matter of fact, I'm pretty sure he dislikes me quite a bit."

"Take it from me, Kate; he may not know it yet, but that man fancies you."

Kate laughed. "I've never heard a person actually use the word fancies in a sentence in real life."

Brenda smiled. "So, what's the bad news?" she asked, tilting her head toward the mountains of paperwork.

"I contacted the IRS and explained the situation with your mom. They have agreed to give us an extension to get the taxes filed for the last five years. After I finish sorting everything, we can start to figure out where we stand. Hey, does this look like a Q or a two?"

"I think it's a 2. Thank God you're here, Kate. All this is Greek to me. I don't know how I would sort all this without you."

"Well, it worked out for both of us because I needed a job. You are a God send, too." Kate smiled as she put her hand on Kate's shoulder. She was starting to really belong in this little town. It was so good to have people in her life who knew at least this version of her.

Griffin looked out over the Inner Harbor in Baltimore. The lights of the buildings reflected off the water's dark surface. He'd been here three weeks and hadn't kicked up a single lead as to her whereabouts. No one had seen her since that day at the bus stop. She hadn't bought a car, plane, train, bus, ticket, or even stayed at a hotel. She'd not used her credit cards or touched her bank account since she left New York. Her cell phone had not been turned on, and she hadn't logged onto her email or Facebook. It was as if she had completely vanished off the face of the earth. He was getting more than a bit irritated now. He was the best at what he did. There was no way some spoiled, rich, crazy princess would slip away from him. His phone rang again; this was the sixth phone call today. He hit ignore and sent it straight to voicemail. He had no news to give the jackass spider in New York, and he really didn't have patience for one of his rants right now. Daily, he felt the web tightening around him. He had to find that crazy bitch soon.

Chapter Seven

Mike ran a hand over his partially balding head and tried to make sense of the gruesome scene before him. In his twenty years as a cop, he had not encountered something like this. He looked at the nine half-buried Styrofoam coolers in front of him. Another cooler had been dug up and chewed on by some animal a little away from the others. Inside each cooler were parts of a woman's body. The place crawled with forensics people documenting and gathering evidence. He had doubts that there was a lot of evidence to gather. As sick and twisted as this was, it was obviously done by an expert. Each body part had been expertly butchered; there was no other word to describe it. This body had been butchered the way one might butcher a pig, each piece cut at the joint with precision. The head had been removed from the body, all the teeth removed, and the fingertips dipped in acid of some kind to remove any prints. Yeah, this was not this psycho's first kill. Mike looked out over the desert and wondered how many other Styrofoam chests were buried, waiting to be discovered.

It was a long, draining day in the desert, draining physically, mentally, and emotionally. All the forensics guys and the other officers in the precinct believed they were up against some freaky psychopath, a Jeffery Dahmer type driven by uncontrollable dark urges and the brain power to see them through without getting caught. Mike couldn't shake the feeling they were dealing with something else entirely. It was all a little too methodical, cold, and emotionless. His gut told him that this woman was dispatched because she had become an inconvenience, an obstacle. Her death had been necessary. There had been no pleasure derived from it, no urge satisfied. No, she had been dealt with as one might a lame horse; her purpose had been served, and there was nothing left but to put her down. Of course, he couldn't prove any of this. Still, his gut was screaming that they were dealing with a very different kind of monster here, a cold, calculating, ruthless killer. It was still early in the game; Dr. Montgomery had just received the body......well, the pieces of the body, and would not start the postmortem for a few days, even with a rush on this case.

Mike was very interested to find out the cause of death. There had been no obvious death-causing injuries. But it had been quite hard to make any real determinations at the crime scene because of the state of the body. Not only was it in pieces, but it was severely decayed, and animals had fed on the head and face. Tomorrow would be the start of a long, frustrating investigation. Mike knew the odds of solving this case were slim at best, but he could not get past how that woman had been thrown away like yesterday's trash. Whoever she was, whatever she'd done, she deserved better than that.

He pulled up to the dark house, it had been four years since his divorce, but he still wasn't used to coming home to darkness, silence, and no one. He'd thought about getting a dog, but it hardly seemed fair to condemn the dog to a life of being alone in the house for only God knew how long. He never knew when he woke up what would happen that day, what time he would get home, hell, if he would even make it home that night. The woman who had loved him and sworn before God and man to never leave him had been unable to take that kind of life. Maybe it would have been different if they'd been able to have kids, but they hadn't. The loneliness eventually drove Melanie into the arms of another man, an IT guy, with a normal 9-5 and four weeks of paid vacation. The last time he had seen her, she was pushing a grocery cart around the local supermarket, glowingly happy, about six months pregnant. Before she could glimpse him, he took his purchases to the register and left the store. It wasn't that he begrudged her happiness, but seeing her like that had only rubbed salt into the wounds of his failure. He unlocked his door, hit the hall light, and headed straight to the shower. He had to wash the smell of the dead off of his body. He turned the hot water full on, scrubbed from head to toe three times, and stood under the steaming water until it ran cold. Mike turned off the water, dried and wrapped the towel around his waist. Living alone meant he could walk around his house any damn way he pleased. He grabbed a beer from the fridge and threw a TV dinner into the microwave. He carried his beer back to his bedroom while his dinner cooked. He threw on his oldest pair of sweatpants and his old college sweatshirt. The fact he could still wear it was a secret source of pride. Other than a little less hair on the top of his head, he was still in really good shape, especially for having turned forty-five last month. The microwave beeped that his food was ready. He made his way back to the kitchen and then to the living room. He put his feet up in the black leather recliner, grabbed the remote, and flipped on ESPN. It was time to veg out and forget the horrors of the day.

Around one am, he awoke in a cold sweat. He'd fallen asleep in the recliner, watching basketball. He dreamed of arms, hands, torsos, legs, feet, and faceless heads spinning like a kaleidoscope around him, blood dripping down and forming shapes as the body parts spun. He kept swatting at the body pieces like you might swat at a fly. But no matter how hard he swatted or how fast he ran, the body parts and blood swirled around him, faster and faster, until he was sucked up into a spiraling tornado of blood and body parts.

Knowing there was no way he was going to be able to fall back to sleep after that dream, Mike threw on his shoes and headed out to his gym. He'd joined as a rookie cop, fresh-faced, with heroic dreams of saving the world. The years had taken their toll, and he no longer dreamed of heroic deeds and commendations. Now his dreams were of retirement and a little fishing cabin up in the mountains of Montana. Seeing so much evil, pain, and senseless death changed something fundamental within his personality. He no longer trusted anyone; everyone was a potential threat until proved otherwise. After a warm-up and some stretches, Mike made his way to the punching bag in the corner. Tonight, he needed to beat on something until he could feel nothing but the sweat stinging his eyes and the complete exhaustion of his muscles.

Griffin hoped to God he'd just gotten an actual lead on the princess bitch, as he'd taken to calling her. He'd been scouring every inch of Baltimore looking for a lead for months. He hated this city now, every blasted foot of it. He'd finally become so desperate he took out an ad in the personal section offering reward money to anyone who could give him information on the whereabouts of a girl matching her description. So far, every single response had been a load of crap. He didn't have much confidence this one would be any different, but he had to follow every lead that came his way. God, he couldn't wait to see New York again.

He pulled up to a rundown trailer in a trailer park in a suburb of Baltimore. He hated trailer parks and the people in them. He'd clawed his way out of one of these hell holes as a kid and swore he'd never set foot in one again, and he hadn't until today; just another thing the New York spider would pay for.

The man who answered the door looked like the embodiment of every white trash stereotype Griffin had ever heard. He had thinning, long, stringy hair, a big beer gut only emphasized by his dirty, stained, used-to-be-white wife beater, and a pair of dirty jeans. He spit a wad of chewing tobacco at Griffin's feet.

"Don't you see the no soliciting sign, you asshole?"

"I'm here because you responded to my ad in the personals about my missing sister." Griffin had to make himself not punch in this guy's face; just the fact this guy was breathing the same air as he was an abomination.

"Your sister, huh? She sure was a hot piece of ass, a hot, scared piece of ass. She paid me extra not to tell anyone anything but seeing how you're her caring "brother" and all, I guess I could be persuaded to tell you what you wanted to know if the price was right." He made a quotation sign with his fingers when he said, Brother. Clearly, the little creep didn't believe his story.

"How do I know you saw my sister and aren't just selling me a lot of crap?" Griffin ignored the idiot's insinuations, instead getting down to the business at hand.

"When she wasn't looking, I took a picture of her. As I said, she's a hot piece of ass, and I've got my own needs." The prick made a fist and jerked his hand up and down a few times. Oh, he was a real class act, Griffin thought ironically. The idiot pulled an old flip phone out of the front pocket of his jeans and pulled up a picture. He flipped the phone around and showed Griffin. There she was. He had his first glimpse of the Princess Bitch he'd had in months.

"I take it from the look on your face that this is your "sister." I think you'd better come in, so we can come to an arrangement."

"I'll stay right here if you don't mind. I'll give you the $500 we agreed on."

"Well, your "sister" paid me a whole lot more for me not to talk to you. I do have standards, you know."

"Let me see the picture again to make sure it is my sister. If it is, I'll give you $1000." He didn't need to see the picture again, it was definitely her, but this guy was a real ass. Griffin wished he'd worn a pair of latex gloves as he reached out and grabbed the phone. God only knew what kinds of bacteria and germs were on it; hand sanitizer would never be enough. He deleted the picture. The prick would have to find something else to jerk off to. He snapped shut the flip phone and handed it back. He resisted the urge to wipe his hands on his pants.

"Yeah, it's her. I'll give you a thousand, and that's my final offer. I suggest you take it."

He looked like he would argue, but one look at Griffin changed his mind. "Alright, fine. Give me the money, and I'll tell you what I know."

Griffin reached into the inside pocket of his jacket and handed over the cash he'd put into an envelope before he'd left his hotel room. He had done this long enough to know the information would cost him double what he had offered in the ad.

"She stopped here, I guess, about three or four months ago. She walked straight up to my door and asked if I would sell the 1989 Honda Civic I had sitting in the driveway. She offered me $10,000 cash. Hell, the car wasn't even worth a grand. I'd 've been a fool not to take it. The only conditions she gave were that she could keep the registration in my name and that I would keep quiet on having seen her."

"So, did she tell you where she was headed?"

"No, nothing like that."

"You just let some strange woman drive off with a car still in your name without any questions?"

"A woman that looked like her, with that kind of money, hell yeah, I let her take the car!"

"What does the car look like? What's the plate number?"

"It's a red Honda Civic hatchback. I've got the plate number inside somewhere; I'll run in and get it."

Once he had the information he needed and was back on the road, Griffin pulled out his cell phone and placed the call; finally, he had some good news to report to the spider.

"I've found her; at least, I've found the way to find her."

"It's about time. People are beginning to ask questions. Get her here ASAP. Do I need to remind you of the consequences if you don't?"

"Don't worry; I know what's at stake for BOTH of us." With that, Griffin hung up. Now all he had to do was find the car, and he'd find the girl. At last, Miss Carina Wythcliff was his for the finding! He had to give her credit; she had given him a run for his money. She obviously had learned from her mistakes the last time she ran away. Unfortunately for her, though she was good at hiding, he was a hell of a lot better at finding. Let the games begin for real, Griffin thought.

Chapter Eight

With this case, Mike felt like he was beating his head against a brick wall. They had not come up with a single clue as to the identity of the woman or the killer. There were no fingerprints outside or inside the coolers, the victim's fingerprints had been burned off with acid, and there were no teeth to identify dental records. The medical examiner had determined that the victim had been a woman in her mid-forties to early fifties. She was probably Hispanic and had delivered children. The cause of death was strangulation with a wire of some kind. That was all they had to go on.

The press had been tipped off to the story and ran front-page stories all week, dubbing the killer The Phoenix Butcher. The public was demanding answers; the commissioner had held a press conference to reassure the public and to ask for their help. A tip line had been opened for people to call if they had information. Now the phones rang off the hook with all sorts of crackpots calling in. Every third caller seemed to be a psychic who had received a message from the universe or the victim. Little old ladies called freaking out because they heard something outside their bedroom windows, it always turned out to be a dog or cat, but every call had to be followed up on. Dealing with the public had never been Mike's favorite thing. Now, he seriously considered breaking his arm just to take a leave of absence and avoid all this craziness. Between the ever-helpful public, brass breathing down their necks, and the hounding of the press, there was hardly time in the day to get any real police work done. This morning there was finally a tip that Mike thought might pay off. If nothing else, it would get him out of the precinct and away from always ringing phones. One more day of that damned ringing, and he would need to be committed.

Mike pulled up to a rundown gas station on the edge of the desert. There were two old-school pumps in front, the type that didn't take credit cards. He hadn't seen those since he was in college. As he entered the shop, the bell above the door jingled, it reminded him of those damn ringing phones, and he wanted to tear it off the door. Behind the counter was a young kid, probably in his late teens or early twenties, with an attempt to grow a beard on his face, those big gauge things in his ears, and wearing an Iron Maiden tee-shirt. God help the kid when he went to get a real job after college, and he had to take those things out of his ears. Didn't he know he would be walking around looking stupid with big holes in his earlobes and them hitting his shoulders? Oh, the foolishness of youth.

"Hi, I'm Detective Mike Choctowsky. We received a call saying you had a tip regarding the woman we found in the desert."

"Yeah, I called."

"What's your name?" Mike took out a notebook to write down the information.

"My name is Tyler Reston."

"Alright, Tyler, can you tell me why you called?"

"I remembered a few months ago, this guy stopped in here three or four days in the same week. He would get gas and head out to the desert, then stop back about two hours later, dripping sweat and loaded up on ice and water bottles. It struck me as odd because I noticed in his earlier stops he always had several coolers in the back of his truck, but he would come back without them."

Mike could feel himself getting excited, finally a real break in the case.

"Do you have any camera's here? Do you have any security footage?"

"We have a couple of cameras, but they are ancient and record to a videotape. My boss records over them every few days. I keep telling him we need to upgrade them into the 21st century; you know, get some wireless ones that back the footage up to a hard drive. But he hasn't wanted to spend the money, the old tightwad."

Mike tried not to show his disappointment. "Would you be able to describe the guy who came in here to a forensic artist?"

"Yeah, sure, he wasn't real memorable; kind of an average guy, in his late twenties, maybe thirties. I'm no good at guessing ages."

"What color were his hair and eyes?"

"His hair was short and dark. I don't know what color his eyes were. He was always wearing sunglasses. One time he came back from the desert in a sleeveless workout shirt. I noticed he had one of those Marine tattoos on his left arm, the one with the eagle, a globe, and an anchor. It said Semper Fidelis. I asked him about it because my stepdad has the same tattoo, so I told him about my stepdad being a Marine. He said he got it back in the day before he shipped out to Afghanistan. Anyway, he didn't talk too much about it."

"Can you describe his truck?"

"Sure, it was a newer model Ford F150, I think. It was blue. I didn't really look at it too closely. The only odd thing was the coolers, like I already told you."

"Thank you, Tyler. You have been a real help. I will need you to come down to headquarters and work with our forensic artist to come up with a sketch of the man you saw."

"Sure, no problem. So, is there a reward for helping catch the guy?"

Mike had to stop himself from rolling his eyes. No one did things to be a good citizen anymore. They always wanted something in return. "You mean besides the warm fuzzy feeling you'll get from doing the right thing? When you come in for the sketch, you will have to talk to someone in our tip department about that. That's not my department." Mike knew there was no reward money, but there was no need to take away the kid's motivation for cooperating.

Mike made his way back to the station with renewed vigor. It was about time they had some movement in this case. It may not be much, but even the smallest tip could sometimes blow a case wide open.

Griffin smiled, finally some progress. Having his contact in the Maryland Department of Motor Vehicles track Corrine's car through traffic cameras had been simple. She was driving in a wandering path, probably to throw him off her trail. It was kind of cute, actually. She'd

driven south to Richmond, VA. He lost her trail again
when she suddenly started driving northwest. His best
guess was that she had headed to Chicago. He would
make better progress once he got his feet on the ground
in the Windy City. Besides, it would be good to finally
leave Baltimore. He booked his flight for the next
morning and began to pack. He almost didn't pick up
his phone when it began to ring. The New York spider
was driving him crazy with his constant phone calls and
threats. He picked up the phone to send it to voicemail
when he noticed it was an Arizona number. Why the
hell would John be calling him? He knew they were on
strict radio silence.

"Hello."

"Hey, Griffin, we've got to talk. We've got a problem,
buddy."

"John, I hope you were smart enough not to use your
phone when you called me."

"I'm not an idiot, Griffin. It's a burner cell."

"Good, so what's this problem?"

"The cops found her out in the desert."

"What the hell do you mean they found her?"

"They found her. The best I can tell, some coyote dug up one of the coolers and started gnawing on the head. A group of extreme sports hikers found it and called the cops. Who the hell goes to the desert for a stroll? They've found all the coolers, too, if the news is to be believed."

"Not only have the cops found her, but now the news people are reporting it??"

"Yeah, they're even calling you The Phoenix Butcher."

"What a colossal screw-up! I told you not to bury those coolers anywhere where they would be found. I'm the best because nobody ever finds the bodies. People pay me the big bucks because I'm discreet."

"There's something else."

"Damn it all, John! What else could there be?"

"They got a sketch out of a guy that looks an awful lot like me. I don't know who they talked to because I sure as hell didn't talk to anybody."

"They have a sketch of you??? Are you sure?"

"It's just a sketch, but it looks enough like me that I recognized it. I saw it on the news tonight."

Griffin was furious. How could John be such a fucking idiot? Now he was going to have to clean up his mess. Good help was impossible to find these days.

"John, don't do anything stupid. I'll find a way to fix this."

"I knew you would, Griffin."

Griffin hung up the phone and immediately called to change his tickets. Chicago would wait. Phoenix could not. He had hoped it would never come to this; John was his only friend left from the old days. But he'd become a liability. Griffin had always lived by one very simple code "Don't get caught." Everything else: friendships, money, housing, everything else was secondary to that very simple rule.

Chapter Nine

The next few months went by in a flurry of activity. Kate was always working at either Brenda's or the motel. She loved being useful again. She was rediscovering her independence, her strength, and herself in many ways. Each day, she grew more comfortable, feeling safer in the little town than she'd felt in years. Ms. Annetta had insisted on teaching her how to shoot a gun. She said you could never be too safe in the motel business. She had shown her where she kept the shotgun and told her not to hesitate to shoot if she was scared. She'd then given Kate a .38 special snub-nosed for personal protection and made her practice with it daily. She told Kate to always keep it on her. Kate knew it was illegal to carry a concealed handgun without a license, but it made her feel a lot better knowing it was in her purse should she need it. It made Kate laugh to think about what her New York friends would think about her now, living in Texas, carrying a gun, and not having had a manicure in forever. Not to mention she had always been anti-gun. Ha! What a difference a psychopath or two could make!

Sheriff Tom had even stopped treating her like she was a criminal, most of the time. She still saw shadows of doubt in his eyes, but he seemed willing to give her a chance to prove herself. For the most part, she avoided him unless there was no way to get around seeing him. He'd even asked her out to dinner to be friendly, but

Kate was uncomfortable with him, and her heart still grieved for the man murdered because of her. Somehow, even talking to the Sheriff seemed to betray his memory. She stretched out on her bed and gave a satisfied smile. Ms. Annetta had told her she could do what she wanted to the room. After a month or so of living at the motel, she could no longer tolerate the peach and mauve. She felt like she'd been locked in a pastel-colored hell. She'd taken her clunker over to the Walmart in Abilene and bought a new comforter set and curtains. They weren't the silk or high-quality Egyptian cotton she had lived with all her life, but they were hers, bought with her own money. The curtains were a slate blue. The bedspread was cream with slate blue flowers and brown vines embroidered along the bottom and sides. It came with pillowcases that had the same detailing. Kate had thought they were beautiful and feminine in an understated way and very sophisticated. She'd even bought a few throw pillows and a soft plush throw blanket that was pewter colored. She threw it over the back of the Queen Anne-style chair in the motel room. She loved to sit at night wrapped up in her throw blanket, her feet tucked under her as she watched TV. She'd never had the time or inclination to watch television in New York. But in Cutler's Gap, life moved at a slower pace, and she was a different person. She enjoyed her solitude; she enjoyed having shows to look forward to during the week. Ms. Annetta would come to hang out with her on Thursday nights to watch Ghosts and Law and Order. Brenda and Lucy had started joining them. It was great to have a girl's night, laughing, drinking wine, and eating chocolate. It was cheap wine and chocolate, but the friendships she was slowly developing were priceless. Kate had never had a group of women friends like this. Back in New York, all her friendships had been shallow relationships cultivated for their business contacts or for her brother. His endless power plays drove her crazy, but he was her only family, so she tolerated it. They had their share of trauma, and he'd tried his best to care for her while she was little. God, what had happened to them? Kate decided instead of her normal microwaved TV dinner, she would make her way over to Uncle Joe's. It was almost a sure bet she'd run into Sheriff Tom, but she couldn't stay cooped up tonight.

The bell rang as she stepped into the diner. Damn, the stupid bells in this town. Every time she heard one ring, she was reminded of the other bells, the terrifying bells. God, what was with her tonight; she just wanted to forget all the blackness of the past. It had been months, and he still hadn't come for her. Maybe this time he would just let her go, she thought hopefully, as she made her way to her favorite table in the corner. It would never happen, but a girl could wish.

It wasn't very crowded tonight. There was no sign of the sheriff, which oddly gave Kate a moment of disappointment. She was coming to enjoy his obnoxious company in small doses. Charlie Benet was sitting at the table across from Kate. He looked up and smiled at her.

"Howdy Kate, long time no see. I hear Ms. Annetta and Brenda are keeping you busy."

Kate had only spoken briefly with Charlie a couple of times over the past few months, but she liked the older man. There was something about him that spoke of deep and lonely sadness. On impulse, Kate said, "Hey do you want some company for dinner? It seems we're both here by ourselves."

"I'd be a fool to turn down dinner with a pretty girl. I may be many things, but a fool isn't one of them."

Kate smiled and slid into the booth across from him.

"So, I hear you are some kind of numbers genius. Ms. Annetta and Brenda are always bragging on how smart you are."

"I'm not all that smart. I just know how to use a computer and don't keep track of my receipts in a coffee can." Kate laughed.

Charlie chuckled along with her for a moment. "Do you have some special fella out there?"

Kate gave him a sad smile. "I used to."

"Well, what's wrong with him, leaving a pretty girl like you by yourself?"

"He died a year ago." Tears welled up in Kate's eyes. She hadn't spoken of Eric to anyone; she had no idea why she was telling Charlie about him. There was something about Charlie that told her he would understand her grief.

Charlie put his hand over hers. "I'm so sorry. There is nothing worse than losing someone you love."

"Hey, Charlie, are you trying to steal my girl before I get the chance to take her away." Tom joked as he walked over to their table.

"Absolutely, it's not my fault if you young'uns don't have the good sense God gave a mule and move slower than molasses when it comes to pretty girls." Charlie joked back.

"I am not your girl Sheriff."

"Oh, Katie-did, I think you protest a little too much." The Sheriff winked.

"Well, Sheriff, it looks like the lady prefers my company to yours. "Charlie noticed how tense Kate had become once Tom had started toward them.

"I can't hang around anyway. I have a bunch of paperwork to catch up on. I have these two old pains in my ass that keep calling me out to their farms for no good reason."

"We have to keep you busy, Sheriff. We wouldn't want you to get bored. Besides, there's always a good reason. Doug is a mean old coot and should have been arrested years ago for how he treated Ella."

"You know that I wasn't even born when the blood between the two of you went bad. Give me a break; try to make peace before one of you really ends up hurt. I like you, Charlie. But this feud between you and Doug is about to drive me crazy. One or the other of you has called me out to your farm three times just this week!

"You're young. You need to stay fresh and on your toes. But I'll try to behave for a while until you catch up on your paperwork." Charlie winked at Kate and gave the Sheriff a mischievous smile.

Kate stifled a laugh and gave Charlie a big smile. "No fair, you never smile at me like that. I'm adorable; ask anyone in town. They'll tell you." Tom said jokingly.

"I guess I prefer mischievous to adorable," Kate said wryly.

Tom tipped his hat and went to the counter to pick up his order. He gave her one of his trademark boyish grins as he left. He really was a good-looking man. If Kate had met him before, she would have been tempted. But Eric had changed her forever. There was just no room left for anyone else.

Kate had a great time with Charlie. He made her laugh and seemed to understand a bit of her that no one else could. Over dessert, Charlie put his hand over hers.

"Kate, my girl, I want to give you a piece of advice that I learned the hard way. Don't shut your heart off from love. I did when my Ella married Doug. I never moved on or allowed myself to love again, and now I have nothing to show for my life. I have no wife, children, or grandkids; I am alone because I was too afraid to allow anyone else into my heart. I was a coward. You don't have to make my mistakes. Be brave, Kate; open your heart up to love. Don't take the coward's way out and end up like me." Charlie looked so forlorn that Kate couldn't bring herself to brush his advice aside.

"Charlie, I don't know if I can. I don't, but I will consider what you said. I promise." Kate squeezed his hand and brushed away a tear that escaped her eye.

"Now there's a good girl. Finish up your pie, you're too skinny, and Miss Doris makes the best pie I've ever eaten."

Kate laughed. "She sure does. I would never waste a slice of her pie." Kate took a big forkful of chocolate mousse pie to prove her point. Charlie laughed as he dug into his own slice of coconut cream.

Charlie insisted on buying her dinner and walked her back to the motel. Kate wasn't used to this southern way of doing things; back in New York, she always split the check with her date. That way, no one had any expectations. She always had caught a cab outside the restaurant. It was so impersonal, she thought as she looked back now. Eric had been the only exception. He had always treated her like she was the most precious woman on earth.

Kate was glad she had gone to the diner for dinner. She and Charlie had arranged to have dinner again next week. She'd never had a grandfather in her life; Charlie is what she imagined her grandfather would have been like had she gotten to know him. He had spent the night making her laugh with stories of his antics through the years. He'd even slipped some grandfatherly advice in toward the end of their dinner. Smiling, she flipped on the cable news channel while she got ready for bed. She half listened as they reported on the murder of a woman in Arizona. Why did people do such evil things to each other? They put a sketch of a person of interest on the screen. He was so normal looking, but that didn't really surprise Kate. She knew firsthand that monsters very rarely looked like monsters. Many times, monsters were even beautiful. Beautiful monsters were the scariest because people instinctively liked and trusted them. Kate shook her head to clear her thoughts. She shouldn't have turned on the news. It had taken the shine off her fun night. She snuggled into her chair with her blanket and flipped through the channels until she came to a Golden Girls re-run. Their shenanigans always made her laugh and forget her problems for a while.

Chapter Ten

Griffin stepped off the plane to the bright Phoenix sunshine. He'd planned to never set foot in this state; he liked to keep as much distance as possible between himself and the waste byproducts created by his job. Griffin didn't like things messy; he was more than a bit obsessive-compulsive about germs, dirt, and keeping things organized. A psychologist would probably say he had to maintain strict control over his environment because he'd been raised in filth and chaos as a child. He couldn't care less what they thought. He knew that keeping his life neat, organized, and compartmentalized made him thorough and good at his job. John was mixing the compartments of his life and making things messy. Griffin couldn't have that. He hadn't brought any luggage, so it only took a few minutes for him to grab a cab and head out.

A cautious man plans for the worst while hoping for the best; Griffin prided himself on being a cautious man. He had been renting a storage unit a few miles from the airport. The storage facility was next to a strip mall. He had the cab drop him at the mall and ate lunch. After waiting thirty minutes and ensuring he would not be seen, he walked to the storage facility. Inside the storage unit was a car he'd registered under one of his aliases, money, a fully outfitted tool kit, and several changes of clothes. He reached into his wallet for the up-to-date registration sticker he'd brought. The little details got you caught, so he ensured all the details were attended to. He had made sure to maintain insurance and registration on all his secreted vehicles; he had several emergency shelters like this around the country. One could never be too careful. He put his tool kit in the car's trunk, double-checked that his return flight was running on time, and called John. He was using his New York burner cell. John would have no idea he was in town. He just needed to ensure John stayed put as he'd instructed.

"Hey John, it's me."

"Oh, thank God."

"I've been working on our little problem. I just want to make sure you are alright."

"Yeah, I'm fine. I'm staying put for now."

"Good, make sure you keep your curtains drawn. We wouldn't want any nosey neighbors getting any ideas."

"Yeah, I have the curtains drawn."

"Good. I'll talk to you again once I've ironed out a few details."

"Thanks, Griffin. I've always been able to count on you."

"No problem, buddy. You'd do the same for me."

Griffin hung up the phone and waited until dark. He parked four streets away from John's house, grabbed his duffle bag of tools, and made his way casually to his destination. He debated going to John's back door but figured that would be more noticeable than just knocking on his front door. He didn't want any suspicious neighbors calling the police.

He rang the front doorbell and heard some shuffling on the other side of the door. After a minute, he heard the deadbolt turn, and John opened the door.

"Wow, I totally didn't expect to see you here. You gave me a scare when you rang the bell. C'mon in, buddy. It's good to see you."

Griffin patted John on the back and went straight to the living room. He hated that John had become a liability; for years, he'd been the closest thing Griffin had to a friend. The mess John had made of this last job left Griffin no choice, but he deserved a painless death. Griffin pulled a bottle of Jamison's out of his duffle bag. He held it up and gave John a wry smile.

"I figured the best way to figure all this out was over some whiskey, just like the old days. Do you have any glasses?"

John laughed. "You bet. They're in the kitchen. You know, I can still drink your sorry ass under the table."

"Big boasts do not a drinker make. Go get those shot glasses. We've got some drinking and talking to do."

John returned with glasses, and Griffin poured them each two fingers of whiskey. After a few shots, Griffin began to slip phenobarbital that he'd ground to a powder into John's drinks. It didn't take too long before the deed was done. Griffin snapped on a pair of latex gloves; all left was to stage the scene. Griffin went to John's computer and typed a confession and suicide note. He wrapped John's fingers around the whiskey and prescription bottles and placed both bottles on the side table next to John, along with the suicide note. He'd wiped down all the surfaces he may have touched before putting on the gloves, washed and put away his shot glass, and placed his tool kit, which he'd thoroughly wiped free of prints, in John's garage. Then he slipped out the back door, returned to his car, and returned to his emergency shelter. He'd have to get a new tool kit for this location, but that would have to wait. He returned to the mall and called a cab to bring him back to the airport. He had a plane to catch.

Mike rubbed his temples; the incessant ringing of the tip lines had only quadrupled over the last week since the sketch of their suspect was released. Every crackpot, nosey neighbor, pissed-off co-worker, and bored housewife from Phoenix to Tucson had called at least twice. Forget breaking his own arm; Mike would gladly chew off all his limbs if it meant not having to talk to one more crazy person that swore the lady in the desert had been abducted by a big pharmaceutical company for drug trials or by the government for weapons testing or by alien robots that looked just like the sketch of their suspect. One lady had called in, swearing that the sketch was of her husband. When Mike had gone to interview her, he'd seen a picture of a young military guy who looked like their suspect. When he asked if the picture was of her husband, she said it was. Finally, a real lead, Mike had thought, until she'd called her husband to come in from the den. She wanted Mike to arrest him right away. The man who wheeled himself into the room was fifty years old if he were a day, weighed around 350 pounds, and was missing his left leg. He may have looked like their suspect twenty-five years ago, but he certainly didn't look like him now. Today he was chasing down what promised to be another false lead, the three hundred and forty-fifth false lead called in that week if anyone was keeping track. Yup, he'd gladly chew off all his limbs if it would get him out of this. But his captain was a sadistic S.O.B. who would probably just give him a motorized hospital bed and send him back out to talk to more nut jobs.

Mike pulled into the parking lot of a small software company. The secretary had called claiming that one of their employees hadn't been in to work in a week, and she realized last night that he kind of resembled the suspect in the sketch. Mike didn't put much stock in this lead, but at least she wasn't claiming it was her middle-aged, amputee husband.

Mike walked into a confusing maze of glass-walled cubicles, big open spaces in the middle of the room with sofas, TVs, and game consoles. It looked like there may have even been a basketball court at the back of the big warehouse space. Did these people work here or have play dates? Mike looked for a receptionist desk, counter, or even a desk plate that said "receptionist." How in God's name were you supposed to find anyone here? Suddenly he heard his name being called.

"Hey Mike, over here.... over here Mike." Mike looked around to figure out who was calling him. When he found the person standing and waving to him, he wished he could pretend he hadn't heard him. It was IT Larry, the man Melanie had left him for. Of all the software companies in Phoenix, he would be sent to the company that employed his wife's...ex-wife's new husband. The man who had given her everything, including the child, that he hadn't been able to give her. The old Choctowsky luck at work again.

As Mike made his way to Larry's cubicle, he put a smile on his face. "Smile, don't punch him. Smile, don't punch him," Mike repeated the mantra over and over in his head.

"Hey, Larry, I didn't know you worked here."

"Yup, I've been here about five years. What brings you to my neck of the woods?"

"Oh, I'm following up on a tip we received. You wouldn't happen to know where I could find Christy, or was it Chrissy? She said she was an office assistant?"

"Do you mean Christa or Kristin? They both work as office assistants."

"Her last name was Starling."

"You want Christy. She's the Office Manager." Mike mentally shook his head. Keeping all the Chris, Christy, and Christins straight around here must be fun. If he were a betting man, he'd lay odds they were all born in the late 70s. He was pretty sure there had been a girl name shortage around that time, and 70% of the baby girls were named something that started with Chris.

Larry led him to a glass-walled office in the front corner of the building. "This is her office. It was good seeing you, buddy." With that, Larry left him and went back to his cubicle. Mike gritted his teeth. The man who slept with and then married his wife was most definitely not his buddy.

Mike knocked on the door before he walked in. Behind a large, ultra-modern, glass and black desk sat a woman who was just as polished and sophisticated as her desk. She stood and extended a delicate hand. "Hello, I'm Christy Starling. How can I help you?" Christy was a tall, slender woman with dark brown hair put up in a twist on her head. She wore a white button-down blouse, unbuttoned at the neck, hipster glasses, and a dark business skirt.

"Hi, I'm Detective Mike Choctowsky. I'm here to follow up on your call to our tip line regarding an employee here."

"Oh yes, like I told the person on the tip line, I'm not sure that John Phillips is the man in the sketch, but I realized last night that he did resemble it a lot. That and his being AWOL this past week led me to make the call. We've tried calling his home phone, cell and emailing and texting him. We haven't had a single response. It's like he's disappeared completely."

"What can you tell me about John?"

"Not much. He's only worked here for about six months. He's a programmer; he works on our web-based applications. I didn't interact with him much besides the initial paperwork when he was hired. Chad Dobkins sits in the cubicle next to his. He may be able to tell you more."

"Could I see his workspace?"

"Absolutely. I'm sorry I couldn't be more help."

"Ms. Starling, you have been a big help. Thank you."

Christy Starling led him through the workspace, her high heels clicking on the polished concrete floor as she walked. She wasn't as tall as he'd originally thought; she wore high, red-soled heels. A person should have to have a permit to wear those things. They looked lethal. She led him to a cubicle near the far-left wall.

"This is where John works. Feel free to look around. I consulted our legal department before I called your tip line. They said we were perfectly within our rights as a company to allow you access to John's workspace. If you don't mind, I'll leave you to your search. I have a meeting to get to."

"Thank you for all your help, Ms. Starling." She smiled, shook his hand, turned, and clicked her way back across the room. God, what an amazing, efficient woman. Why couldn't everyone he interviewed be like her?

Mike turned his attention to the cubicle. He started sifting around some paperwork before he noticed a picture frame sitting on the back corner of the desk. It was a picture of a young man with short brown hair fishing on a pier; he had an open fishing box and a beer sitting next to him while he smiled widely at the camera. Mike felt a chill run down his spine. The man in the picture was wearing a sleeveless shirt, and tattooed on his left arm was the official seal of the Marines. They had not released that detail to the press. Mike's gut told him that he was looking at the face of his prime suspect.

The cubicle next to John's had been empty, but a little mole-like man was sitting in it now. He had a steaming Styrofoam cup with the paper tab of a tea bag hanging over the side. Mike smelled clove or cinnamon or something like that. He must be drinking one of those herbal teas that Mike's sister loved so much.

"Detective Mike Choctowsky, Phoenix PD, would you mind if I asked you a few questions about your co-worker, John Phillips."

"Chad Dobkins, good to meet you. I'll tell you what I can, but quite honestly, we didn't talk all that much. He's only worked here a short time and kept mostly to himself."

"Can you tell me if he had any family in the area, a wife or girlfriend maybe?"

"I don't think so, but we didn't talk much like I said. The only person he ever mentioned was an old Marine Buddy. He took off a few days a couple months back. He said he was helping an old Marine buddy with a project."

"Did he mention this buddy's name?"

"No, honestly, we just talked about work stuff. We didn't have anything in common. I asked him to go for drinks after work a few times, but every time he said he had plans. Quite honestly, I was relieved. I'd much rather hang out with my girlfriend than some ex-military type who talked about fishing." Chad spat the word fishing out like an epitaph. Mike shook his head internally. How did a guy like Chad Dobkins, with his round head, beady eyes, thick glasses, and nasally voice, have a girlfriend? He hadn't had a date since he took that girl Gina out six months ago. He'd met her at the gym. They'd had exactly two dates, and he hadn't even gotten lucky.

"Can you remember anything else that stuck out to you?"

"Not really, he annoyed me. He kept throwing paper away instead of recycling it and drove this big, blue truck. Do you know how bad those are for the environment; I mean, why not just suck on an exhaust pipe and call it quits?"

Mike had a chill go up his spine; John was a Marine with a blue truck. This could be their guy.

"Here's my card. If you remember anything else, please give me a call. Thanks for all your help Chad."

Chapter Eleven

John lived in a Spanish-style bungalow in a middle-class neighborhood outside of Phoenix. Everything about John Phillips was average. The only thing that stood out about him was that he was average in every way. Mike made his way to the porch, and he noticed that mail was sticking out of the over-full mailbox. He rang the bell, waited a minute, and rang it again. He knocked and called, "Mr. Phillips, It's Mike Choctowsky with Phoenix PD. Your co-workers were concerned for you and asked that we check on you." There was still no answer.

Mike made his way to the backyard. There, parked under a carport, was a newer model, blue Ford F150. Mike's adrenaline kicked into overdrive. His gut was screaming that this was their guy. Mike pulled out his phone and placed a call to his captain.

"Hey, Captain, I think this may be our guy. He may have already flown the coop, though. He has at least a week's worth of mail piled up, all the lights are off, and his truck is still parked in his carport."

"I'll call a judge and get a search warrant now. Do not make a move until backup and that warrant arrive." Captain Kirkland's voice was emphatic.

"I'll wait."

"I'm serious, Mike. This must be by the book. Don't go pulling any of that rogue hero cop crap."

"I'm not a rookie. I'll wait for the warrant before I go in." Mike was a bit irritated that he still had to prove himself.

"You better." Captain Kirkland hung up without another word. Mike decided to spend his time poking around the outside of the property while waiting for the warrant. His least favorite thing in the world was waiting.

Griffin stepped onto the curb outside Chicago's O'Hare airport and hailed a cab. It was good to be in a real city again. He had a lot of contacts here. Whatever rock Carina Wythcliff had crawled under, he'd find her. First things first, he was going to check into The Waldorf Astoria and then call Elaine. She ran the most exclusive, discreet escort service in the city. Tonight was his night to relax; a luxurious hotel room, a five-star restaurant, and a highly skilled whore were just what the doctor ordered.

Griffin stood under the hot, pounding pulse of the shower. God, it had been a crazy couple of months. If he'd known helping that spoiled, rich bitch escape would mean he would be stuck traipsing all over the country after her, he'd have just let her rot in that dark little room. No, she was not going to ruin tonight for him. Tonight was his night off. Carina and that obsessed bastard in New York could go screw themselves.

Griffin wore his silk robe while waiting for the hotel to return his pressed suit to his room. He looked in the mirror and smiled. He'd been described as angelically beautiful his whole life, not handsome but beautiful. He had curly blond hair, golden skin, piercing blue eyes, and classic features. His angelic looks had been a curse when he was growing up, alone and unprotected in the filth and rubbish of a backwoods trailer park in Georgia. His mom had left him with his alcoholic father, who had only paid him any attention when he was shit-faced and beating Griffin with anything that happened to be handy. More than one "protector" volunteered to keep him safe for just the pleasure of his young body. He'd been ashamed, disgusted, terrified, and eight years old the first time, but he'd learned that being a victim didn't suit him. By the time he was ten, he'd learned to turn his weakness into his strength. No longer would he be prey for smelly, beer-bellied, sleaze-ball rednecks. No, he was the hunter, using his looks as the bait; he would lure more distinguished, important sleaze-balls into his web. He would lure them in and use their own lust against them. Then they paid and paid until he'd earned enough to escape the hell hole he'd been born into. By the time he was sixteen, he was on his own, headed for New York. At eighteen, he joined the Marines, and they honed his hunting skills. His angelic looks were now the perfect camouflage, hiding the master hunter he'd become. His suit arrived at seven o'clock, just as he'd requested. He'd made reservations at TRU for 8 o'clock, and it wouldn't do to be late.

She arrived promptly at 8:15, just as he'd requested. She stood at his table, not saying a word, while he inspected her. He always thoroughly inspected any purchase he was about to make. He motioned for her to turn around by rotating his finger. She did as he instructed without question.

"You'll do." He motioned for her to sit in the chair across from him.

She smiled and tossed her long black hair over her shoulder. "Hi, I'm...."

"I don't care what your name is," He interrupted. "Please order whatever you like. I have quite the night planned for us. You're going to need your energy." He smiled a cold, emotionless smile. They dined in silence, just the way he liked it. He had never understood why people insisted on ruining a good meal by babbling through it. It was only when you were doubled over in pain because of your hunger pangs and when you grew so weak from hunger that standing up took a concerted effort and all your concentration that you truly learned to appreciate the eating experience. Once they had finished their dessert and were in the cab headed back to the hotel, he laid out the ground rules.

"Tonight, you are my property. You were bought, at quite a price, I might add, to perform certain services. I am not looking for anything else. You will not speak to me, and I will not speak to you other than to instruct you. You are in the business of sex, and tonight I want sex. I don't do safe words. Nod your head if we have an understanding; if not, get out of my damn car." The girl looked a bit confused but nodded. She then turned her head and watched the city lights fly by the cab's window, lost in her own thoughts. Griffin smiled quietly to himself. Nothing pleased him more than a plan flawlessly executed, except plenty of money.

Chapter Twelve

Kate took off her glasses and rubbed the back of her neck. She'd been working twelve-hour days trying to get Brenda's taxes sorted out. The IRS had extended the deadline, but the further she got into the books, the more of a mess they became. Tonight, she was going to knock off early. Friday nights, she had dinner with Ms. Annetta and Tom. They had never made a production of setting up an official weekly dinner date. Since her first Friday in town, they continued to arrive at the diner every Friday night and sit at their table. It was just another of the no-muss, no-fuss things she loved about her new life. Her old life had been so formal, stiflingly so. For the first time since she arrived, Kate almost skipped going to Friday dinner. She was bone weary. All she wanted to do was curl up with a pint of Death by Chocolate ice cream, a bag of pretzels, and a Lifetime movie. Maybe she would duck out of dinner early, but she wouldn't skip it. The Sheriff was beginning to trust her. It wouldn't do to start changing the status quo now.

Joe's was swamped, as it always was on Fridays. Kate couldn't believe she'd come to love chicken fried steak and collard greens; the champagne and caviar girl she'd been had completely disappeared over the last several months. The Sheriff was already at their corner table, but Ms. Annetta hadn't yet arrived. Kate made her way to the table.

"Howdy, Sheriff."

Tom laughed. "When did you start saying 'Howdy'? You're more the 'How do you do' type."

Kate smiled. "You know what they say, "when in Rome.... besides, you have no idea what type I am."

"A thoroughbred doesn't become a field horse just because it gets tied to a plow. You are most definitely a thoroughbred, Katie-Did. That is written in everything about you, down to the way you walk."

Kate shifted in her seat uncomfortably. Tom played the part of the affable, small-town Sherriff well enough, but he noticed everything. If you took the time to look past the boyish good looks and awe-shucks attitude, you noticed the laser-like focus and determination in his steely grey eyes. And why was she noticing his eyes anyway? She huffed aloud before she caught herself.

"Where's Ms. Annetta?" She quickly changed the subject.

"She sends her regrets. She said she was tired and was going to bed early tonight." Kate again shifted in her seat and sighed slightly. "What, you aren't scared to have dinner with me alone, are you, Katie? I promise not to bite unless you ask real nice."

Kate rolled her eyes. "You don't scare me, Sheriff; annoy me, yes, but scare me, no way."

Tom grimaced. "Just what every guy wants to hear. "You don't make me nervous. You just annoy me."

"You know what they say, "if the shoe fits," and all that jazz," Kate smirked.

"I have an idea; why don't we have a real conversation instead of exchanging quips and insults? You do know what a conversation is, Katie, don't you?"

Kate rolled her eyes. "Why no, I don't, Sheriff. Why don't you educate me, the brainless, useless female that I am?" Kate's voice dripped with sarcasm.

"Alright, if you insist. In a conversation, I ask you a question about yourself, and you answer it. Then you ask me a question about myself, and then I answer. We continue in this way until we finish our meal. Hopefully, by the end of dinner, we will both have been entertained and know each other just a bit more. What do you say, shall we give it a try Katie-Did?"

"Fine, we'll conversate on one condition; you stop calling me Katie-Did. My name is Kate."

"Okay, *Kate*, first question; what do you like to do when you aren't taking over Cutler's Gap, one accounting gig at a time?"

Kate breathed an inward sigh of relief. If he stuck to questions like this, dinner could be fun. "Hmmm, let me think.... My favorite way to relax is to take a steaming hot bubble bath. My secret guilty pleasure is watching Lifetime movies. I never really watched TV much in the past, and now I think I may be addicted to cheesy movies."

"Now it's your turn to ask a question, Kate. Remember, that's how this whole conversation thing works." Tom teased.

"Yeah, yeah. Tom, what do you do to relax?"

"I love to go hiking. When I worked for Denver PD, I would hike every weekend I wasn't on duty. But I miss the two weeks a year that I would load up a pack, grab my sat phone, and head off into the wilderness, as far from the hiking trails as possible. Two weeks of just me and nature, no crime, office politics, or relationship drama. Those were the best two weeks of my year."

"I love to hike too! When I was younger, my brother would take me hiking in..." Kate stopped herself. In her excitement, she almost talked about hiking in the Alps with Grant. Normal people did not fly to Switzerland to go hiking. This whole conversation thing was a lot more dangerous than she had thought. It was too easy to be at ease with Tom, to forget that he could ruin her life with just the click of a mouse. God, Carina, not Carina, Kate, she was Kate now. Get it together. "Well, wherever we were at the time."

Tom noticed her pause and the change in her voice when she finished her sentence. Whatever Kate had been about to say, she had changed her mind. But she had mentioned a brother. That was more information than he had ever gotten from her. He had no doubt she would clam up again if he pushed now. No, he would play it close to the vest for now.

"See, we do have some common ground. My turn to ask a question; what was your favorite place you've ever hiked?" he asked as casually as he could.

"I've hiked a lot of places, but I think my favorite was after I graduated from college. A friend and I backpacked around Europe. I know it's the stereotypical thing everyone does, but it was nice to be stereotypical for a little while. We went over to Scotland for a couple weeks. I loved hiking in the highlands." Kate smiled at the memory.

"I've never hiked in Scotland. I will have to add that to my hiking bucket list." Tom didn't mention that most people did not hike around Europe after college. Just another piece to add to the puzzle, Kate came from money.

"I'm supposed to ask you another question; why'd you choose law enforcement?"

"Mostly because it made sense after I got out of school. I went to community college and took criminal justice courses. Once I got into it, though, I found out I was good at it. I've always loved solving puzzles; once I made a detective, that was my job. Granted, not all the puzzles were all that interesting or hard to solve. Most criminals aren't all that bright." Tom smiled and winked as Kate chuckled.

"So why did you become an accountant or whatever it is that you do?"

"Because it was what was expected of me. Fortunately for me, I actually really love numbers, and I'm good at my job. Numbers make sense when nothing else does." Kate started to get that distant look again. Tom decided to try and lighten the mood again.

"Well, you can do my bookkeeping anytime. Numbers have always bored me to death." Dinner flew by; Kate was surprised at how much she enjoyed Tom's company. He was funny and goofy, but he had real depth too. They didn't talk about politics or religion or anything controversial. It was just a light, fun dinner.

They walked in companionable silence. What a difference a few months made, Kate thought, remembering the first time Tom had walked her back to her hotel. The cold war that had been declared that night seemed to have ended sometime over the months.

It was only a matter of minutes before they were at the door to her room. Kate turned and smiled. "Thanks for dinner, Tom. I had a surprisingly good night. I'm glad we can be friends."

"Friends wasn't exactly what I had in mind, Katie." Tom gently put one hand on each side of Kate's face and pulled her in for a gentle kiss.

Kate was too surprised to do anything at first. Once the shock began to wear off, she started to push him away, but it felt so good. It had been so long since she had been held by anyone. Besides, the kiss was so tender and sweet that there was no danger in enjoying it for a few minutes. Kate felt herself relaxing, leaning in further to deepen the kiss. God, this was so good, so right.

Tom felt all his rational thought fly away. What was left was pure emotion. What was it about this woman that he couldn't get enough of her? She tasted spicy and sweet, so Kate. Tom put his arms around her and pulled her tight against him. He deepened the kiss. God, he wanted so much more of her. By the way, she relaxed into him, clinging to his shirt and kissing him back. It seemed like she was right there with him.

Kate felt the passion stirring deep inside her. It had been almost two years since she'd felt this way. The last time was the night before Eric had.......The panic came out of the blue. Swamping her, drowning out any passion and replacing it with uncontrollable terror, grief, and guilt. She started pounding on the chest she was pressed against. She had to escape the arms that bound her; she shoved and kicked. God, she had to get away, NOW. She had to run and run some more until the panic and pain receded, and she was numb again. Damn it, she was going to be sick. She kicked her jailer hard in the shin and pushed him back with all her strength, taking advantage of the momentary slackening of his grip. This was her chance. Blindly she ran, tripping, almost falling but still stumbling forward. She could not stop. Branches and underbrush slapped across her skin, leaving welts and bleeding scratches. She barely felt any of it. She had to get away.

"Hey Kate, wait up. I'm sorry. I didn't mean to freak you out. Stop Kate, really, I won't kiss you again." Tom had no idea what had just happened. One minute he was kissing Kate, and she was enjoying it. He'd swear to it. The next, she attacked him, biting his lip, hitting him, and kicking him in his bad knee. What the hell was going on here? Whatever it was, she was flat-out crazy with fear; that much was clear.

Kate ran until nausea forced her to stop. She dropped to her knees and doubled over, vomiting in the bushes. Dear God, what had she done?? Eric would never forgive her for kissing someone else. Suddenly, she was back in that room on that night from hell. Eric was tied to a chair, beaten so badly she could barely recognize him. The beautiful devil just kept hitting him, over and over, while strong arms held her immobile from behind, making her watch every sickening blow. The sounds of crunching bones and pummeled flesh were intermingled with Eric's screams, now turning into pathetic moans. Then there was blessed silence, except for the sounds of fists hitting flesh. Eric had finally succumbed to unconsciousness. The demon hit him a few more times for good measure, then pulled a knife out of his jacket. His beautiful mouth smiled cruelly at her, and then he drew the blade quickly across Eric's throat. The blood sprayed everywhere, on the walls, the demon, her hair, and her face; even the air she breathed was coated in blood. She screamed and screamed until her voice was gone.

Kate was rocking on her hands and knees, screaming screams that sounded barely human. Her eyes stared blindly in front of her. Wherever she was, it wasn't here, now; whatever she saw was not the trees in front of her. She was locked in her horrific nightmare, and he could not reach her.

"Kate, c'mon Katie, look at me. You're okay. It's over. You can come back now, Katie. You're safe with me."

"Leave me alone! Stop it!" Kate was still rocking back and forth. Tom brushed her hair back from her face.

"Come back to me, Kate. I've got you. It's okay. You're safe."

A voice began to slowly intrude upon the darkness of Kate's memory. The voice was strong and safe. It didn't belong in this place of blood, evil, and pain. She wanted that voice; she needed that voice. She grabbed hold of that voice with everything she had. It was her safety, her tether to good, to safety, to reality. It took every bit of strength she had, but she pulled herself out of the abyss, and she was back, kneeling in a puddle of her own vomit, rocking, while Tom held her.

"It's all my fault. It's my fault." Kate was babbling in between her sobs.

"It's fine, Kate. This isn't the first time a girl turned me down. It's the first time I caused one to throw up, but it's fine." Tom mentally kicked himself at his clumsy attempt to lighten the mood. Kate was obviously deeply traumatized. What was wrong with him? He just couldn't stand to see her hurting.

"There was so much blood. It was everywhere. It was on the walls, in the air, in my hair; oh God, I could taste his blood. Eric, I'm so sorry. It's entirely my fault; you died because of me!!" Kate kept rocking and sobbing and babbling incoherently. Tom knew what PTSD looked like. He'd seen it before. Hell, he'd experienced smaller attacks. He'd seen hell, but whatever Kate had been through was a different level of hell and evil. God, what had this woman seen? He wanted nothing more than to take it all away from her.

Kate suddenly reached up and grabbed his arm, looking straight into his eyes, tears streaming down her face. "I killed him, Tom. I killed him." Her voice was broken and choppy through her sobs, but her words were clear nonetheless. What was she telling him? Was Kate a murderer? Tom looked at the broken woman, sobbing into her own vomit at his feet; she was so vulnerable and defenseless right now. She couldn't have killed anyone, could she? Kate was in no shape to answer any of his questions tonight. He would have to wait until she was more coherent. His gut told him the woman at his feet was no killer; his heart told him he was well on his way to falling in love with her. But the cop in him knew you couldn't always trust your heart or gut. For tonight he pushed aside the cop. He would deal with that later. For now, he needed to make sure Kate was okay. He needed to hold her. He knelt down beside her and picked her up. She tried to slap him away, but he just held on to her more tightly and rocked while he ran his hand over her hair.

"It's going to be okay, Katie. You're safe. I've got you. I won't let anything happen to you." He softly whispered comforting words into her ear. She slowly began to calm down, her sobs turning into soft mewling sounds. Tom slowly stood and carried her back to her room. Her room was locked, but Ms. Annetta was standing outside it. She was in her housecoat, her purple hair in rollers, with a key and shotgun. God, he loved that old lady. She'd heard Kate's screams and had run to protect her. She looked at him worried, her eyes asking him what was happening. He shook his head and mouthed, "Later."

She nodded. Tom carried Kate into the room and tried to lay her on her bed, but she held onto him.

"It's okay, Kate. Ms. Annetta's here. You'll be fine." Kate looked at him with red, tear-filled eyes and held on tighter. She reminded Tom of a terrified, small child burying her head in the chest of anyone bigger and stronger than the monsters of her nightmares.

"Do you want me to stay for a while?" Tom asked softly

Kate nodded.

"Okay, I'll stay. Just let go of me one minute so we can get your shoes off." Kate held on tighter. Ms. Annetta just waved at him to stay put. She bent down and took off Kate's shoes and socks. She went to Kate's dresser and pulled out a pair of sweatpants.

"Lift her up, Tom. I'm going to get her out of those pants." She unbuttoned Kate's jeans. "Turn your head, boy." Tom obediently turned his head. It was reassuring in a ridiculous way to have Ms. Annetta worrying over propriety at a time like this. He heard Kate's pants being unzipped and pulled down and the sweatpants being pulled up. "You can turn around now."

Then she went to the bathroom and got a cold, wet washcloth. She sat in the chair beside the bed, wiping Kate's face with it. She filled a water glass and sat it on the bedside table. Kate hid her face in Tom's shirt and continued making soft mewling sounds like a kitten that had been beaten. Tom felt completely helpless to help her. His heart was breaking to see Kate this way. He looked at Ms. Annetta for answers. With tears in her eyes, she said, "You're doing the only thing you can for her."

After about an hour, Kate fell into an exhausted sleep. Tom tried to ease away from her, but even in her sleep, she clung to him. Ms. Annetta covered them with a grey throw blanket, turned off the light, and left the room.

Kate slowly awoke. She felt like she had a hangover, her head was pounding, and her mouth was dry. She was surprisingly warm, and something heavy rested across her stomach. Instead of making her feel claustrophobic, she felt safe. She opened her eyes slowly and sat up with a start. Sheriff Tom was asleep next to her, his arms around her waist. His dark lashes were like fans resting on his cheeks. The events of the previous night flooded back to her. Oh God, she'd had a panic attack, and Sheriff Tom and Ms. Annetta had witnessed the whole thing. She remembered Tom had kissed her, and she'd freaked out, run away, and thrown up. She couldn't remember anything that had happened after that. What had she said to him? She tried to wiggle out of his arms, but they tightened around her.

"Go back to sleep, Kate. You were up most of the night. You need your rest." Tom's voice was deep and thick with sleep; she felt his chest rumble as he spoke.

"I'm so sorry, Tom. I don't remember everything that happened last night, but what I remember is humiliating." Kate tried to sit up again. The shame of her breakdown made her want to flee this place and never return. But the arms again tightened around her, keeping her in bed.

"Kate, I'm not awake enough to talk about this now, but you have nothing to be embarrassed by. Just stay here, close your eyes, and get some more sleep. You really need it, and quite frankly, so do I."

"I need to get up, Tom. Brenda is expecting me this morning." Kate pushed his arms off her and started to get out of bed. Before her feet hit the floor, she was dragged back into bed.

"Brenda knows you aren't coming in; Ms. Annetta called and took the day off for you. Please, Kate, lay back down. You scared me half to death last night. I need you to know you're okay. If you won't rest for yourself, do it for me." Tom's gray eyes were grave, and his voice was more serious than she'd ever heard him.

"Fine, I'll stay here a bit longer." Kate sighed jokingly. "But I won't promise to stay long." Kate looked up at Tom, the worry still clear in his eyes. "Thank you for everything you did for me last night. I'm sorry I freaked out on you; that hasn't happened in a long time." Tears started to fill Kate's eyes, and she looked away.

Tom gently lifted her chin so that she was again looking into his eyes. "I'm not going to pretend that I know what last night was all about but Kate, whatever it is, I'm here. You don't have to deal with it alone. You have people who care about you and want to help. Let us help you, Kate."

Kate sighed. She would have to leave this place, this home she'd created, these people who'd become family to her. She would have to leave soon, but for now, she'd enjoy a few minutes of safety and peace in Tom's arms. Kate put her arms around Tom's neck and pulled his head down into a tender kiss.

"You're right, Tom. I don't want to talk right now." She smiled and kissed him again, more desperately this time. She wouldn't allow herself to think or plan. She would allow herself the joy of just feeling for these few minutes. Once she left, she'd always have these few minutes of freedom and passion to remember.

Tom groaned. "Katie, stop. Last night, I freaked you out by kissing you. You don't owe me anything. I stayed because I was worried. You don't owe me anything......just stop. Please stop." Tom groaned as Kate continued to lay feather-light kisses on his jaw, neck, and ears.

"I don't want to stop. Just don't hold my arms and let me be on top" Kate smiled coyly at Tom and unbuttoned his shirt, following her hand with her lips. "As a matter of fact, I'm quite enjoying this."

"Kate, you're killing me. I'm trying to do the noble thing here."

"I've always thought nobility was overrated." The last button of his shirt popped open, and Kate began to push his shirt open wider. God, he was beautiful. His muscled chest was a real piece of art. Kate smiled and began to pull her shirt over her head. She couldn't believe she was being this bold. She'd only ever been with one man in her life, Eric, and she'd been reserved. Sex had been fun, but she could take it or leave it. With Tom, it was entirely different. She couldn't wait to get her hands on him. She felt powerful and sexy and, most importantly, in control.

Tom stared in amazement at the woman above him. Good God, she was even more beautiful than he'd imagined. Her milky skin was smooth with thin silvery scars at odd places across what he could see of her breasts and torso. He gently traced each mark, giving her a solemn, questioning look.

"Tom, I don't want to talk about those. They are there, a part of my past. Today, I don't want to think about being broken. Right now, I want to think about us. You make me feel whole and sexy. Let me forget about the past for a few minutes. Please." Kate gave him a small, sad smile.

He growled low in his throat and pulled her face down for a deep kiss. "Two can play this game. You aren't going to have all the fun, Katie." Tom kissed her again deeply. The passion of the kiss left them both shaking. His hands slowly caressed her arms, shoulders, torso, and stomach, always avoiding her still bra-clad breasts. He kissed her eyelids, cheeks, the tip of her nose, her chin, and his mouth began caressing the places his hands already had. Kate was squirming. She needed more. She wanted his mouth on her breasts, to touch and tease him the same way he was teasing her, but her hands were still bound up in her jersey knit shirt above her head. Tom laughed, a wickedly delicious sound that vibrated through her, making her even more desperate. "Oh, Katie, you better get comfortable. I've been making a list of things I wanted to do to you since the day I met you; I intend to do everything on that list." Tom slowly moved back up her torso to unclasp her black lace bra.

Kate leisurely stretched. She couldn't remember feeling more relaxed as Tom snored softly beside her. She smiled at the memory of their morning and then afternoon lovemaking. Tom was a fun lover. She'd never laughed during sex before today. It added a level of intimacy that she wasn't completely comfortable with. He had a way of keeping her unbalanced enough that she never knew what to expect. It was a shame she had to leave him. He wouldn't take that well. Kate knew instinctively he wasn't a love em' and leave em' kind of guy. He was everything she wanted and never knew she needed. He would never leave her to fend for herself.

He was all cowboy, a little alpha male for her normal taste. She couldn't let him protect her, so she had to go. Her sadness at the thought of leaving caught her off guard. With tears pricking her eyes, she leaned down on impulse to kiss his cheek.

Tom awoke with a smile and stretched.

"Damn girl, you've worn me out. If you want to play more, I need something to eat." He looked more closely at her " Hey, what's wrong?" He touched the single tear that had escaped down her cheek.

"I'm just happy." Kate tried to laugh it off. "You know us girls, we cry over just about anything."

"Don't treat me like an idiot Kate. I know you well enough to know that something is upsetting you. You don't have to tell me if you don't want to but don't lie to me." Tom was angry. What did he have to do to get her to trust him?

"I'm sorry, Tom. I don't think you're an idiot. Let's go get some breakfast" Kate looked out the window. "Err, I mean lunch," she said, pointing to the afternoon sky.

Tom gave her a wry smile. "Well, we certainly will give the purple hairs something to talk about, walking into Uncle Joe's Diner at this time of day, looking satisfied.

Tom pulled her down and gave her a hard kiss. "Alright, woman, I need food. Let's hit the shower and then head out for lunch."

"I don't think taking a shower together is a good idea if you want to leave this room anytime soon," Kate said wryly.

"Oh, I think taking a shower together is a very good idea. Think of all the time we'll save by scrubbing each other's backs" Tom looked her up and down playfully "and various other body parts. Besides, it saves water, and I firmly believe in doing anything I can to save our planet."

Kate rolled her eyes. "Sure you are." She swung her legs over the side of the bed and started toward the bathroom, sashaying her naked hips as she went. She looked over her shoulder and motioned for Tom to follow her with a seductive smile.

An hour later, they walked into Uncle Joe's diner. The shower hadn't saved them time, but it was worth every second. Kate smiled a secret smile up at Tom. He pulled her close and kissed her hard right in the middle of the diner. If anyone doubted their relationship, they certainly didn't anymore.

Lucy saw Sheriff Tom kiss Kate, and she felt a pang in her heart. She'd tried for so long to get his attention but had never even been able to get a date out of him. Kate shows up in town, and he starts chasing her around almost from day one. It wasn't that she begrudged Kate's happiness. Lord knew that girl needed something good in her life, but Lucy longed for it to be her turn to fall in love. She fixed a smile on her face and started over to get their order.

Lunch was casual; she wasn't sure what she ate. She was simply enjoying Tom's company. With him, she could be who she was. It hadn't been that way with Eric. He'd never asked her to be anything, but she'd been so terrified of losing his love that she'd become what she thought he would want. Their relationship had ended so suddenly, so tragically, she would never know if they would have grown to this place of ease and comfort she and Tom had. Somehow, she doubted it. Her experiences since Eric's death had given her the desperation to break free, to hell with the consequences.

"You know we need to talk, Kate," Tom said as they returned to the motel.

Kate had been dreading this talk since she'd awoken this morning. She'd hoped she would have come up with some explanation for her breakdown last night without giving Tom any more information. It didn't help that she couldn't remember exactly what she'd said to him. This was going to be a touchy conversation. Maybe she could distract him long enough to leave town.

"I know we do, but let's enjoy today. Tomorrow will be here soon enough. I want one day before we talk about last night." Kate pleaded quietly

Tom shook his head. "That's not going to work, Kate. I'm a cop, remember. I know when someone is trying to distract me or is planning to run. That's what you're thinking, right? You're planning to sneak away without saying a word to me. It won't work, Katie. I will find you wherever you run to. You will still have to tell me what's going on, and it will seriously piss me off to have to track you down." There was hurt and suppressed anger in Tom's voice. Kate didn't bother to deny his accusations; there was no point. They were true, and they both knew it.

"I'm sorry, Tom. I don't know what I said last night, but I should have never said it. The more you know, the more danger I will be in."

Tom couldn't believe she didn't even deny it. "That's all you have to say to me after last night? When are you going to start trusting me, Kate? One day you are going to have to trust someone. Why can't that someone be me?" Tom was seriously pissed off now. Kate stood before him with a scared rabbit look in her eyes but still stubbornly refusing to say a word. If she wanted it this way, he could play hardball too.

"Kate, this is your last chance. Tell me what the hell is going on!" Tom was yelling at her in the middle of Main Street.

"No." The finality in Kate's voice pushed Tom over the edge of reason.

"Fine, if this is the way you want it, Kate. Kate, whatever the hell your last name is, you are under arrest for suspicion of murder." Tom grabbed the cuffs off his belt, where he always kept them and put them on her wrist.

"What the hell are you doing, Tom?" Kate shouted back.

"My job. I gave you a chance to tell me what's happening, but you refused. Now I have no choice but to arrest you. You did say you killed someone last night."

"I will not be threatened into doing what you want." Kate was beyond furious. She felt betrayed. Any secret guilt she had for planning to run away was swept away in a torrent of rage and hurt.

"You have the right to remain silent. Anything you say can and will be used against you in a court of law........" Tom continued to read Kate her Miranda rights. Run away from him, would she? Not while he had anything to say about it, he thought with satisfaction.

"You bastard! You just wait until Ms. Annetta finds out what you've done!"

Tom laughed derisively. "In this instance, I think she'll be on my side when she finds out you were planning on running off."

"Grrrrrr! You are impossible!!! You have no idea what you are doing, what kind of hell you are inviting to rain down on this town. Let me go, damn it! Do you think I want to live like this, always running, never having anyone in my life? Do you think I enjoy the thought of leaving you after last night? You have no idea the hell I live every single day! Leave me alone and let me go before it's too late!!" Kate was on the verge of hysterics. For a moment, Tom wanted to forget the whole thing; to scoop her up and tell her it would all be okay. Then he remembered her doubled over, vomiting and hysterical, and he wanted to shake the truth out of her. Kate was the most stubborn and infuriating woman! Why couldn't she just trust him? No, she was going to talk to him, and she was talking to him today. He continued marching her down Main Street toward the station. God, he hoped she would forgive him for being such a dick someday. If he was a betting man, he'd say a snowball in hell had better odds than he did right now.

Chapter Thirteen

Mike heard sirens off in the distance; it was about damn time. His preliminary yard search hadn't turned up anything other than the truck. He knew in his bones that this was their guy. He was itching to get in that house. What was taking those guys so long? It seemed like the minutes were going by in slow motion. Finally, he saw this first patrol car rounding the corner. The games were about to begin.

Mike groaned inwardly when he saw the leggy redhead exiting the first car to approach the scene.

"Wells, I thought you were still on vacation," Mike said, not bothering to disguise his dislike for the woman.

Mike wasn't a sexist, but Vanessa Wells was one of the females that gave all women a bad rap. She'd been climbing the ranks as fast as she could spread her legs over the past few years. That wasn't gossip. It was a stone-cold fact. She'd even tried it with him, but he hadn't been interested. He'd sooner stick his dick in a blender; it would be safer, that's for sure. Once she'd slept her way to the top, lo and behold, she was pregnant. After the dust had all settled, the commissioner divorced his wife, Audrey, and married the piranha in front of him. Audrey, his sister's best friend growing up, had been his first crush. She had known him only as the bratty little brother of her friend, but he had loved her as only a twelve-year-old boy could. She'd left for college, and he had lost track of her, other than little mentions of her attending this or that event with the commissioner in the paper. It killed him to see her dragged through the news, publicly humiliated the way she had been when the story broke about Vanessa and that bastard, the commissioner.

"Maternity leave is not a vacation, Mike. I had another two weeks of leave, but staying home doesn't suit me. I was itching to get back on the job." Vanessa smiled a saccharine smile and straightened her green suit jacket.

He should have known she would show up today. The Commissioner had made her the department's head media liaison before the scandal of their affair. Since taking the position, this would be her first major case; it guaranteed major media exposure. The sad thing was that Vanessa was quite suited to the position and would have probably been promoted to it after putting some time in. Instead, she'd chosen to cheat her way to the top, leaving a trail of destruction and broken families in her wake. There was no helping it. He'd have to simultaneously work with her and protect the investigation from her. One thing was for damn sure, Vanessa Wells would compromise this investigation in a heartbeat if it meant she got her five minutes of fame. Mike squinted into the sun. Sure enough, just behind the squad cars, a news van was pulling into the neighborhood.

"Shit! Vanessa, you couldn't wait until we entered the house and found out if anything was happening?"

"The mayor wants this situation contained, Mike. People are becoming panicked. It's been months since that woman's body was discovered in pieces throughout the desert. We need to put this to bed ASAP. You did say that your gut was telling you this was our guy. Everyone knows that you have great gut instincts. You just suck at the rest of life." Vanessa's smile was sharp enough to flay the skin from your bones.

"And it doesn't have anything to do with the fact that it's an election year?" Mike scoffed derisively. "Here are the ground rules. I'm the lead investigator on this case; I will not allow you to compromise it. You will keep all the media behind the barriers. You will release only the information I have cleared for release, and you will not set foot inside that house. So, help me if you overstep, even once, I will have your ass thrown out of here so fast, it will leave skid marks on the pavement, commissioner's wife or not."

"Of course, Mike. After all, we want the same thing. Let me get some uniforms on setting up the perimeter and barriers." Her smile was all peaches and cream, but her eyes said she'd stab him in his sleep if she ever got the chance. Mike didn't bother to mention that the perimeter and barriers had already been set up.

"Hey Mike, are we ready to do this thing?" Bear Chambers thumped Mike on the back as he headed toward the front porch. Bear's real name was Doug, but no one ever called him by it. He had been a rising football star in college when a car accident brought all his NFL dreams crashing down. Years later, he was still built like the linebacker he once was. At 6'4 and 250 pounds of muscle, just walking into a room often had suspects shaking in their boots. Underneath the booming voice and gruff exterior, he was a big old softy, a teddy bear; over the years, it had been shortened to just Bear.

"Oh yeah, Bear, I'm ready! I can feel it down in my bones. This is going to blow the desert case wide open."

"Mr. Phillips, it's the police. We need you to open the door. We have a warrant." Mike called out, just for good measure. When there was no answer, he motioned for two officers to break down the door.

The smell of death hit Mike as soon as the door was breached. He entered the house, ensuring no one disturbed the crime scene. It didn't take long to discover the source of the smell; to his right, in what looked like a den, a very dead John Phillips lay back in a leather recliner. Mike went over to the body and did a quick visual inspection. Sitting on the table next to the chair was a shot glass, an empty bottle of whiskey, an empty pill bottle, and what he assumed was a suicide note.

"Call forensics and no one touches a thing until they arrive. Make sure the house is clear, and then everyone out. No one says a word to anyone about this. Understand?" Mike motioned for everyone to leave the crime scene the same way they entered. "Johnson, you are to protect the crime scene. Don't let anyone into that house unless I have cleared them."

"Yes, Sir." Johnson was the youngest member of Mike's team. In his late twenties, he proved to be a real natural when investigating crimes. He was moving up the ranks quickly but remained humble and ready to learn from the more experienced detectives. Mike liked the kid. More importantly, he trusted him. Mike pulled him aside. "I know this goes without saying, but do not give any information to the media or the media liaison." Mike nodded in the direction of Vanessa.

"I read you loud and clear, sir. No one will get by me." Johnson gave Mike an understanding nod. I really like that kid, Mike thought.

Vanessa lost no time cornering Mike as he walked toward his car. God, why'd he ever give up smoking? Cigarettes helped get the God-awful stench of death out of his nose better than anything else.

"What can I do for you?" Mike asked as politely as he could.

"What the hell is going on in there? No one will tell me a damn thing! And don't bother trying to play innocent. I know you told them not to talk to me." Vanessa was steaming mad; red color crept up her neck to her face. Mike almost laughed out loud, wondering if her head would fly off if the color made its way to the very top. The thought of Vanessa's head flying off her shoulders and through the air, her mouth still yelling at him, made him smile. Many would find his sense of humor dark and disturbing, but it helped him get through scenes like todays. The way he figured it, it was better to laugh at what you could because otherwise, all the darkness would become trapped in your soul until it was hard to tell the difference between yourself and the sick bastards you chased.

"They aren't telling you anything because there is nothing to tell. Once we know something, you will be one of the first to know." Mike started back toward the house, ignoring the middle finger Vanessa flashed his way.

It was well into the early morning hours before forensics finished the scene. Though it hadn't been officially decided, it was the consensus that John Phillips had killed, butchered, and disposed of the woman in the desert. Then in a moment of guilt, he took his own life.

It was all there, the alcohol, the pills, the confession, and the suicide note. They'd even found a murder kit hidden in the garage. The mayor had given Vanessa the go-ahead to release a statement to the press at 8 am stating that there was a person of interest in the Butcher case. There was no longer thought to be a threat to the public.

Still, something was eating at Mike; something was off, and he couldn't put his finger on what. It was all a little too tidy. Too many loose ends had been tied up too neatly. He made his way one last time through the house. Nothing stood out to him, but something was bothering him. He just didn't know what it was yet. He'd been working for 36 hours straight; he needed a shower, something to eat, and a few hours of sleep. Hopefully, then he'd be able to figure out what was teasing at the back of his brain.

It had been three days since discovering John Phillips's body. The mayor, desperate to have this case sewn up and packed away, had pushed to have the postmortem rushed. The ME had determined that John's death was consistent with a suicide. That, combined with the suicide note and the evidence in the garage, had closed John's death and the Phoenix Butcher case in one fell swoop. The mayor was delighted; the public was safe, and his campaign was back on track. Still, Mike couldn't shake the feeling something was off. He'd revisited the crime scene several more times and was now pouring over the photos. He kept being drawn to two photos in particular; one of the kitchen cabinets and one of the tables next to the chair opposite the one John was found in. Something was off in these photographs, but he'd be damned if he could see it. He took another gulp of his lukewarm coffee; damn, that was the last of it. He could use a minute to stretch his legs anyway. He walked over to the coffeepot in the corner of the squad room. Damn it, the coffee pot was empty again. Why couldn't the jerk who had the last cup just start another pot? Seriously, it wasn't that difficult. And would it be too much to ask that they throw away their own trash? Every time he came over here, he had to throw away a bunch of coffee stirrers, paper towels, and empty cups. He instinctively started to straighten the cups when suddenly it hit him. He knew what was wrong with those two pictures. He stopped what he was doing and rushed back to his desk. He magnified the picture of the kitchen cabinet on his computer, and there it was, the answer he'd been looking for. It was the shot glasses. They were all wrong. All the other cups and glasses in the cabinet were placed haphazardly; coffee mugs were next to glasses and plastic cups from the local BBQ joint; there was no real rhyme or reason to the cabinet except for the shot glasses. They were lined up exactly three inches between each glass, color coordinated, and on their own shelf. There was even an empty space for the shot glass that John had been drinking with.

Mike flipped over to the den photograph. It was the same thing there. The room was in a comfortable state of chaos except for the table next to the chair across from John. All the coasters on that table had been stacked very precisely. The framed photograph of John with a pretty blonde was exactly three inches from the coasters and three inches from the lamp on the other side. Not a speck of dust was to be seen, though the rest of the room looked like it hadn't been dusted in a month. Mike looked at the table next to John's chair; it had been dusted, and the suicide note, whiskey bottle, shot glass, and prescription bottle were exactly three inches apart. Mike scoured the rest of the crime scene pictures, and not another place in John's house had this same OCD stereotyped behavior. His closet was a mess; all his clothes were hung haphazardly on different hangers, facing different directions, and nothing was even about the spacing. In fact, the rest of the house looked exactly like his closet. For a former marine, he was pretty sloppy.

Mike felt a chill go down his spine. He knew without a shadow of a doubt that somebody else had been in that house with John. His gut was telling him that person was their real killer and John was just a convenient fall guy. There was no way in hell that anyone in the department was going to listen to his hunch based upon some shot glasses and dust, especially since the mayor had already declared the case closed to the entire world in a news conference. He was going to have to come up with some proof. Mike needed a new angle because whoever had been in that house with John might as well have been a ghost. From what he could tell, he had left not a fingerprint, shoe print, or even a damn eyelash; whomever he was chasing was damn thorough.

Life in the precinct went back to normal, no damn tip line phones ringing off the hook, no news van parked outside the precinct 24 hours a day, just the normal stream of gangbangers killing each other and drug overdoses. Officially the Phoenix Butcher case was closed, and the world had moved on. The world may have moved on, but Mike couldn't. He spent every spare minute he could find going back over his notes from the case, re-interviewing witnesses, and looking at the crime scene photos. So far, he had come up with exactly nothing. He had a gut feeling that the favor John did for his Marine buddy was tied into this whole mess. Still, no matter how hard he tried, he hadn't found any trace of this buddy; no old pictures from boot camp, no phone number, no name; it was like this guy was a ghost. He had requested John's old military records in hopes he'd find some clue of this guy's identity. But they were characteristically dragging their feet in releasing them to him. He was impatient but couldn't apply pressure because the investigation was officially closed. He had to tread very carefully, or his neck would be on the line.

He was on his way to see Danny in the Traffic Bureau; if he was lucky, maybe they could get something off one of the traffic cameras near John Phillips's house. He grabbed a case of Danny's favorite beer and a pair of tickets to the next Sun's game. Danny was the best in the department; he had earned the nickname eagle eye because he could spot the most obscure things on the camera feeds. It was freaky how much he saw. Once, he'd identified a suspect in a convenience store holdup by the reflection of her face off a CD she had hanging on her rear-view mirror. Mike didn't know what idiot had decided hanging a CD would get you out of speeding tickets because that was a load of BS. However, their suspect's stupidity led to her arrest, her stupidity, and Danny's eagle eye.

"Hey, Mike. How's it going, man?" Being the best meant Danny was allowed his eccentricities. He came to work in khaki shorts, Hawaiian shirts, and deck shoes daily. He only broke out his uniform for court appearances or funerals. He always looked mildly rumpled, with a perpetual five o'clock shadow.

"I'm good, Danny; how about you? Are you still dating that girl from Italy, Spain, or wherever she was from?"

"Nah, that was over months ago. I'm not ready to be tied down, you know that. I'm a playa'" Danny thumped his chest, like Tarzan.

"Yeah, so you've told me. Hey, I brought you a few presents." Mike handed Danny the brown paper bag. Danny peered inside and whistled, "You must want something big if you're giving up these Sun's tickets."

"Nothing too extreme, just your amazing eagle eyes looking over some traffic footage." Mike tried to sound nonchalant.

"Sure, no problem. What footage do you need me to look at, and what am I looking for?"

"I was wondering if you would pull all traffic cams in a mile radius of John Phillips's house for the 36 hours before he died. See if you can spot anything out of the ordinary."

"Just a small favor, huh? I thought that case was all sewn up." Danny raised a questioning eyebrow.

"Officially, it is, so I'd appreciate it if you could keep this between us. I have a couple of loose ends teasing the back of my brain. I need to tie them up, so I can sleep at night. You know how it is." Mike gave Danny a self-deprecating smile and shrugged.

"Yeah, I know how it is. I'll do my best, but I can't promise anything."

"You're the best, so if you don't find anything, there isn't anything to find. About how long will this take you?"

"I've got a pretty heavy load this week, so it may be a little while." Danny caught the look of frustration that crossed Mike's face briefly. "Look, I'll do my best to finish it in three or four days. No promises, though."

Mike gave Danny a friendly pat on the back. "Thanks, Danny. I owe you big time for this."

"Yeah, you do. Don't think a couple of Suns tickets and a case of beer makes us even, either." Danny joked as Mike started towards the door.

"I'll name my firstborn after you if you find me something on one of those feeds."

"Ha, you'd have to get laid for that to happen, so I won't be holding my breath," Danny called after Mike as the door closed behind him. He laughed as Mike flashed him the middle finger through the crack in the rapidly closing door.

Chapter Fourteen

Chicago had turned out to be a bust in terms of tracking down Carina Wythcliff. Still, he had enjoyed being in a real city again, with all its amenities. Griffin sat at the coffee shop, an open map spread across the table, a cup of steaming espresso on his left. His computer had different map programs, which sat conveniently at his feet in its black carry case. Sometimes he needed to go old school, to have a tangible, physical map spread out before him. There was something about being able to trace his fingers along the highways and byways that got his juices flowing. He'd been sure she would head to the biggest city where she could blend in and disappear.

Carina Wythcliff was used to a certain standard of living. The last time she'd run, he'd found her in an upscale bed and breakfast on the coast of Oregon; true, it had been remote, but it had been the kind of remote that panders to the wealthy and famous. But she was proving herself more resourceful this time around. Maybe he was looking at this all wrong. Maybe she had truly gone off the grid. The car she'd paid cash for had been a piece of crap. Maybe she was taking her whole life in the crap direction. If that was the case, she'd be heading to some no-name town out west or down south. The tension was back in his shoulders. He hated those little backwoods towns and their idiot redneck inhabitants. Just the thought of them made him angry. He'd fought too hard to get away from those hellholes to be forced to go digging through them again. Maybe she'd headed for LA or even Vegas. No, his gut told him he'd find her in some little shit-kicker town where even the air stunk of failure, poverty, and desperation. In other words, the exact opposite of her real life.

Damn her, he should have just let her stay drugged into oblivion with that sick prick in NY. He'd been right to let her escape. She was his bargaining chip to get out from under the thumb of that psychotic bastard. Griffin had learned early on how to leverage others' weaknesses and turn them to his advantage. Carina Wythcliff was his big payday, retirement plan, and escape route all rolled into one bratty package. Griffin ordered another espresso and pulled his cell phone out of his cashmere Burberry suit. A man was only as good as his suit, and Griffin always wore the best. It was time to bring in some reinforcements. If he had to search every hellhole in the country, he would need more manpower.

Kate stared at the cinder block walls of the small cell that Tom had tossed her in. The past 24 hours had upended her life on levels she couldn't yet process. She wanted to scream and rage. Tom had held her and comforted her through her panic attack, they'd become lovers, and the sex had been amazing. They had laughed. She had trusted him more than anyone in a very long time. Then he publicly humiliated and arrested her. His betrayal had broken the small corner of her heart that hadn't already been destroyed. She should be crying or screaming; instead, she stared blankly at the wall. There was nothing left except soul-deep numbness.

Tom paced the office. Why couldn't he have fallen for some nice, simple girl instead of the woman cursing him from here to eternity in the other room? He hadn't officially booked her yet, though she didn't know that. What a mess, he'd taken her prints, but he hadn't run them; he was afraid of what he would find. Besides, he really wanted Kate to trust him enough to tell him what was going on herself. His gut told him she was a victim, not a criminal. The bell above the door out in the vestibule rang, and in marched Charlie Benet, madder than a bull in a China shop, followed by Ms. Annetta, carrying her shotgun.

"Start talking, and you best have a good reason for being an ass other than pure male stupidity. Kate trusted you, and you betrayed her. Don't think that badge on your chest will stop me from changing you from a rooster to a hen." Ms. Annetta nodded towards the shotgun in her hand.

"Hand me the gun before I have to arrest you too. What is wrong with you, marching into a police station and threatening the sheriff?"

"I wouldn't care if you were Sam Houston himself! That girl just started to trust us. She was making a life for herself here. Then you go and act a fool!" Ms. Annetta started to lunge for him, but Charlie held her back.

"Sheriff, what the hell are you doing arresting that sweet girl and marching her through the streets of town?"

"Calm down, both of you. You know I can't discuss an active investigation."

"The hell you can't. I'm Kate's lawyer."

"C'mon, Charlie, you aren't a lawyer. I know Kate would appreciate you sticking up for her, but you don't understand the situation."

"I sure as hell am a lawyer. I haven't practiced in years, but I sure as hell passed the bar in 1961. I've made sure to renew my license every year. I never know when I will need it with that old mean old coot that lives next to me."

"Really, Charlie, you passed the bar exam, and instead of practicing law, you have devoted your life to feuding with your neighbor? I'll never understand you." Tom shook his head incredulously and rubbed his temples, hoping to relieve the headache that was quickly forming.

Charlie straightened his overall strap and stood tall. "Annetta. I'll let you know how Kate is. You ought to go before I have to defend you too."

"You tell Kate that I was here. I'll only go if you promise to call and let me know she is okay. Otherwise, I'm staying right here."

"I promise, Annetta. You know I love her too." Charlie patted Ms. Annetta's arm

"Alright, Sheriff, I'd like to see my client now."

"Sure, Charlie, I'll bring you back to her. Maybe you can talk some sense into her." Tom grabbed his hat and started to make his way back to the holding cell.

"Out of curiosity, what's she charged with, Sheriff?"

"Suspicion of murder." Tom almost smiled at the look of shock and confusion that crossed Charlie's face.

"Are you crazy, Tom? There ain't no way Kate is a murderer any more than I am!"

"I'd like to believe that, Charlie, but she confessed to the crime."

Charlie muttered something about, "damn fool, Sheriff. Who wouldn't know a good thing if it bit him in the ass" at Tom's back as they made their way to the holding cell.

"Hello, Kate. I hope you've had a few minutes to calm down. Your lawyer is here to see you." He unlocked the holding cell and motioned for Kate to follow him.

A look of utter panic crossed Kate's face. "I don't have a lawyer."

"You do now." Charlie made his way around Tom.

A brief look of relief crossed Kate's face when she saw Charlie, but quickly she became expressionless once more. "I appreciate the offer, Charlie, but I don't need a lawyer."

Tom led them to the interview room. It was a small, plain room. Three of the four walls were plain drywall, painted institution white. On the fourth wall, there was a large two-way mirror. Besides the wooden table, two folding chairs, and the camera mounted high in the left corner, the room was empty and stuffy.

"I'd have to disagree with you there, girl. Suspicion of murder ain't something you handle without a lawyer." Charlie sat in one of the chairs and waved for Kate to sit in the other. "Now, Sheriff, I'd appreciate it if you left me and my client alone so's we can talk."

Tom nodded and walked back to his office. Hopefully, Charlie would be able to get Kate to be reasonable.

"Okay, girlie, you need to tell me what's going on here. I'm your lawyer, so anything you say to me will be completely confidential."

"Charlie, I'm telling you I don't need a lawyer. Thanks for the offer. You should go."

"Kate, I don't know what's going on with you, but I am not leaving this room until you tell me what's happening." Charlie reached across the table to touch her hand gently.

Tears began to well up in Kate's eyes. Kindness always made her weepy. She brutally brushed them aside. Now was not the time for sentimental emotionalism. Now, she had to be strong and protect the people she cared about.

"I'm serious, Charlie. I'm not telling you anything. You should leave." Kate tried to sound as dismissive as possible.

Charlie just smiled, pulled a pipe out of the front pocket of his overalls, grabbed a pouch of tobacco out of another, and started to pack his pipe. He didn't say a word, just leaned back and took a deep draw on his pipe after he'd finished packing and lighting it.

"Just go, Charlie. I don't have time for this and don't want you."

Charlie stretched, smiled, and looked at his beat-up pocket watch. "I don't got anything better to do, and you certainly don't have anywhere better to be." Charlie looked around the room pointedly and continued to puff on his pipe silently.

As minutes ticked by at a snail's pace, Kate became more and more fidgety. She'd always hated sitting still; it drove her nuts. It infuriated her that Charlie was so calm, puffing on his damn pipe and quietly watching her.

Kate stared at him sullenly, her fingers tapping on the table, her foot tapping a counterbeat on the floor. Oh, the young had no clue how to be still. Aging gave you an appreciation of sitting still and allowing the moments to happen. Now her youth was working against Kate, and his age was working for him. Yeah, she didn't stand a chance; she'd be telling him her story sooner or later.

Forty-five minutes went by, then an hour, then two hours, and after four hours, Kate was ready to pull out her hair. Charlie sat in the chair across from her, alternating between puffing on the infernal pipe and taking cat naps. The man had the patience of a saint.

Tom watched the scene playing out in the interview room with amusement. Kate looked like she was about to go crazy, and Charlie was just sitting patiently. Finally, someone who may be more stubborn than his Katie. Hell, if Charlie could live next door to his worst enemy for sixty years to annoy the shit out of him, Kate didn't stand a chance holding out against him. He laughed and decided to stir the pot a bit.

A knock sounded outside the door. Tom walked in like he owned the place, the confident, backstabbing bastard.

"I'm headed to Uncle Joe's for dinner. Can I grab you two anything?" He gave Charlie a conspiratorial wink.

"I sure could use some chicken fried steak, mashed potatoes, and a slice of Miss Doris's key lime pie. What about you, Kate?"

"I'm not hungry." Kate knew she was sulking like a child, but she really didn't care at this point.

"She'll take the same as me, Tom," Charlie said with a smile.

"I said I don't want anything to eat, and I don't want any lawyer! Are you both deaf?" Kate was really fed up with being treated like she wasn't there.

"Did you hear something, Tom?" Charlie said, looking around with mock curiosity.

"Yeah, I heard an annoying mosquito buzzing around my ear." Tom joked back.

"Grrrrr, you two are impossible."

"I'll be back in a few minutes," Tom called as he walked out the door whistling.

Another three hours clicked slowly by. Kate laid her head on the desk and closed her eyes. It had been an exhausting 24 hours. She'd had a major panic attack, slept with Tom, made love to Tom for hours, been arrested by Tom, and was now being stared down by the most stubborn lawyer she'd ever come up against. He was wearing overalls and smoking a pipe. Dear Lord, her friends in her former life would be laughing at the utter ridiculousness of it all. She was asleep within minutes of laying her head down.

Charlie listened to Kate's soft breathing; he had grown quite fond of this girl. He imagined if he'd ever had a daughter, she would have been a lot like Kate, quick-witted, smart, and too stubborn for her own damn good. Once he was sure Kate was asleep, he silently crept out of the room to talk with Tom.

"Alright, that girl in there is scared to death of something, and don't tell me you haven't noticed. What the hell is going on?" Worry and exhaustion had deepened the wrinkles on Charlie's face. Tom had to admire how he'd outlasted Kate at his age. He had to be pushing 80.

"Honestly, Charlie, I have no idea. She had a huge breakdown last night. I mean full-out PTSD shit. I stayed with her all night to calm her down. She kept saying she'd killed him. I have no idea who he is."

"So let me get this straight, that terrified woman in there had a breakdown. You SLEPT with her and then arrested her? I never thought of you as such a bastard Tom." Charlie was clearly furious with him. He shook and pointed a gnarled, arthritic finger straight in Tom's face.

"Yes, but it wasn't like that. I'm in love with her, Charlie. I asked her what was going on because I wanted to help her. Instead, she tried to put me off; I've been a cop for a long time. I knew she was planning on running. She didn't even deny it. She wouldn't even give me her real name. How the hell am I supposed to help her when she won't trust me? So I arrested her, hoping she would come to her senses. I haven't even officially booked her. I took her prints, but I haven't run them yet." Tom sighed and rubbed his temples again. God, this woman was putting him through the wringer.

Charlie put a wrinkled hand on Tom's shoulder. "I still think you are acting like a jackass, but run the prints,

Tom. We've got to know what we're dealing with here. She needs our help and is too scared to ask for it."

Tom nodded, ran his hand through his tousled hair, and went to the computer. Charlie returned to the interview room. He didn't want Kate to awaken alone.

After a few minutes, Tom came into the room looking shocked.

"I know who she is, Charlie." His voice quivered with emotion.

"Sit down, boy." Charlie got up from the folding chair and motioned for Tom to sit. "From the look of you, you need to sit. So, who is she?"

"Her name isn't Kate; it's Carina Wythcliff. Damn it, I knew I recognized her when she first came to town." Tom was obviously shaken.

"Who the devil is Carina Wythcliff, and why did you recognize her?"

"Do you remember that big news story from about two years ago? The one where the New York socialite was kidnapped along with her boyfriend. Her boyfriend was killed, and she had a breakdown after being released. It was all over the news."

"Oh yeah, I remember something vaguely about that."

"Yeah, well, Kate is that girl."

Kate had awoken during their conversation. She was now sitting up straight as a board with a look of absolute horror.

"You ran my prints, didn't you?" her voice shook, and her whole body tensed as if preparing to flee.

"Yes, CARINA, I did. Since you wouldn't talk to me, I had no choice."

"Oh God, Tom, you have no idea what you have done. He'll send them for sure now. There will be no stopping him. And my name is Kate." Kate started rocking back and forth, moaning quietly. "Now, no one is safe."

Charlie went over to Kate and put his hands on her shoulders. "Kate, we'll protect you from whatever you're afraid of. Me and Tom ain't gonna let no one get to you."

"Charlie, I'm not scared for me. He won't hurt me. He will burn this town to the ground to find me, though."

Tom swallowed his pride and put his feelings aside. It didn't matter that Kate had lied to him from the moment he met her. It was his job to protect her and find out what was happening. "Kate, I need you to be straight with me; who are you running from? Why do you think they are coming for you?"

"You probably already know what happened."

"I know the official story, but I'd like to hear it from you."

Kate paused, deciding how much of the story she should tell him. The official version was the best shot she had at keeping them safe. Sometimes ignorance was bliss. "Two years ago, my boyfriend and I decided to escape the city. We found a Bed and Breakfast on the coast of Oregon that looked perfect. I had always loved quiet, beautiful places away from everything. This place fit the bill. It was an old Victorian-style house built on a bluff overlooking the Pacific Ocean." Kate paused, wishing that the trip really had been a romantic getaway. Instead, she remembered the frantic packing, the driving across the country, always looking in the rear-view mirror, and the feeling of relief when they thought they had escaped. She shook her head to clear the memories and continued with the official version of events.

"We had been there a few days when Eric arranged a day of sailing. I have always loved sailing. Once we were out in open water, he dropped sail and suggested we eat. He had brought a gourmet picnic packed by the owner of the B&B. We sat right on the deck and ate. It was lovely. At the end of the picnic, he served dessert with champagne, and at the bottom of my glass was an engagement ring. It was corny and sweet and perfect." Kate stopped again, brushing a tear from her eye. This part of the story was true. After all, they had been through, Eric wanted to marry, protect, and love her. They had even dreamed of having kids out on the water, thinking their worries were behind them, clueless about what awaited them back at the B&B. Kate cleared her throat, brushed aside another tear, and continued, "We spent the day sailing, enjoying our happiness. It was dark when we got back to the B&B. We really weren't paying a whole lot of attention to what was going on around us. We were walking up the garden path when someone grabbed each of us from behind, covering our mouths, and injected us with what I assume was a sedative."

Kate's fingers were now nervously tapping the table. Her eyes had gotten that frightened deer in the headlights look, and she was starting to rock back and forth. Tom wanted to be jealous of the man who had obviously made Kate so happy, but watching her now, all he could feel was pity for him. He couldn't stand seeing Kate this way, so he moved around the table and knelt beside her chair, grabbing both hands.

"It's okay, Katie. I'm here... look at me, Kate, it's going to be okay." Kate snatched her hands away from him and cleared her throat.

"I'm fine, Sheriff. I got through this without you the first time. I certainly can get through the telling of it without you." Tom felt like she'd stabbed him through the heart. Gone was the funny, quick-witted woman he'd fallen in love with. Instead, she was now cold and aloof. Kate, the mysterious accountant, had been replaced with Carina Wythcliff, the high-powered New York businesswoman and debutante. This woman had little to no use for him. That was clear.

Tom went back to the folding chair across from her. Charlie had pulled in one of his old wooden office chairs at some point. Tom hadn't noticed when.

"I'm sorry, my mistake, Miss Wythcliff. It won't happen again. Please continue your story when you're ready." He could play it the same way if she wanted it to be this way. He knew how to be all cop and no lover.

"I awoke sometime later in a car. I have no idea how much time had passed, some type of cloth had been shoved in my mouth, and a piece of duct tape was put over it, my hands secured behind me, and my legs taped together. I was laid down on the back seat, and the chain from the cuffs on my wrists was tethered to the door somehow. I couldn't move more than a few inches. I couldn't make a sound, my throat was deathly dry, and I had no idea where they had taken Eric. I was terrified. There were two men in the front seat. I could hear them talking. Nothing important, just game scores and what actress was hotter, normal guy stuff, like they were just out for a Sunday drive, not two kidnappers who had a woman incapacitated a few feet from them. It was surreal.

We drove that way for what seemed like forever. I know that the sun set at least once. I can only assume I had been unconscious for the entirety of the night before."

"Eventually, we stopped. I didn't have any idea where. I was blindfolded before they removed the duct tape from my legs and made me walk into a warehouse building. I had no feeling in my legs. The circulation had been cut off so long my legs wouldn't hold me. I fell a couple of times as they tried to make me walk to where they were leading me. Every time I fell, one of them would yell at me, kick my ribs and drag me up again. This repeatedly happened until the blood finally started circulating in my legs. According to the ER records, they treated me for five broken ribs. This would have been when they broke them," Kate paused to collect her thoughts.

"Finally, we made it into the building, and I was forced to sit in a chair. I wasn't bound to it. I still wonder why. They ripped the duct tape off my mouth, pulled the rag out, and one of the kidnappers pried my mouth open and poured water down my throat until I gagged. He then bent down and shoved his tongue down my throat. That's when I heard Eric yelling for him to stop. The kidnapper laughed and stepped away so that I could see Eric. It was awful. He was sitting in a chair across from me. His legs had been duct taped to the legs of the chair that bolted into the floor. Eric's hands were taped behind him. There we sat, staring at each other in horror." Kate stopped talking and was rocking back and forth. Charlie tried to hold her hand, and she jerked it away. The tears were flowing uninhibited down her face.

Tom sat in his own chair in shocked horror. He'd followed the news story and read the official report, but none of it had prepared him to hear the gruesome tale from the woman he had come to care about. The fact she had survived was a miracle. The fact she was able to function and live a normal life was beyond miraculous.

He needed a break. He understood PTSD. He understood that you had to distance yourself from the atrocities to survive. But listening to Kate recite such horrors like she was retelling her trip to the mall was killing him. He cleared his throat. "I am pausing this interview for a few minutes."

Without another explanation, he left the room. Once the door closed behind him, he started to run. He ran through the office, out the front door, and didn't stop until he reached his house twenty minutes later. He stood in his living room and screamed, kicked, threw things, and even cried. He cried for Kate, the man she'd loved and lost, and he cried for himself because hearing this story, he knew the Kate he knew was gone. Actually, she'd never really existed. After he calmed himself, he took a shower, changed his clothes, and walked back to the station. It was time to finish this damn interview and figure out what the hell had Kate so spooked now.

"Here you go" Tom handed Kate a water bottle and tossed a second one to Charlie. He noticed that Charlie had moved his chair close to Kate, and his plaid shirt now had a large wet spot on the shoulder. It looked like Kate still needed a shoulder to cry on, just not his.

"When you're ready, please continue, Miss Wythcliff." Tom had his professional composure firmly in place now. At least, he hoped to God he did.

Charlie reached over and grabbed Kate's hand, which she promptly squeezed as she gave Charlie an appreciative smile.

"I will never forget how the one kidnapper laughed as Eric begged him to leave me alone. The more Eric begged, the more he hurt me. He cut the clothes off my body, drawing blood with each slash of the knife. Once all my clothes had been stripped away, I was sure he would rape me. Instead, he turned his attention to Eric. He started beating him. He hit him with a metal pole and kicked him with his boots. But his favorite thing to do was punch him like he was a piece of meat. He just kept pummeling him. Eric screamed and screamed. His blood was everywhere. He screamed until he lost his voice and finally fell unconscious. His attacker hit him a few more times, looked me straight in the eye, and smiled the most chilling smile I had ever seen. I begged and begged him to leave Eric alone. I told him I would do anything he wanted and offered my body in every way I knew how. I offered money and promised him anything. After I had begged for what seemed an eternity, he spat on me and said I didn't have anything he was interested in. He then nodded at the guy behind me, who tightened his hold on my arms. He pulled a knife out of his belt. It was different than the one he'd used to cut my clothes off. He laughed as I struggled, took a handful of Eric's bloody hair, and pulled his head back. He slashed the knife quickly across Eric's throat. I remember how the blood sprayed everywhere. It coated my body, my hair. I even breathed it in. I screamed and screamed until I had no voice left. At some point, I must have passed out. The next thing I remember is waking on the side of the road naked, bleeding, and cold. It took a few tries, but eventually, I stood up and started walking. After just a few minutes, a car stopped, and the couple tried to help me. I wouldn't let them touch me, but they called the police and an ambulance. The rest is yesterday's news, quite literally. From what I was told, the kidnappers had contacted my brother and demanded a ransom. He is well known. You may have heard of him, New York Senator Grant Wythcliff? Once he had paid, they let me go." Kate was far away from him, somewhere deep inside herself. It was like she had to lock herself far away from the world to survive, even telling the story. She wasn't crying or screaming or rocking. She was just staring blankly at the wall behind Tom's head. This was even more disturbing to Tom than when she had the breakdown. He didn't know this woman who sat before him. All the life had gone out of her, leaving an empty shell.

"If it's okay, Sheriff, I'd like to go back to my cell unless you are going to release me. If so, I'd like to return to my room." Kate never made eye contact with him, just continued to stare blankly at the wall behind him.

Tom cleared his throat to push down the emotion that was climbing his throat. "You're free to go." Tom paused. Something bothered him from the original police report. "Just one last question, can you describe the men who kidnapped you?"

"Like I told everyone who interviewed me, I never saw their faces. They had those ski masks with the eyes and mouths cut out of them."

When she had her breakdown, Kate described her attacker as a beautiful demon, which implied she had seen at least one of her kidnappers. Why would she lie about such an important detail? Tom had to wonder. Did she not want her attackers caught? Tom decided now was not the time to press her. He'd do a little digging on his own first.

"Thanks, Miss Wythcliff; I'll walk you back to your room now."

"That won't be necessary. I'm sure Charlie won't mind dropping me off on his way out of town." With that, she stood and gracefully walked out of the room without a backward glance at him.

Tom hated the idea of Kate being alone. Everything in him wanted to hold her, for his sake and hers. It was his fault that he couldn't. He should never have slept with her after that night, or he shouldn't have arrested her. He sure as hell shouldn't have done both. Since he couldn't be there, he would make sure someone was; he called Ms. Annetta; she would make sure Kate was okay tonight.

Chapter Fifteen

Charlie pulled into the motel parking lot and parked outside the room that Kate indicated.

"I'd feel better if you let me check your room out before you went in." Charlie had seen more than his share of human depravity in his lifetime. He'd been in the Korean war, seen the bruises on Ella's face over the years, and his father was known to be heavy-handed with the belt with his mother and siblings. Still, none of it had prepared him for Kate's story. The worst thing was that he was sure she hadn't told them the worst of what had happened. He didn't doubt that things had happened as she described them. The emotion had been too raw, the trauma too real. No, it was just at the end of the story he could tell there was more. Something was still terrifying that poor girl. Charlie knew that checking her room tonight wouldn't accomplish anything, but it made him feel better if nothing else.

Kate's room was perfectly fine, so Charlie dropped her off, waited to hear the lock click into place, and then went to find Annetta. They needed to come up with a plan to make her feel safe.

Kate shivered as she vigorously ran her hands up and down her arms. She felt numb and chilled, cold to the very depths of her soul. She grabbed her sweats and headed to the shower. She turned the hot water tap all the way on and stood under the steaming deluge. The minutes ticked by, and she stood staring at the shower wall, the hot water slowly cooling as it pounded her skin. Once the hot water had turned to ice, she turned it off, dried herself, and threw her sweats on. She looked at the bed but couldn't bring herself to lay in it after.... well, just after. It was best not to think about the last night and afternoon she'd spent in that bed. She curled up in a ball on her chair and pulled her chenille blanket over her. There she sat, staring blankly at the empty screen of the television until the first rays of the sun began to creep onto the horizon. They were coming, there was no doubt. She began to pack up her few belongings. She had to leave before they got here. It would be better for everyone.

She silently slipped out of her room and made her way to her battered old car, a suitcase in each hand, an overnight bag over one shoulder, a backpack, and her purse over the other. She popped open the hatchback to put the bags representing her life inside when she heard someone clear his throat behind her. Her full hands made it impossible to get to her gun. Of course, it was just her luck that after months of making sure she could always get to her weapon, the one moment she made the mistake of having her hands full, he'd find her. She dropped the bags into the open hatchback and slowly turned around.

"Where are you heading, Katie-did?" Tom drawled lazily, a steely glint in his grey eyes.

Finally, she had shown her hand; the man in the gray, pin-striped Kiton suit smiled a malevolent smile. It was about time. He'd begun to think she may be dead, which simply wouldn't do. He smoothed invisible wrinkles, running his hands over the breast and sleeves of his suit jacket. It was an unconscious tick he'd developed in boarding school; neatness was next to godliness, after all. He would never presume godliness, but neatness he had down. It only took half a dozen licks from the priest's leather strap. Many other boys hadn't learned as quickly, but he had always been superior to most people. He went to his desk and retrieved the burner phone from its secret compartment. Griffin had been a big disappointment in his handling of this situation.

After he brought in Carina, his usefulness would be at an end. This is one case where he would enjoy doing his own dirty work. Griffin had been a very expensive thorn in his side for too long.

"Hey, call me when you get this. I know where she is." He slammed his phone closed. He was sick of Griffin ducking his calls; it was insulting to his position to have to continually chase down the hired help. He tossed the phone back into the desk and locked the compartment. He would deal with Griffin in due time. For now, he had a press conference to address. He smoothed his suit again, tightened his slate blue silk tie, and buzzed his assistant into the office to take a quick dictation.

Mike was startled awake by the buzzing of his cell phone. Damn it, he'd only fallen asleep...he looked at the time flashing on his cell phone before answering it... two hours ago. He'd spent most of the night reviewing John Philip's neighbors' witness statements. He hoped to find something he had missed the other hundred times he'd gone over them.

"What?" Mike didn't bother trying to not sound surly. He was damn tired, and whatever idiot was on the other end of this phone call would know he was pissed to be awakened.

"Well, hello to you too, sunshine." Danny's joking, cheerful voice made Mike want to punch him in the face.

"Who died, Danny? Tell me they had it coming so I can go back to sleep."

"No one died."

"Great, I'm going back to sleep."

"Hey, wait up. Remember those camera feeds you asked me to go over. You know that favor you asked for?"

"Oh yeah, sorry about snapping at you. Did you find anything?"

"I think I may have. I have it down here if you want to come and take a look."

"Thanks, Danny. You're the man!" The exhaustion was swept away with a renewed excitement. Hopefully, this was his chance to catch the bastard behind John Phillips's murder and the dismembered woman they had found in the desert.

"Hey Mike, Vanessa walked into my office while I reviewed the traffic footage. She asked what I was doing. I told her I was reviewing the daily footage looking for idiots running the lights, but I don't think she bought it. She asked me what you wanted when you came to my office. I don't know what you did to piss her off, but she is looking for your head on a spike. Just thought you'd like a heads up." Danny started laughing at his own pun.

"You're hilarious, Danny," Mike's voice was laced with sarcasm. "Thanks for the warning and for covering for me. I'll come down to your office in about an hour."

"Alright, just watch your back, dude."

"I will." Mike hit end call and rolled out of bed. It was going to be another long day. He went to the kitchen to start the coffee brewing; it would be ready when he finished showering and dressing. He'd been hoping to sleep in, hit the gym, and actually take his day off, well, off. But he couldn't wait to follow up on this lead, especially if Vanessa was out for his blood. He'd known she'd be out for his hide after he'd kept her out of the crime scene; she wasn't the type to forgive and forget. Still, it had been worth seeing her sputtering mad and unable to leak any more case details to the press. He'd cross that crazy bitch bridge when he came to it. For now, he was going to track down a killer.

Mike walked through the maze of office cubicles towards Danny's office. Another perk of being the best was that Danny got an office with an actual door that closed, albeit the size of a utility closet. Geniuses and their quirks, he shook his head. Mike knocked on the door and walked in, not waiting for Danny to answer; he always had his headphones on, listening to that thrash metal trash he loved so much.

He tapped Danny on the shoulder, causing him to jump. Danny grinned. "Hey, man. How's it going?"

"It really depends on what you've got to show me."

"Ah, you're a no foreplay kind of guy; straight to the deed and no extra conversation. That could explain a lot about your lack of female companionship."

"You are one twisted bastard, Danny." Mike laughed.

"Yeah, so you've told me. It's part of my genius." Danny gave him a devilish smile. "So let me pull up the file I found." Now he was all business. That was Danny's way; half the time, he was like a fifteen-year-old kid, horny and crude, and the other half, he was all business and the best there was.

Danny flashed through several computer screens that meant nothing to Mike, and suddenly the traffic footage was playing.

"So, what am I looking at?"

"This is from about 4 hours before Phillips's approximate time of death at the intersection of Grant and West Lake, about two miles from his house. Okay, watch closely. It is coming up......right about......now! Do you see the guy in the Camry wearing a dark hat and sunglasses, stopped at the light?"

"Yeah, what about him?"

"Doesn't it strike you as odd that he is wearing sunglasses at dusk?"

"I guess so, but people wear sunglasses at crazy times of the day all the time."

"I know, but look what I found six hours later, around midnight."

"It's the same car, the same guy wearing the same hat and sunglasses going in the opposite direction."

"It is a bit off, I suppose."

"Yeah, it struck me that way too. So, I decided to run his plates. Everything looked perfectly in order at first glance. It's registered to Otto Armstrong from Phoenix. Still, something wasn't sitting right, so I dug a little deeper, and guess what I found?"

Mike shrugged and motioned for Danny to continue. "Otto Armstrong died in 1989 when he was fifteen. They have the same social security number and the same birthday. I must say old Otto looks really good for being dead more than 30 years."

Mike would bet his retirement, house, and car that this was the real killer. He leaned closer to the screen, trying to memorize every curve and indentation of this, his killer. He was strangely calm as he memorized the little of this man's face he could see. For the first time, he knew who his target was. Now all he had to do was find him.

"Danny, my man, I owe you big time. Finally, a break!"

"It's Daniel Roosevelt Carter."

"What?" Mike asked distractedly

"For when you name your firstborn after me." Danny laughed

"Roosevelt, really?"

"Yeah, my grandmother was a staunch yellow-dog democrat. My father and uncles all had Democratic presidents for their middle names. Uncle Harry Kennedy, Uncle Bill Truman, and of course, my dad, Phillip Roosevelt." Danny smiled, shrugged, and went back to the computer screen.

"This explains so much about you, Dude." Mike laughed and started for the door. "Thanks again. You really came through for me."

"Came through, how?" Vanessa pushed into the room and made her way over to Danny's desk.

"I just asked him if he had any Sun's tickets I could buy," Mike said the first thing that came to his head. He looked over at Danny's computer monitors and was relieved to see the feed they had been watching was gone.

"Oh well, that's good. I would hate to think you were wasting police time and resources on an already closed investigation. An investigation, I might add, the mayor wants long forgotten before the election rolls around."

"I'm beginning to think you're stalking me, Vanessa. You always show up where I am, asking everyone what I'm doing." Mike arched his eyebrow in mock surprise.

"I hate to tell you, girl, but he's just not that into you." Danny cracked sarcastically, causing Mike to laugh and Vanessa to start steaming.

"If you keep harassing me, I'm going to have to file a restraining order. A sensitive guy like me feels threatened by so much attention." Mike continued sarcastically.

"In your dreams, Choctowsky. I only sleep with males of the same species." Vanessa retorted. "You better watch your step. I will find proof of what you're doing, and it will be your neck on the chopping block. I will laugh as your entire career gets flushed down the drain." She turned sharply and left the room, the cloying scent of her perfume lingering long after she had gone.

"Mike, seriously, watch your back. That is one tiger that isn't afraid to dig her claws into your back."

"Yeah, I know. Hopefully, I'll be able to fly under the radar long enough to find this guy. Somethings are more important than a career, and finding this guy is one of them."

"Hey, could you print out a blow-up of that guy's face for me?"

"Sure, just give me a minute here." In a matter of a few seconds, Mike heard the whir of the printer.

"Thanks again, Danny. If you find your nuts in a vice with Vanessa, you tell her what I had you do. I'm the ranking officer. There is no reason for us both to go down over this."

"You're good people, Mike." Danny gave him a dismissive half-smile and then lost himself again in his virtual universe.

Mike returned to his desk, studying the fuzzy face on the printout in his hands. A baseball cap covered the suspect's hair, and dark sunglasses covered his eyes. All Mike could see was that the suspect was a Caucasian male with a square jaw. He pulled the vehicle registration in the database and jotted down the address. It wouldn't hurt to take a drive past the house listed.

Mike rolled the window of his truck down; the Phoenix heat was hell, but he wanted the feel of the wind on his face as he drove. He input the address he'd scribbled on a blue post-It back in the office into his GPS. It brought him only a few miles from the airport. He turned up the 80's radio station and drove with the wind blowing through the open windows. Nothing made him happier than tracking down a killer and nailing him to the wall. He glanced in his review mirror and noticed that the same black Cadillac had been following him for five miles. He recognized the car. Vanessa was doing a lousy job of tailing him, he decided to have a little fun with her. He looked for the nearest gas station, quickly crossed two lanes, and pulled in without warning. He parked parallel to the road and waved at Vanessa as she drove past, unable to get over to follow him into the gas station. Before she could turn around and pick up his trail, he darted down a few side roads, making his way toward the airport on the back roads. It wouldn't do for Vanessa to figure out what he was up to today.

It took an extra ten minutes, but he eventually reached the address the car was registered to. He looked at the building and then at the GPS. Making sure he hadn't made a mistake. He called Danny and had him read the address from the original vehicle registration to be sure he hadn't copied it wrong. No, he was at the right address. It wasn't a house; instead, it was a rundown self-storage business. The office was open, so he figured he'd see if the employee recognized their suspect's blurry photocopy. It was a long shot, but you miss every shot you don't take.

The old bell above the door rang as he walked through. There was no one at the counter as he approached, but after a few seconds, a middle-aged woman made her way from the office to the counter. She had frizzy bright red hair, the color red that could only be bought in a box. She wore a skin-tight leather miniskirt and a black shirt at least two sizes too small.

She eyed him up and down and smiled a seductive smile. "Well, what can I do for you, good-looking?"

Mike cleared his throat and pulled his badge from his back pocket. "Hi, ma'am. I was wondering if you could help me?"

The smile vanished when the aging vixen caught sight of his badge. "Oh, what can I do for you, officer?"

"I'm Detective Mike Choctowsky. Could you look at a picture and tell me if you recognize the man?"

The woman visibly relaxed when he pulled the picture out of the folder in his hand. "Sure, I'll have a look." The woman leaned over the counter, her ample tits stretching the limits of the small shirt, and grabbed the paper he held out.

"It's blurry, so I'm not certain, but that might be Mr. Jones."

"I'm sorry, I didn't catch your name, Ms.?"

"I'm Freda Wright. I've been the manager here for the last twenty years."

"Ms. Wright, how do you know Mr. Jones?"

"He has rented one of our units for the last" Freda stopped to remember for a moment. "I guess it's been about ten years or so."

"Ten years, wow. Is there anything that sticks out about him to you?"

"Actually, I've only ever met him the one time I rented him the unit. Every year we get a money order for the entire year's rent. I don't think I've seen him come to the unit since he rented it."

"Thank you so much, Ms. Wright. I don't suppose you could show me which unit is his."

"It's number 12. If you want more than that, you'll need a warrant. Our clients expect a measure of privacy, you know."

"Absolutely. Thank you so much for all your help, ma'am." Crap, there was no way he would get a judge to sign a warrant on what he had. He would have to figure something out. He had to get into that storage unit. His gut told him he would find some of the needed answers inside.

Vanessa slammed the car door shut. Damn Mike Choctowsky, the self-righteous prick. A few years ago, she'd flirted with him. She knew she had a reputation. She made no apologies. She had grown-up dirt-poor, eating government cheese and wearing Salvation Army rejects. Her mother had worked two minimum-wage jobs to afford even that. Vanessa swore she would never be poor again. She would do whatever or whoever it took to never again feel hunger pains or smell the stench of a second-hand store.

When she had flirted with Mike, she'd been attracted to him, not for anything he could offer her career but because he excited her. He was a little older than her, but he was hot, and he didn't give a damn what anyone thought. Mike did what he knew was right, no matter what it cost him. He refused to play the politics of the job because all he cared about was getting his man. It made him a damn fine detective, but he would never be anything more.

She'd tried to kiss him late one night at the precinct. Instead of being flattered, he'd pushed her away. Then he laughed and said he'd sooner kiss a scorpion. No one treated her like that, no one. She'd never forgotten the humiliation of that night, but now she would get her revenge. He was up to something with that computer geek. She was sure of it; now she had to prove it. She'd been sure she would get her proof today when she followed him, but he'd spotted her and then had the nerve to wave at her as she drove past. What an arrogant jackass! Well, she had her own ways of getting what she wanted. She smoothed her tight black cocktail dress over her hips, grabbed a compact out of her purse, and fixed her red lipstick. Yeah, she had her own assets, and so far, Mike had been the only man to turn them down.

Danny stretched at his desk; it had been a long day. Thank God tomorrow was Sunday; he planned to sleep in, grab a quick workout, and then he was going to sit his ass on his sofa and play Call of Duty. It was going to be an epic day. He took off his headphones and started shutting down his computer. Suddenly soft hands were messaging his shoulders, making him nearly jump out of his skin. He quickly spun around to see who was behind him. It was Vanessa in some skin-tight, short get-up. Yeah, she looked hot, and she knew it. She ran her hand down her waist and pouted at him with plump, fire-engine-red lips.

"Danny, I was wondering if you could help me."

"Wha" Danny cleared his throat. "What do you need, Vanessa?" Danny tried to avoid looking at her, but were those tits real?

"Well," she ran one red-tipped finger down the buttons on his shirt. She stopped at his belt buckle. "I need to know what Mike wanted you to find for him. It is important, so I could make it worth your while." she smiled a pouty smile and absentmindedly flicked her finger a little lower on his belt buckle.

"He just wanted some game tickets, li, like he told you." Danny was having difficulty focusing on the conversation; beautiful women were his kryptonite.

Vanessa slid her finger into the waistband of his pants. She leaned over to whisper in his ear, her breast pushing against his arm. "C'mon, baby, tell me what he really wanted. I can tell you want me as much as I want you." She blew a long, hot breath into his ear and stood straight, removing her finger from his waistband. Danny groaned. God, he was only a man who could resist only so much temptation.

"He didn't want anything big; he just asked me to look at some traffic footage." He reached out to run his hands up the outside of her dress. When his hands were right below her tits, Vanessa put her hands over his "Do you want to touch those?" Danny groaned. "Well, you need to show me exactly what he wanted to look at."

Danny felt like a traitor, but he turned around and started his computer back up. While the computer was booting up, Vanessa began leaning over him, her arms wrapped around him, unbuttoning his shirt. After his shirt hung open, she began to flick his nipples with her fingernails and ran her tongue along the shell of his ear. "That's it, baby. Show me what I need to see, and I will give you your prize."

Danny could barely type as he got into the system and pulled up the feed he had shown Mike not too many hours before. His hands were shaking, and his breath ragged. He knew she was playing him, but God, she played him like a pro.

"What's so special about this feed, Danny baby?"

"It's the guy in the car at the stop light. Mike thought he looked odd."

Vanessa looked at the screen and saw a guy in sunglasses sitting at a red light. His registration wasn't even out of date.

She turned Danny around in his chair, undid his belt, and pulled his shorts down. She knelt in front of him and licked her delicious red lips. "Tell me everything" She dropped her face into his lap. "And I won't stop doing what I'm doing."

With that, Danny told her everything he knew, some things a man couldn't resist.

Griffin meticulously packed his tool kit. He would have to drive to the small town where Carina Wythcliff was. What he had in this bag would not make it through airport security. He should send the local yokel cop a bottle of bourbon for running her prints through the system. Griffin laughed at the irony of law enforcement making it possible for him to carry out his oh-so-illegal plans. It had been a stressful few months hunting her, but the hunt was almost at its end. Then he would be done with her and that bastard in New York forever. There was an island in the Pacific calling his name. He could almost smell the sunblock and taste the rum. He ensured he had enough of the tranquilizer to knock out a herd of elephants, plenty of ammunition, his trusty K-Bar knife, Glock, a shotgun, a small coil of piano wire, his gloves, plastic sheeting, duct tape, and a bone saw. Always be prepared was the motto of every Boy Scout and serial killer. He whistled as he triple-checked his preparations; the ritual of preparing always relaxed him. He smiled as he straightened the bone saw and a box of latex gloves. They had shifted as he was packing them, and that wouldn't do. Everything has a place, and everything in its place. Satisfied that everything was in order, he locked the car, left his storage unit in Chicago, and returned to his hotel. He would have one more night of luxury before leaving in the morning for Cutler's Gap, which promised to be some small west Texas hell hole.

His cell phone rang as he entered the lobby of the Waldorf Astoria. He looked at the number and sighed as he answered it.

"Griffin here." His tone was clipped. This bastard was the last person he wanted to talk to tonight.

"Do you have her yet?" The sick bastard sounded like he was foaming at the mouth in anticipation.

"You only called me a few hours ago with her coordinates, so I don't have her yet. Calm yourself, take a cold shower, lift a car, and do whatever rich bastards like you do when you have a hard-on. Leave me alone to do my job in peace! I'll call you once I have her."

"Don't talk about her that way; it's sick. Also, remember that this entire mess is due to your incompetence. If you lose her again, I will not be as patient as I have been." The threat was clear in his voice. The spider may have to be dealt with sooner rather than later.

Griffin was a smart man; his caution had saved his life more than once. He took every threat seriously, no matter how seemingly inconsequential it was. He dealt with every threat quickly, dispassionately, and without mercy; a man in his line of work couldn't afford to leave his enemies alive.

He kept his voice steady and unaffected. It wouldn't do for the Senator to become more paranoid than he already was. "I'll get her and have her back home sweet home soon. I'll call you when it's done." He ended the call. Griffin knew most polite society would consider him an evil man; he didn't care what they thought. The way he saw it, he had a set of skills and provided those skills to others who could afford to pay for them. He did his job, did it well, got paid, and walked away. He didn't get any particular pleasure in doing the work; it was just a job. But the Senator was another kind of evil entirely. His good looks and pep school manners may fool most people but not Griffin. When he looked into the Senator's eyes, he saw a predator, the kind that enjoyed torturing small animals to death, or scared women, as the case may be. Griffin rubbed the back of his neck. He needed to relax before he started the hunt. He called Elaine; with any luck, the girl he'd rented the first night in town would be available. She had pleased him.

Chapter Sixteen

Mike opened his eyes, instinctively reaching for the remote as he picked up his ringing cell phone. He'd fallen asleep in the recliner watching ESPN again. He muted the TV as he answered his phone.

"Choctowsky." His voice was rough with sleep.

"Mike. It's Danny. I have shit news."

"Oh God, what now?"

"You know how I warned you that Vanessa was nosing around?"

"Yeah, she tried to tail me earlier today. What's she done now?"

There was an uncomfortable pause, and then Danny cleared his throat. "She came back to my office right before I headed home. She was, uh, real, umm, insistent that I tell her what you were looking into."

Mike silently sighed. "It's alright; I figured this might happen. How much did you tell her?"

Danny went quiet again, then cleared his throat. "Well, um, at first I tried to just tell her the bare minimum, but she has ways of making you talk."

"What did she threaten you with?" Mike felt his blood pressure rising. That bitch had been a thorn in his side for too long. But he had no way of getting rid of her.

"Well, she didn't exactly threaten me." Danny sounded sheepish on the other end of the call.

"Danny, tell me you didn't sleep with her!" Mike groaned.

"To quote our great former president, Bill Clinton, I did not have sexual relations with that woman."

"Danny, do you know where that woman's mouth has been?"

"Well, I know one place." Danny's old humor was back.

"This may be good for you, though, Mike."

"How will this be a good thing for me?" Mike asked incredulously.

"No, seriously, Mike, listen up. There are a few things about me that Vanessa doesn't know. One is that I am one paranoid SOB."

"Danny, the whole office knows that about you."

"Yeah, the whole office except Vanessa. She didn't know I existed until a few days ago."

"Where are you going with this, Danny?"

"I think you know exactly where I'm going with this." Danny retorted.

"You suspicious, horny, genius; you have your office wired, don't you?"

"I figured I couldn't be too careful; with a body like this, you never know who will get their panties in a twist when I turn them down. Never thought I would be the one sexually harassed." Danny laughed at the irony

"It doesn't sound like a lot of harassment involved," Mike said sardonically. "However, she is technically a superior officer. Let's see her get out of this one. If nothing else, it will keep her off my back for a while." Mike started up the stairs.

"Thanks, Danny. I need to run. I have to do something before Vanessa can make a move."

"Don't do anything stupid, Mike."

"I think you're the one wearing the dunce cap tonight. I'd get tested to ensure she didn't infect you with her evil."

"I'm a weak man Mike, but I have to say all her practice has made her an expert."

"I'll have to take your word for it because there is no way I will ever find out." Mike hung up the phone.

He looked at the clock. It was quarter to nine. He should get to the storage unit by eleven if he left now.

He took the stairs two at a time to his bedroom, changed into his black sweats, grabbed a pair of latex gloves in his uniform pocket, and a lockpick set his ex-wife had bought as a gag gift years ago. He put on his black baseball cap and put sunglasses on his sweatshirt. He'd take a few tips from his mysterious man on the traffic footage.

Mike pulled into the parking lot of the old shopping center next to the self-storage units. He'd noticed earlier that day that the fence on that side of the storage units was old; in some places, the fence was permanently bent up, leaving a space for someone to bellycrawl through. He quickly looked around, and seeing no one, he jogged to where he was least likely to be seen. After one last look around, noting it was clear, he dropped to his stomach and scooted through the small hole. It took him only a few seconds to clear the fence and get back on his feet. Soon he was walking towards the units to find unit number twelve.

The storage unit wasn't hard to find. It was the twelfth from the gate. Go figure. He was relieved to see it had a closed shackle padlock. He would be able to pick it instead of cutting it off. It took him several nerve-wracking minutes to pick the lock. Finally, after what seemed like an eternity, the lock clicked, and the shackle popped free. Quickly, he rolled open the unit's garage-style door. He felt around for a light switch and clicked it on.

He blinked, his eyes taking a moment to adjust to the bright light. Once his eyes could focus, he began his survey of the unit. Shelves lined the walls. Plastic storage bins lined each shelf, each labeled and exactly three inches from the one beside it. In the middle of the unit sat a tarp-covered car. He rolled the unit door back down and walked to the car. Mike had chills go up his spine as he uncovered the vehicle. He read the license plate number aloud, checking it against the Post-it he'd stuck in his notebook. Sure enough, the numbers matched.

He tried to open the car doors, but they were locked. He'd bet a week's pay that he'd find the keys in this storage unit. He opened the plastic bin nearest him.

It was labeled 'Plastic Sheeting"; inside was a pile of perfectly folded plastic. He'd need forensics to test it and compare it to the desert plastic to know for sure, but it was the same density and color. His gut told him it was the same stuff. No keys. He moved to the next bin. Jackpot! Sitting on top was a set of car keys. Under the keys was an Arizona driver's license.

He had barely glanced at it when he noticed a quiet beeping; he glanced around, trying to figure out where the noise was coming from. He bent to the ground and looked under the car. He saw a flashing light attached to what appeared to be a bomb. The light started to flash faster; Mike ran to the storage unit door, quickly pulled it up, and ran.

He hadn't quite cleared the fence when the world exploded around him. Mike felt the heat where he lay halfway through the fence. As soon as the ringing in his ears subsided, he sprinted to his truck. He could not be found near this place when the fire department arrived. He drove only on backroads, like a bat out of hell, hoping to avoid traffic cameras. He had just pulled into his driveway when his phone rang.

"Choctowsky."

"Mike, I hate to call you in, but we've just had an explosion at an old storage unit facility near the airport; we're calling everyone in on this one."

"Were there any fatalities?"

"We don't know yet. They're still trying to get the fire controlled. From neighbor reports and the shrapnel they found around the property, they are sure it was a bomb. I want you on the scene so you can get a look at the crime scene as soon as the bomb squad has cleared it."

"Good God, what's happening to this town? I'm on my way, Chief." Mike hung up, took the stairs two at a time, changed his clothes, and headed back out. He went the direct route this time, ensuring the traffic cameras recorded his whole trip.

Griffin smiled a half smile. Whoever had set off the alarm at his Phoenix storage unit just received quite the surprise. He had wired all his units to send an alert to his cell phone if they were compromised. He could send a text and blow the unit to hell. No, they wouldn't be recovering any evidence from the unit. Still, it also meant that his identity in Phoenix was blown, no pun intended. That wasn't as big a deal as it would have been if he still had a contact there. With John gone, there was nothing to draw him back to Arizona. In his own way, he was going to miss John. John was his last link to his past; maybe not all his past, but his military past. John had been the closest thing to a friend Griffin allowed himself. The whore that was busily bobbing her head in his lap looked up when he sighed and lifted her head when she noticed him studying his cell phone.

"I didn't tell you to stop," Griffin said softly, violently shoving her head back into his lap. She wasn't nearly as satisfactory as she had been the first time he'd hired her. He hated not getting his money's worth out of anything he bought. Just the thought frustrated him enough to lash her back with the belt he held in his hand; strict discipline was the only way for a whore to learn. He locked his phone screen and laid his head back against the back of the chair. The girl was earning her keep now, the tears flowing down her cheeks and the welts rising on her back finally excited him. He might as well enjoy it while it lasted.

Mike saw the flashing lights of the fire trucks long before he pulled up to the scene of the bombing. Surveying the damage, he realized how lucky he had been to survive the explosion. The storage building that housed unit 12 was completely gone; only the concrete slab of the foundation remained intact. Debris from the explosion was everywhere, some of it still smoldering. Several other storage buildings had sustained serious damage. Though most of the fire was out, smaller blazes still burned here and there and were being put out by the firefighters on the scene. The cloying smell of smoke, burning plastic, rubber, and chemicals made breathing hard. Mike searched the scene and found Chief Conway sitting on a collapsible chair. Soot covered his face, his eyes irritated and red from the smoke.

"Hey, Mike," Chip Conway's voice was exhausted, "I'd say it was good to see you, but honestly, I would rather be asleep in my bed than dealing with this mess." His bloodshot eyes surveyed the destruction before him

"It's been a long time, Chip. What in hell is this city coming to?" Mike was still shaken from his narrow escape. No one knew how close he had come to having his body parts scattered amidst the smoldering debris.

"Do we know if there were any casualties?" He silently prayed that no one had been injured or killed because of him.

"It's too soon to know for sure, but so far, it appears the building was empty when it went up. An old, dilapidated storage facility gets bombed in the middle of the night," Chip shook his head. "If I were a betting man, I'd wager the owner was trying to ditch the building and claim the insurance. Of course, that's purely a guess at this point, so don't quote me." Mike just nodded as he leaned against the chief's truck, watching little flames dance across the ground.

"Hey, Chief, look what we found over by that fence." A young fireman came running over towards the truck Mike leaned against. He felt his stomach drop when he realized what was in his hand. He must have still had the license in his hand when he ran away from the storage unit, and he had obviously dropped it during the blast. At least he'd been wearing gloves so his prints wouldn't be on it, but that was his one-real lead to who the killer, now bomber, was. Now his one piece of solid evidence would be buried in this investigation. He hadn't even gotten a good look at it before he had to run for his life.

"Hey, Chief, can I get a look at that." Mike tried to sound as casual as he could

"Sure," Chip handed it to him. "Mean anything to you?"

"Not right now." Mike studied the face in the picture, dark hair slicked back, green eyes, and a slight scar on the left cheek. The man was good-looking enough. He memorized the face before him. He would find him, whoever he really was.

Chapter Seventeen

Kate huffed as Tom led her back to her room. Why couldn't the man leave her alone? She needed to get out of this backwoods town today. Even then, it may be too late.

"You didn't really think you could ditch me that easily, did you?" He gave her one of his infuriating wry smiles and a wink.

"Sheriff, I didn't realize I couldn't leave town. I thought I'd been cleared of any crimes."

"Well Katie-Did, that is a matter of opinion. See, I know that there is something you still aren't telling me, something that still terrifies you. Until I am sure you aren't in danger and aren't a danger to others, I will keep an eye on you. It is my job, after all."

"Tom, I have to go. I can't explain any more than that. You have to trust me when I say it will be bad news for everyone if I don't leave." Kate tried to sound rational, not letting the sick panic in her throat break through her voice. Tom would never let her go if he heard the terrified screaming inside her soul that had started two years ago and had never stopped. It had grown quieter for a few short months when she had deceived herself into thinking she could have a real life here in Cutler's Gap. That delusion had been smashed into a million jagged shards of pain and disappointment that embedded deep into her heart when Tom ran her fingerprints through the national database.

Kate was physically shaking, though Tom doubted she realized it. She was trying so hard to hide how terrified she was. His heart broke with hers. Why wouldn't she trust him, even a little? He would move heaven and earth to protect her, even if that meant protecting her from herself.

"Okay, here's the deal. If you really want to leave, you can. I won't hold you here. Just give me ten minutes to pack my bags."

"What do you mean "pack your bags'? I don't remember inviting you along for a road trip. I mean, the sex was great and took the edge off, but it wasn't that great!"

Tom laughed, he actually laughed, out loud, at her, like she had said something ridiculous! Kate stiffened her spine, no one and nobody laughed at her. She stood up, jerked her arm away from Tom's hand, and stormed towards the door.

Tom called after her, "Katie-did, you're forgetting something." He dangled her keys from the fingers of his other hand, laughing all the harder.

"Grrrr, you are the most infuriating man I have ever met!" Kate stomped back towards him, trying to grab the keys he easily kept out of her reach. Finally tired of trying to get her keys back, Kate stomped her foot and fell into the chair in the corner. Tom smiled and waved at her.

"I'll be right back. We'll take my truck; I'm pretty sure your car will fall to pieces the moment we hit a pothole." With that, Tom opened the door and walked through it.

"Har-de-har. You are hilarious." Kate called after him, but the door had already closed, and she saw him walking away through the window. He was the most narcissistic, irritating man she'd ever met. It would show him right if she hotwired her car and left anyway, not that she knew how to hotwire a car. Somehow, she'd missed that class in prep school.

There wasn't anything she could do about the situation right now. At least she was getting away from the town, and though she would never admit it to him, having Tom along did make her feel a little safer, almost as much as it terrified her. She could not handle having another death on her conscience. She had barely survived the first one with her sanity intact. In the distance, Kate heard church bells chiming. It was one of those quaint little small-town things that most people loved about Cutler's Gap. A shiver went down her spine. Those church bells made her want to scream every morning. They reminded her of other bells, bells that chimed every hour on the hour. Kate reached for the blanket on the back of her chair only to realize she had packed it and left it with her bags in her car's trunk. She sighed, laid her head against the back of the chair, and closed her eyes. She pushed aside all the bad memories and willed herself to grab a few minutes of dreamless sleep.

Tom looked at his watch. He had already been gone from Kate for more than the ten minutes he'd promised. Having returned to his office, he realized that he couldn't simply pack up and go but couldn't keep Kate in town. She would run as soon as he turned his back. He needed her to be safe, but how could he care for her and the town? He leaned back in his chair, pulled his hat low over his eyes, put his boots on his time-scarred desk, crossed his legs, and twirled Kate's car keys around his finger as he thought of a solution to his dilemma.

The bell above the door clanged noisily, interrupting his thoughts. He pushed back his hat and saw Charlie, mad as a hornet, rounding the front counter and heading towards his office. Tom sighed. He really didn't have time for Charlie and Doug's nonsense today. He had a town to watch over and a girl to save from herself.

Charlie pushed open the office door and didn't even stop to catch his breath, "Tom, he's been at it again! I'm pressing charges this time, and I expect you to go out there and arrest him."

Tom sighed loudly, pointedly. "Charlie, breathe. You'll give yourself a heart attack, rushing around, mad as a bull, red in the face. You're too old for this. Have a seat," Charlie started to protest, but Tom interrupted him, "Have a seat and take a minute to catch your breath. My day is already booked, and I can't fit "Give Charlie CPR and save his life" into my schedule. Once you've calmed down, tell me what's going on. I'm assuming the 'him' you're referring to is Doug."

Charlie flopped into the chair across from Tom and loudly took a few deep breaths as he stubbornly glared at Tom. The older Charlie and Doug got, the more they acted like a couple of kids. He now understood why his mom would count to twenty when he was a kid. He'd always thought it was for his and his brothers' benefit to instill the fear of God in them. Now he knew it was to give herself a minute to regain some patience because he found himself counting silently, hoping that Charlie would miraculously disappear before he got to twenty.

"Alright, I'm done 'breathing.' Of course, I'm talking about that old coot, Doug! Do you know what he did while I was helping you with your girlfriend, which you made a mess of? I wouldn't be surprised if she never spoke to you again! Anyway, while I was helping you, Doug cut my new fence lines and let his cows into my wheat field. They've destroyed half the field!" Charlie was up, out of the chair, pacing the room, his face red once again as he recounted the story.

"Do you have any proof that Doug cut your fence line?" Tom asked in as reasonable a voice as he could.

"Who else would it be? That man has been a thorn in my side for sixty years!" Charlie's voice was getting louder with every word he spoke.

"Be that as it may, your history isn't grounds for me to arrest him. I need proof that he did it." Tom explained as patiently as he could.

"Getting proof, ain't that what you're paid for? You're the sheriff of this town, aren't ya? Why don't you go take some fingerprints or something?"

"You want me to get fingerprints off a barbed wire fence? If Doug cut the fence, he would have worn work gloves when he did it, don't you think?"

"Well, sure, he's a mean old coot, but he ain't an idiot," Charlie responded as if Tom were an idiot to even ask.

"If he wore work gloves, he wouldn't leave fingerprints, now would he?" There was an edge of frustration in Tom's voice. He didn't have time or energy for this today.

"Don't speak to me like I'm the dunce of the class. I was a lawyer before you were born!"

"What would you like me to do, Charlie? I have a town to protect, the woman I love is in trouble, and she won't tell me what it is, and I have to figure out a way to protect her while still doing my job. I don't have time to be settling 60-year-old feuds today!"

"Well, it's your own fault she won't speak to you. What did you expect would happen after you arrested and interrogated her?" Of course, Charlie would be on Kate's side. The two of them deserved each other as far as he was concerned. Suddenly Tom had a brilliant idea that would solve both of his problems at once. This idea was so brilliant that he should be nominated for the Nobel peace prize or something!

"You're right, Charlie. It is my fault that Kate wants nothing to do with me, but I still have to keep her safe." Tom said with as much humility as he could muster. He pretended to think for a minute, scratching his five o'clock shadow for effect. Then he slowly started speaking, like an idea had just dawned on him. "She loves you, though. I bet I could convince her to stay at the farm with you. Then you could keep an eye on her while I focus on solving the mystery of your cut fence lines." Tom had to bite the inside of his lip to keep from laughing as Charlie pondered his proposal.

"Well, I guess that would work. Kate would be safer out at my farm, and you could do your job and get proof on Doug. Of course, this is just temporary. I don't want her feminizing the place up or anything. But Kate is good company." Charlie stuck out his hand and shook hands with Tom. Along with his Nobel prize, he deserved an Oscar for that performance, he thought as he shook hands with Charlie.

"It's a deal. I'll round up Kate and her things and bring her by your place in a bit." Charlie grunted, seemingly satisfied, and left, the bell tingling as the door closed behind him.

Now to convince Kate of the plan, but he didn't have a doubt that she would go along with it. After all, if she had to choose him on her ass all day, every day, or Charlie, she'd choose Charlie. If his woman was gonna be pissed at him, he might as well make it work to his advantage. Tom stuck his boots back on his desk, leaned back in his chair, his hands crossed behind his head, and smiled a satisfied smile; two frustrating birds, one spot on stone, just how he liked things.

The noon sun glared through the window, waking Kate from her exhausted sleep. She turned her head and glanced at the red digital numbers of the alarm clock; 12:30, twelve thirty her foot. Where was Tom? She needed to get out of this town; like an approaching storm, she could feel the dark presence of evil speeding toward her. She should already have a few hundred miles between Cutler's Gap and herself.

As she stretched, she noticed a long body stretched out on her bed, sandy hair tousled on her pillow, and gray eyes looking at her intently. How dare he just show up and think she would be okay with him lying in her bed after yesterday? Kate fumed. She reached for the remote on the side table beside her chair and threw it at his arrogant head. It missed the mark and hit the wall behind him. Tom jumped as the remote clattered to the floor behind the bed. "Now, Katie, don't be like that. You enjoyed seeing me in your bed not all that long ago." Tom smiled; the intensity was gone as if it had never been there. Would she ever understand this man? Underneath the easygoing cowboy exterior was a man with strength, intelligence, and strong emotions. She never knew what to expect from him.

"Hello, sleepy head. Are you ready to go, or would you like to join me?" Tom gave her a wolfish grin and patted the bed next to him. Kate didn't even answer as she glared at him. "Oh well, your loss." He swung his long legs out of bed, picked up the bag she had carried back into the room earlier, and was at the door in three easy strides.

"Where exactly are we going?" Kate crossed her arms, leaned back in her chair, and looked at him suspiciously. She didn't trust that easy-going act he was throwing her way; he was up to something. She'd bet her last dime on it.

"You said you had to go, and I said the only way that would happen is if I went with you. So, let's go," Tom continued opening the door.

"I'm not going anywhere with you, and that's a fact." Kate glared at him across the few feet that separated them.

"Well, I guess we are at an impasse because you've got to go, I won't let you go without me, and you won't go with me." Tom was irritatingly calm.

"Tom, be reasonable. You barely know me. Your life is here. Just give me my keys and let me go. It's better for everyone." Kate tried to sound as reasonable as he did.

"Sorry, Kate, it would be irresponsible of me to let someone who claimed to be in danger leave without protection. I would never let the woman I love leave without me. So, I guess we'll just sit here until you make up your mind what you want to do." Tom put her bag down, took the three steps back, swung his legs back up on the bed, crossed his booted feet, and reached for the remote.

"You do not love me! You barely know me!! You have no right to keep me a prisoner here or to come with me! I am a grown woman who makes my own choices and decisions. I choose to leave. I choose to leave you. I don't love you and don't want you or your damn protection. Just leave me the hell alone! I will never let another man decide anything for me!!" Kate was screaming, and she didn't care. She was tired of men trying to impose their will on her. The last man that tried it had admitted her to a psychiatric hospital. When they had released her, he had kept her drugged in a bed for over a year. Tom would never control her. No man would.

"Kate, you're wrong. I do love you. It may not be what you want to hear, you may not feel the same way, and it may have happened suddenly. I don't expect anything from you. But I am a grown man, and I know my own feelings. You aren't the first woman to turn my head, but you sure as hell are the first woman I've loved. It's insulting for you to insist that I don't know my own mind and heart. As for controlling you, I have no desire to control you or decide anything for you. One of the things I love most about you is your independent nature and strong will. I want a life partner, not a doormat. I understand you aren't there. I'll wait for you to make up your mind about me. I'm in no hurry. I'm not expecting anything from you, but I will be damned if I let whatever it is you're running from hurt you because you're mad at me. If you don't want to be with me, that's fine. Go stay with Charlie, he'd love to have you, and honestly, it will keep him out of my hair for a while. He's a lonely old man living on a ranch out in the middle of nowhere. No one will find you there, and you will be rid of me. The other two options are you stay here in town where I can look out for you, or we load up and leave together. You decide. It's your choice, but you will not leave this town alone to run from some danger you will not even explain."

Tom was angry, very angry. She'd been wondering what lay underneath that intense stare, well now she knew, and she wished she didn't. Her feelings for Tom were confusing and frustrating. He was funny, smart, infuriating, and arrogant. She felt safe with him, but he betrayed her trust when he arrested her. She didn't have the luxury of figuring this out or falling in love. She needed distance between the two of them. If moving in with Charlie would make Tom happy enough to leave her alone, she'd move in with Charlie. Besides, she could get away from Charlie much easier than Tom.

"Fine, I'll go to Charlie's ranch for now." Kate sounded defeated, but Tom didn't trust her for a split second. She'd be gone from Charlie's before the dust settled from him dropping her off. "That's alright; I've got your number Katie-did." Tom smiled to himself.

"Alright, if that's what you want." He slid off the bed again, picked up her bag, tossed her the keys, and held the door open for her.

Kate caught the keys midair, a confused and surprised look on her face. She'd expected more of a fight from him.

She marched to her car, Tom behind her. He loaded her bag into the hatchback and stepped back, giving her a small wave. Kate turned the key to start the engine; all she got was a sputtering sound. She tried to start it again, and the engine sputtered again, making a coughing noise, and died. She tried a third time, but the same thing happened. Great, just flipping great. The car had been on its last legs since she bought it back in Baltimore, but she hoped to get to Colorado before switching it for another beater.

Tom motioned her to roll down her window. "What's the problem?"

"I have no idea," Kate sighed. "I knew she was on her last legs, but I thought she still had a little life left in her."

"If you pop the hood, I'll have a look. I'm no mechanic, but if it's something simple, I may be able to get it going." Tom walked around to the front of the car, and she popped the hood latch.

"Thanks' I appreciate it." Kate blew out a long breath. She so didn't need this right now.

Tom poked around under the hood for a while, every few minutes yelling for her to "Try it now." all to no avail. The car would not start. "There is nothing obvious that I can see, but like I said, I'm no mechanic. You could have Graham over at the garage look at it for you."

"I doubt that there's anything he can do. She's been dying for a long time now. I'll have him take a look, but I don't have a lot of hope for this old girl. You wouldn't happen to know anyone selling a used car, would you?"

"Sorry, I don't, but I can ask around. How about I give you a ride out to Charlie's for now? If Graham can't fix your car, someone will hopefully sell something."

"If it isn't too much trouble, I'd appreciate that." Kate gave him a half smile. This is just what she didn't need, another delay in leaving.

Tom had to force himself not to whistle as he loaded Kate's few bags into the back of his truck. So far, his plan was going perfectly. Pouring that ten-pound bag of sugar into Kate's gas tank had been an act of mercy; really, it had been. The poor thing should have been laid to rest ages ago; now, it happily raced around that giant racetrack in the sky. The fact that Kate had one less escape route, well, that suited him just fine. He'd already told Charlie to hide his truck keys in the barn. This is what made him so good at his job; he always saw at least ten moves ahead. He had developed the skill in high school, where he had been the state chess champion for three years straight. He smiled at Kate as he climbed into the driver's seat of his truck. She scowled at him and turned toward her window, her thoughts a million miles away.

Chapter Eighteen

Kate stared at the stark landscape as the miles flew by the window. There were long, barbed wire fence lines, on either side of the road, with an occasional tumbleweed pushed up against them. Behind the fences was a wilderness of scrub, dust, and rock; the desolation was only broken by the scattering of cows and an occasional goat. A large plateau loomed in the distance, creeping steadily closer. This west Texas landscape was simultaneously foreboding and beautiful.

After driving for nearly an hour, Tom slowed the truck and turned down a dusty, dirt road. A rusted metal arched ranch entrance proclaimed, "Benet Ranch." The large B and R were in fancy script, a twisted, metal lasso wrapping loosely around the name. The gate stood open. At one time, the entrance must have been painted white. But the harsh west Texas wind and dust had long ago stripped away most of the paint, leaving the whole entryway rusted with small bits of peeling dirty white paint. Kate couldn't help but think the ranch sign captured Charlie perfectly, old and tired, worn down by time and life storms, but still showing bits of its former glory.

Like the entrance, the long dirt road to the ranch house had seen better days. Tom swerved back and forth to avoid crater-sized potholes; the constant jerking and swerving made Kate sick to her stomach. She was so relieved when they finally pulled up to the ranch house that she considered kissing the ground as she stepped out of the truck. After seeing the condition of the entrance and road, Kate had been apprehensive about the house's condition. To her delight, the ranch house was in good repair and surprisingly homey. Like most ranch houses, it was a single-story house. The wood siding was stained a dark brown. A large porch ran the length of the front of the house, and three fans spaced equal distances apart whirred quietly overhead. Charlie sat in one of several rocking chairs spread haphazardly around the porch. Other than a large American flag and an antique Coca-Cola vending machine, the porch had no other decorations or adornments. Charlie smiled as she walked up the porch steps while Tom grabbed her bags from the truck's bed.

"So, you've come to keep me company for a spell" Charlie held an old pipe in his. The smoke silently curled around his head before the fan dissipated it.

"I really appreciate you having me, Charlie." Kate swallowed the lump of emotion in her throat. She was unused to people being kind, with no ulterior motive, people that genuinely cared about her with no secret desire to get something in return. Cutler's Gap was full of good people, and Charlie was one of the best.

"You know you're always welcome here, girl. It ain't five-star lodgings, but it's clean, and I cook a good steak." Charlie stood up, grabbed a bag from Tom's hand, and motioned them to follow him inside the house.

Kate looked around as she stepped through the door. There was a large central room with a hallway on either side; a large, two-sided fireplace stood in the middle of the room. She looked around the living room with its worn leather sofa and recliners. On the left wall were bookcases overflowing with books. The books were in no particular order; there was a large book on criminal law besides a paperback mystery novel next to a farmer's almanac. The coffee table sat on a large, tanned cowhide. The walls were decorated with antique cowboy paraphernalia, rusted spurs, lassos, cattle skulls with long horns, canteens, and even a large wooden Texas star.

There was a small television in the right corner; it had to be thirty years old if it were a day. Kate took a minute to take it all in. Though the room was cluttered and lived in, it was clean and bright. The sun from the large windows made patterns on the ceiling as it reflected off the glass of the old lanterns Charlie had sitting all over the room. Kate smiled. This place felt like a real home, the kind of home she had never experienced before. She had lived in several houses, each bigger and grander than the last. They were beautiful showpieces, with art hanging on the walls; cold, austere art, bought for its ability to impress the "right" people and for its investment value. Large fundraisers and social functions were hosted in those houses. They were pictured in the society pages of the best newspapers, and their summer house had been featured in an architectural magazine. Yet, none of them, not one, had ever given her the sense of peace and relaxation that this ranch house did. They had all left her cold, alone, and desperate to escape.

"Charlie, your house is beautiful." Kate gave Charlie a genuine smile.

"It ain't much, but it's home." Even as he shrugged off the compliment, Kate could see the pride in Charlie's eyes. He truly loved this house.

Kate and Tom followed Charlie as he led her toward her room.

"I sleep on the other side of the house, so you'll have this whole side to yourself. The bathroom is across the hall, and here is your room," Charlie motioned her to enter the room as he laid her bag down.

It was a simple room with an antique wrought iron bed and an equally antique quilt spread across the bed. A nightstand beside the bed had an electric alarm clock and an old water pitcher with a bouquet of wildflowers. When Kate saw the bouquet, Kate couldn't hold back the tears. Charlie had gone out and picked those just for her, to make her feel welcome. That kind of caring generosity was her undoing. She turned and gave Charlie a hug.

"This is the most beautiful room I have ever had. Thank you so much for the flowers, Charlie. I love them."

"See, son, if you want a little sugar, you need to treat a lady right." Charlie teased Tom as he patted Kate on the head. He may pretend to be a gruff old man, but he had the heart of a teddy bear.

"Yeah, Charlie, there is a lot I could learn from you." Tom was only half teasing. He looked over Charlie's shoulder into Kate's eyes.

"Well, I'm gonna give you a minute to settle in." Charlie gruffly patted Kate's back one last time, leaving the room and down the paneled hallway.

Tom cleared his throat. "So, do you think you'll be okay out here?"

"Yeah, I do. Thanks for bringing me. Even if my car hadn't died, I don't think I'd have ever found my way here alone." Kate gave a small laugh and a half smile.

"Charlie does live out in the middle of nowhere, that's for sure. The first time he called me to his ranch, I got so turned around it took me three hours to get here" Tom gave her another uncomfortable smile.

"I guess I'm going to get going unless you need something. You know you can always call me if you change your mind about being here or need anything."

"Thank you, Tom. I appreciate all you have done." Kate reached out and touched Tom's arm, then jerked her hand back as if she'd been burned. She wished to God she had never slept with him; she needed more complication in her life like she needed a hole in the head.

"One of these days, you will stop resisting me Katie-Did. It is hopeless; I'm irresistible. My mamma told me so." He gave her one of his most dashing smiles and wiggled his eyebrows suggestively.

Kate picked up a pillow off the bed and threw it at him as she stifled a laugh at his antics. Tom could always make her laugh. It was one of the things she liked about him. "Get out of here, you egotistical goofball."

She teased as he dodged the pillow and started down the hallway.

Kate settled into a kind of routine over the next few days. She would wake up early to help Charlie with feeding the ranch animals. He had resisted her help the first day, but now he just nodded at her and handed her a cup of surprisingly good coffee. After the morning feeding, Kate would work on Brenda's books. She could kiss Brenda for finally relenting and buying the scanner. She had scanned all the receipts into the computer, which made Brenda happy because she now had her dining room back. More importantly, it made Kate's job a hell of a lot easier. Now that she was at Charlie's, she could still work on Brenda's books with just her laptop. She'd have to get used to using dial-up internet again. What was this, the dark ages?

She took over cooking dinner at night. Charlie was great at cooking exactly four things: bacon, eggs, biscuits, and steak. Kate's arteries could only handle so many meals like that. Charlie had run to town and grabbed groceries from Kate's list. He had grumbled at what he called "damned female food" until he'd tasted her rosemary-roasted chicken and rice pilaf with asparagus. From then on, he hadn't raised a single complaint about her taking over his kitchen. In fact, he would ask what they were having for dinner every morning. When she would tell him, he would grunt and go back to doing the daily crossword in the paper, but Kate didn't miss the slight smile he tried to hide. Charlie didn't say much; spending the last 60 years living alone, he was accustomed to silence. Kate enjoyed the companionable silence, having time to get lost in her own thoughts. She surprised herself at how quickly she adapted to ranch life. She did miss her friends and their weekly TV show marathons. She missed Ms. Annetta's no-nonsense affection, Lucy's laughter, and Brenda's gossip. She missed Tom in the moments that she forgot he had betrayed her.

However, overall, she was the most content she'd ever been here on the ranch. Out here, surrounded by cows and tumbleweeds, she could almost forget that danger was coming; she could almost believe she would be safe. The only people who knew where she was were Tom, Charlie, and Ms. Annetta. Ms. Annetta had not been happy when she saw her loading her things into Tom's truck. She'd been mad as a wet hen until Tom whispered something in her ear. Kate didn't know what Tom said, but whatever it was, Annetta calmed down. Then she hugged her and told her to always keep her gun on her because you never knew when you'd come across a snake in the scrub. Kate knew that between the three of them, they would never purposely reveal her location. Ms. Annetta had told Brenda and Lucy that she was safe and would be back to stop them from marching down to the Sheriff's office and running Tom out of town on a rail. They figured she'd left because Tom arrested her and marched her through town. He had gone from the handsome and much beloved Sheriff to persona non-grata in their books. Kate had never had real girlfriends before, the kind that would storm the jail to give the Sheriff a piece of their minds for hurting their friend. She hoped to tell them how much that meant to her one day. She rubbed the back of her neck and closed her computer. Ranch life had her going to bed almost before the sun these days; she would fall into bed exhausted and sleep peacefully. She hadn't realized it until now, but she hadn't had a single nightmare since moving to Charlie's.

Griffin was almost happy to pull into the two-horse town known as Cutler's Gap. It had been a hellacious drive from Chicago. Over 18 hours of driving time, not counting the times he stopped to piss or eat. He'd grabbed a few hours of sleep at a shitty rest stop. He prided himself on keeping things professional, but Carina Wythcliff had made his life complicated in the last five months. She would have to pay for that when he finally got his hands on her.

Usually, he tried to blend in as much as possible when he was on the job; that would be impossible in a town the size of Cutler's Gap. The old biddies had probably started calling each other the moment he drove past the rundown *Welcome to Cutler's Gap* sign. God, he hated shit-kicker towns like this; he hated the smell. He hated the nosey neighbors. Hell, he even hated the mangy-looking dogs.

Like every other piss-ant town, Main Street was a straight, pothole-infested stretch of road through the center of town. It had a scattering of rundown, mostly empty storefronts, a motel that hadn't been painted since Carter was President, and a café named Uncle Joe's. How was it that every shit-kicker town had a Main Street, and they all looked the same? Was there a Shit Kicker Town convention where all the mayors gathered every year and made sure everyone kept their shitty town to the same shitastic standard? He found a parking spot on the street between two dust-covered, well-used Ford trucks. Another thing he hated about these towns was the damn pick-up trucks. He parked his sedan, locked it, and approached the café.

"Hey, son, you won't need to lock your car around here." Griffin had to do a double take at the old man who called to him. He was tall, maybe 6'2, with a broad chest. He stood straight in a plaid button-down shirt, Wrangler jeans, a thick leather belt with an engraved metal buckle, and worn cowboy boots. In his hand, he held a battered cowboy hat. If it weren't for the deep wrinkles on his weathered face and hands and the thick white hair on his head, Griffin would have thought him a man in his prime.

Griffin forced a smile, "Yeah, I've been living in the city too long. Sometimes I forget what a safe town is."

"Name's Doug Jenkins. What brings you to these parts?"

"Gary. I'm just driving through to visit my sister." Griffin purposely didn't give a last name. It would just complicate things if it was different than whatever name Carina had given herself.

"If you're hungry, you can't do better than Joe's here in Cutler's Gap. I recommend the steak, but they also make a good meatloaf."

"Sounds great. I'm hungry enough to eat the whole cow."

"In that case, you'll want a piece of Miss Doris' pie. She's known all over these parts for her pie."

They walked together towards the café. Doug opened the door, holding it as Griffin walked in. Oh yeah, he hated Southern manners too. In Chicago, people would let the door shut right in your face. They were so busy with their own lives they had no time to notice you. He loved that about big cities; he felt safely cocooned by that kind of anonymity.

"Enjoy your meal, and welcome to town." Doug made his way to a booth in the back of the café.

Lucy caught her breath. The man that just walked into the café was the most gorgeous man she'd ever seen. Strike that he was the most beautiful person she'd ever seen. He looked like a piece of artwork with his short blonde hair, blazing blue eyes, perfect nose, and sexy-as-sin jaw. He was dressed well in khakis, a polo shirt, and loafers; he stood out like a peacock among Wrangler-clad ducks. Lucy patted her hair to make sure it was still in place in the braid she'd thrown it in that morning, reached in her apron pocket for her tinted lip gloss, quickly swiped it on, grabbed a menu, and made her way to the Adonis waiting to be seated.

"Hi. I'm Lucy. I'll be your waitress. You can sit anywhere you like." Lucy blushed as she looked up at the man before her. Gee-gads, he was tall too. And that polo shirt didn't hide his muscular arms. A human should not look this perfect.

Thanks, I think I'll sit at the counter where I'll have the prettiest view in the house." Griffin winked at the flustered girl before him. He could turn on the charm when he needed to. His looks, and charming young waitresses, were just more tools in his toolbox. He may prefer the more direct approach to dealing with things, but he could also play this game.

Griffin ate slowly, being sure to make friendly conversation with the waitress, even flirt a little. She was cute enough in that small town, girl next door way; all the ways that set his teeth on edge. But he was here to do a job, and do it he would, one way or another.

"Gary, what brings someone like you to Cutler's Gap?" Lucy blushed scarlet. "I er meant, well, Cutler's Gap is so country and out of the way, and you're obviously not from the country." Lucy groaned inwardly and blushed an even deeper shade of red. 'Ugh, could you not stick your foot down your throat and babble like an idiot to the hot guy,' she chided herself silently.

"It's okay. I knew what you meant." The blonde god smiled at her, making a thousand butterflies take flight in her stomach. "Actually, you may be able to help me." He dug in his pocket and pulled out a photograph. "Could you look at this picture and tell me if you've seen this girl. It's my sister. She left a while back, and no one in our family has heard from her. We're really worried. Dad is sick, and I promised Mom I'd do my best to find her."

"That's so sweet of you! Of course, I'll help if I can." Lucy reached for the photograph and almost dropped it when she saw the face smiling back at her. It was Kate, her hair was different, and she was dressed like a million bucks, but it was definitely Kate. "That's Kate! She's my best friend! At least, I thought she was, but she never said anything about a brother or a family. She left almost a week ago. She didn't even tell me she was going!"

Griffin smiled. He was closing in. Fly away as fast as you can. You can't outfly me.

"That sounds like our Kate. She's never been reliable. She's a free spirit who goes where the wind blows her without a thought to those she may hurt by leaving. I'm sorry she ditched you too. You wouldn't happen to have a guess as to where she might go next? Maybe a place she said she wanted to visit?"

Lucy shook her head, "Kate was always so quiet; she didn't talk much about herself at all, now that I think about it. She left after she and her boyfriend, Sheriff Tom, had a fight. I don't know what it was about, but it was a doozy, right on Main Street. The Sheriff actually put her in handcuffs and marched her to the jail. Of course, she was out in just a matter of hours. I guess a lover's spat when your boyfriend is the law can go all kinds of weird places. It's been the talk of the town for almost a week. Anyway, if anyone knows where she is, it would be him or Ms. Annetta over at the motel. She lived there and worked for Ms. Annetta since she came to town."

Griffin hated small-town life and the trusting fools who lived it. However, they sure made it easy to gather intel. He would head over to the dump of a motel as soon as he finished eating. He had no intention of introducing himself to the sheriff.

The bell above the café door jingled. Griffin slightly turned his head to see who was coming in. A tall man in jeans, a cowboy hat, boots, and a tan buttoned-down shirt, with a sheriff badge pinned to his chest and a gun holstered on his belt, entered. He had expected the sheriff of this beat-up town to look as old and rundown as it did. Instead, the man who stood in the doorway was young, with sharp eyes that had already settled on him. Well, this could add an unneeded complication to his plans.

"Hi, Lucy. Are you talking to me yet?" Tom kept his voice casual as he called out to Lucy, but the man sitting at the counter had his senses on high alert. He had noticed the strange car parked in front of the café and gone over to check out the visitor. He couldn't take any chances that whoever Kate was afraid of might make an appearance. The stranger had done his best to blend in; khakis, loafers, and a polo. But his face was anything but average; how had Kate described her tormentor... beautiful. Yes, she had called him a beautiful demon. The man in the café could be described as beautiful. He reminded Tom of a Botticelli painting. He didn't know God made people that actually looked like that. Despite the beauty of his face, the guy's eyes creeped him out. They were blue, a bright blue that reminded him of the warm seas of the Caribbean. Yet, they sent a shiver down Tom's spine. Those eyes had seen death. Those eyes were death.

"Sheriff." Lucy's voice held none of her usual friendliness. It would appear that she would not forgive him any time soon.

"I'm still mad at you for being a jackass and running off my best friend. Speaking of Kate," Lucy motioned with her head towards the guy at the counter as she started walking back towards him, "this is Kate's brother. He's looking for her because their dad is sick. I told him she had been here until you made her run away. Now you can explain yourself while I go get you your usual." She huffed. She had no idea why she used to think Tom hung the sun and the moon. Sitting next to hunky Gary (what a dorky name for such a hot guy), he looked like any other guy. When she saw Kate again, she would give her a piece of her mind. First, she left without so much as a whispered goodbye. Then to find out she had a Greek god for a brother! How could she have such a gorgeous brother and not mention him? Kate was lucky she was such a forgiving best friend; a lot of other friends wouldn't forgive this kind of foolishness.

"Howdy, I'm Sheriff Tom Fletcher. Lucy says you're looking for your sister? I'll help you if I can." Tom tried to play it cool. He didn't want to let the guy sitting in front of him know he was on to him. He didn't know who he was, but one thing was for damn sure, he was not Kate's brother.

Stupid, interfering waitress! Griffin silently seethed; he'd had wanted to avoid the Sheriff. Things just got a hell of a lot more complicated.

"Gary. The waitress, Lucy, I believe was her name, said you may know my sister, Kate." He took the picture from his pocket. He casually passed it to the cop with suspicious eyes. He would play the caring brother, looking for his lost sister. It was a good thing that she had gone from this town. At least when he caught up with her, it wouldn't be in a town where the local Andy Griffith knew what he looked like. The sheriff looked at the photograph for a few seconds longer than was necessary.

"Yes, I knew Kate. Unfortunately, she left town a week ago without a word to anyone. We've all been worried about her." The Sheriff's eyes didn't tell him anything. He was too cool for a small-town donut eater. Griffin didn't like it. "I'd appreciate it if you knew where I could look for her next.

"Wish I could help, but she left me without a word. We'd argued, so I figured this was her way of leaving me." If he knew more than he was saying, the sheriff wasn't giving anything up.

"Well, thanks anyway. I'll wander over to the motel and see if they know anything over there."

Lucy appeared with the Sheriff's to-go order.

"I'll see you around. Let me know if you find Kate. It would ease my mind to know she was okay." With that, the sheriff nodded at Lucy and left.

Griffin waved down the waitress. He wanted to get out of this town as quickly as possible. Before he could leave, he had to stop at the broken-down rat-infested motel he passed on the way in.

Chapter Nineteen

When he left the café, Tom fished his cell phone out of his pocket and called Ms. Annetta. He needed to warn her that trouble was heading her way. He walked around the corner and went in Uncle Joe's back door.

"Hi, Miss Doris."

"Hey Tom, what brings you to my kitchen? You know I can't stand it when people get underfoot while cooking."

"I know, Miss Doris. I'll be out of your hair real quick. I need to keep an eye on someone for a minute."

"You go right on ahead. Just keep yourself out of the way. I can't be having you mess up my flow."

"Yes, ma'am." Miss Doris was not a woman to be trifled with. She was in her late 50s and stood damn near 6 feet tall with flaming red hair and arms covered in tattoos. She'd been raised in Cutler's gap but had moved to San Francisco after graduating high school. According to Charlie, he was her uncle; she'd led a colorful life in California. She'd been a park ranger and tour guide for twenty-odd years before returning to Cutler's Gap. She bought the café from Uncle Joe, and the rest was history.

Tom stood to the side of the swinging doors to the dining room and watched the stranger through the small window. He seemed in a hurry to leave, which suited Tom just fine. He said something that made Lucy blush clear to the tips of her ears, paid his bill in cash, and left. Tom immediately went to the counter and grabbed his glass with a napkin.

"Tell Miss Doris I'll return it when I finish it," Tom said when Lucy gave him a questioning glance. He needed to return to the police station, call Charlie to tell him what was happening, and print this glass. There was no time to waste.

Ms. Annetta was waiting when the bell rang, announcing the city slicker Tom had called about. She had her shotgun within arm's reach just in case she should need to rid the world of another rat. Anyone who wanted to get to Kate would have to get through her first, which was no easy job. At 235 pounds, she was a substantial obstacle to move.

"Good afternoon, ma'am." Just the sound of his voice made Annetta's skin crawl. He had a pretty enough face, but his eyes were devil eyes. She'd looked into the eyes of her own devil years before; once you've become acquainted with evil, it was easy to spot no matter how nice the face it hides behind.

"Sorry, we're full up. I don't have a room to rent you."

Griffin doubted that very much. From the look of this place, it hadn't had a paying guest in twenty years. He forced himself to smile and switched on the charm. This day was wearing his nerves thin. He liked to keep his jobs short and sweet with as little collateral human interaction as possible. First of all, talking to idiots grated on his nerves. More importantly, the more people who saw or spoke with him, the more likely he was to get caught. He had one rule "Don't get caught."

"That's no problem, ma'am. I'm actually just here to ask you a few questions. You see, I'm looking for my sister. She is a free spirit who comes and goes as the whim hits her. Normally we wait for her to contact us when she gets around to it, but our father has fallen ill. He's asking for her. I have a picture if you'll take a quick look." The big woman behind the counter continued to puff on her cigarette, but she reached for the picture.

"Sure, she worked here a few weeks. I didn't know her real well. I minded my business, and she minded hers. She left a week or so ago." She turned back to the old television mounted high in the corner, completely dismissing him. What an old bitch. Griffin cleared his throat.

"I'm sorry to bother you again. Did she give you any idea of where she might head next?"

The purple-haired, chain-smoking bitch shook her head no, seemingly too engrossed in whatever show was on the television to turn around.

"Nope, just collected her pay and left. Like I said, I didn't know her real well."

"Thanks anyway." Griffin left and made his way back to his car. That purple-haired bitch was lying. The chatty waitress had said that she and Carina, Kate, or whatever she called herself now, were close. Now, why would she lie about their relationship? What had Carina told her? He may have to arrange an accident if she'd told the old biddy anything incriminating. He'd find out once he found the little princess. He had ways to make her talk.

Tom immediately dusted the glass and lifted the prints. He ran them through the state database but didn't find a match. He ran them through IAFIS, the FBI's national database; after twenty minutes, he had a possible match, Sergeant Conrad Griffin, no criminal history. He was a member of a couple of national law enforcement groups. He would post this guy's info and see if anyone else had something on him. There was no way he was completely clean.

Chapter Twenty

It had been a week since the explosion at the warehouse. Mike felt like pulling out his hair. Everyone was focused on insurance fraud for a motive to the exclusion of all else, it seemed to Mike. To top it all off, Vanessa had filed a complaint against him with the chief. She claimed he was harassing and slandering her, creating a toxic work environment. He had to hand it to the bitch; she knew how to make a preemptive strike. He had a meeting with Captain Thomas at three this afternoon. Until then, he was going to search a few law enforcement sites. They weren't official, but maybe he'd get lucky and find a lead on his guy.

After several painstaking hours, Mike hit pay dirt. Some sheriff in Texas had posted on a confidential law enforcement forum for information on a Sergeant Conrad Griffin. The name meant nothing to Mike, and he almost skipped over the posting. Then he noticed the picture. The guy's hair was blonde, not dark, eyes blue, not green, and there was no scar, but despite all that, there was no mistaking that face. Without a doubt, this was his mysterious driver and licensee. Unfortunately, it was time for his meeting with the captain; he'd have to wait to contact this Sheriff Fletcher.

"Good to see you, Choctowsky. Have a seat." Captain Ed Thomas stood and offered Mike his weathered brown hand. He was a slight man, rail thin, standing around five and a half feet tall, with a shock of curly, white hair circling a mostly bald head. It would be easy for someone to dismiss him as a pushover except for his intense brown eyes. He had been on the force for forty years, working his way up and earning the respect of his fellow officers in a time when the force had been a good ole' white boys club. The job and politics had jaded Mike; he now respected few men. Captain Thomas was one of those few.

"Sir, it's good to see you again." Mike returned his firm shake and sat in one of the two chairs across from the captain's desk.

"I assume you know why I scheduled this meeting." Captain Thomas was straight to business, as was his way.

"Yes, sir; a false harassment accusation was filed against me with HR," Mike responded candidly.

"We take such accusations seriously. We will be opening an investigation. Until we have concluded that investigation, you will be placed on administrative duty. This is not a reflection upon you; it is simply procedure."

"Sir, I will go stir crazy on administrative duty. I have quite a bit of unused vacation time. Would it be possible for me to use that instead of being placed on desk duty?"

"That will be fine. Just be sure to give your statement to IA before you take your vacation time. Considering the nature of this claim, I don't think it will take too long to clear up."

"Thank you, Captain. To be clear, I did not do what I was accused of."

"Speaking off the record, I've known you a long time Mike. You can be reckless and bullheaded sometimes, but you operate by a strict code of ethics.

Your character speaks for itself. However, we will follow the procedure here."

"I appreciate your vote of confidence. I want them to investigate this. I have worked too hard to have something like this hanging over my head." Mike stood to leave.

"Catch some trout for me. I'm assuming you're heading up to Montana to fish again."

"Actually, I think I'm going to visit a friend in Texas."

"I figured you'd want a break from the heat. I hope you have a good time, despite the humidity."

Mike laughed. "I don't expect to be there long. Maybe I'll still find some time to head up north to fish."

After shaking hands with the captain, Mike headed straight to IA to give his statement. Forget calling that Texas Sheriff. He was going to catch the first available flight there.

Charlie sat on the porch cleaning a rifle, six more leaning against the house behind him, and several handguns sitting on the table beside his rocking chair.

"So, what's with the arsenal? Are you expecting a war or something?" Kate joked as she sat in the rocker beside him, sipping sweet tea with lemon.

"Nah, it's just gun cleaning day," Charlie said nonchalantly

"Want some help? Ms. Annetta taught me how to shoot and clean guns." Kate offered

"Of course she did. Can't understand how you got to be as old as you are without knowing such basic life skills. Ms. Annetta's good people."

Kate laughed. "Back in New York, I campaigned for stricter gun laws. The idea I'd one day be sitting on a front porch with an old codger like you, preparing an entire armament, would have never crossed my mind." Kate giggled at the thought. It was nice to mention her old life now that Charlie knew who she was.

"You just weren't raised to know better. Now that you're in God's country, we taught you better."

"Why don't we go do some shooting. Nothing is better for relaxing than shooting things." Charlie grinned mischievously at her.

"Sure, why not. Let me go grab the gun Ms. Annetta gave me. She told me to keep practicing anyway."

"I got plenty of guns out here. You might as well get used to shooting more than one kind of gun. Pick you a rifle and a handgun, then we'll head on out to the shooting range." Charlie grabbed a couple of boxes of ammo sitting beside his rocker on the porch.

"You have a shooting range here on the ranch?" Kate was incredulous.

"Of course. How else is a man supposed to relax and blow off steam? It ain't much. Just a little something that I rigged up in my spare time."

"Charlie, you never cease to amaze me." Kate shook her head and laughed.

Charlie fell into his usual silence as they got into his beat-up Dodge truck and drove over the worn dirt "road" to somewhere on the ranch. If you asked her to take you back, Kate wouldn't be able to tell you; one tumbleweed looked pretty much like the next to her.

Charlie glanced over at Kate as he drove. Tom had called him earlier in the day and said some guy was in town looking for her. Tom didn't know much about him other than he was not the brother he claimed to be and that he was military-trained. He'd bet the ranch that it was no coincidence he'd showed up in town not even a week after Tom had run Kate's prints.

Charlie wasn't a violent man by nature, but he'd spent his life trying to defend the weak and abused. So far, his efforts to protect the women he loved had been in vain, Ella had died young at the hands of that abusive jackass Doug, and he'd been too young to defend his mother from his father's fists. He had done the best his little eight-year-old self could, but his dad had just smacked him out of the way and continued on with beating his mom. After that night, his father took off, never to return. It had been a relief to Charlie. Though he and his mom had been dirt poor and went to bed with empty stomachs more than one night, at least they went to bed free of bruises and blood. It wasn't until nearly forty years later, when his mom was dying that he found out what had really happened to his good old dad. His mom put up with being beat on herself, but when his dad had hit him, she'd taken matters into her own hands. She buried him in the back forty, and no one was ever the wiser. Charlie suspected that the old sheriff hadn't investigated too hard. The whole town knew exactly what kind of a drunk his dad had been.

Now another bad man was coming for a woman he'd grown to love like the daughter or granddaughter he'd never had. He'd be damned if he let anything happen to her. Tom was going to send someone out to set up security cameras around his property. He would come himself, but he was afraid the stranger, whoever he was, would follow him.

Mike's plane taxied down the runway. He'd finally landed in San Angelo, Texas. Thank God! He hated flying; he always got airsick and had to take Dramamine. He needed to caffeinate and grab something quick to eat before picking up his rental car. According to Google, he still had to drive another three hours before reaching Cutler's Gap, Sheriff Fletcher's town. He couldn't risk losing his lead on the real Phoenix Butcher by stopping for the night.

Griffin had developed an even deeper hatred of Texas over the last few days. He'd set up a rudimentary camp in the scrub over the ridge from the motel. He could see all of Main Street from this position, but he was camouflaged and far enough that no one could see him. He was miserable between the heat, fire ants, and other biting insects. He had to kill three snakes in the last two days. Why did people choose to live in this hell hole? Despite his misery, Griffin lay on his stomach, on a tarp, watching the motel through his binoculars. That purple-haired old lady knew something more than she was saying. He only had to be patient; hopefully, she would lead him to his prey.

When he arrived at his office in the morning, Tom was surprised to see yet another stranger sitting on the steps, presumably waiting to see him. What was going on in Cutler's Gap? Since Kate had arrived, they'd had more visitors than they had had in the entirety of the five years he'd been sheriff. When the man stood, Tom got a good look at how big he was. Tom was tall, six foot one, but this man had a good three or four inches on him, and he was built like a boxer. Tom instinctively put his hand on his sidearm.

"Hi, sorry to surprise you this early in the morning. My name is Mike Choctowsky. I'm a detective with Phoenix PD. I was wondering if I could talk to you about Conrad Griffin?" Mike extended his hand.

Tom relaxed and shook the hand of the man standing on his doorstep.

"Nice to meet you, Mike. I'm Tom Fletcher. I must admit that when I posted looking for information, I didn't expect an in-person visit from Phoenix PD. Come on inside, and we'll talk." Tom unlocked the precinct door. Well, precinct may be a bit grandiose to describe the small clapboard building that housed his office, a holding cell, a reception area, and an empty desk for the officer they had never bothered to hire. He was a Sheriff without a department.

"Have a seat while I brew a pot of coffee." Tom motioned with his head towards his office.

"I want to be upfront. I'm here on my own, not on the department's behalf. I don't want to misrepresent anything."

"I appreciate the heads up." Tom counted the scoops of grounds as he poured them into the coffee filter. "I hope you don't mind old-fashioned drip coffee."

"Anything is better than what they serve at our precinct. It's thick as tar and usually left over from the last shift." They both laughed. Some things were universal; bad coffee in stations was one of those things.

Tom filled the machine with water and hit the brew button. He made his way over to his desk and sat down.

"So, if you aren't here on official business, what brings you to Cutler's Gap?"

"I'm unofficially here on officially closed business."

Tom arched a brow, waiting for Mike to continue.

"A few months ago, we had a particularly brutal case. A woman's body was found dismembered, buried in coolers out in the middle of the desert. The killer had removed all identifying features, teeth pulled from the skull, and fingerprints burned off with acid. The face had been eaten by animals. We still haven't identified her. All we know is that was is a slightly overweight middle-aged Hispanic woman."

"I think I saw something about this on the national news. I thought y'all had found the guy who did it."

"That's what they say, but I was the lead investigator on that case, and things didn't add up. So, I kept digging and came across this guy on my own time." Mike handed him a computer printout of a scanned Arizona license; the hair and the eyes were different, but there was no doubt that this was Conrad Griffin.

"Why are you looking at him?" Mike sipped his coffee as he asked

"He came into town asking about my kind of girlfriend, pretending to be her brother. It's a complicated situation." Tom wasn't sure how much he could trust this Mike guy. His gut told him that he was one of the good guys, but he wasn't willing to risk Kate's life on a feeling.

"If this is the guy asking about your friend, then you have a real problem on your hands. If he did everything I think he did, he is real bad news. Besides the woman in the desert, I think he killed his partner and blew a storage unit to hell."

"Blew to hell, as in blew it up with explosives?" Tom asked incredulously.

"Yeah, almost got me too. My ass still feels the flames."

"You were there when it blew? If he did all this, why are you here unofficially?"

"Because officially, the partner committed suicide and worked alone, and they are investigating the storage unit explosion as insurance fraud. This guy is a ghost. He leaves no evidence behind. What I've found is based on a few anomalies, nothing that would stand up in court. Add that to the fact that I'm off the reservation on this one. Well, I came out here hoping you had something more."

"Nothing concrete. In fact, I have less than you." Tom gave Mike a measured look. He didn't want to put Kate in more danger, but if what Mike was saying was true, he would need all the help he could get. After a long minute, Tom knew what he had to do.

"So, have you made up your mind about me?" Mike asked, completely unoffended. He liked a man who took his time and weighed his options; it was the opposite of how he worked, but he understood the need for thinkers like Tom.

"Actually, I have." Tom's expression was grave. "What I'm about to tell you is on a need-to-know basis only. Nothing I say can leave this room. If word gets out, the woman I love will pay the consequences. However, I don't have a choice if this man is who you think he is. I'm going to need all the help I can get. Right now, I am the only lawman for nearly 100 miles. The only backup I have right now is a stubborn old man, a purple-haired old woman, and a mule-headed, terrified woman."

Mike nodded. "You have my word that what is said here stays here. I only ask for the same courtesy. I was pretty far out on the ledge while investigating this guy."

Tom held out his hand, and Mike took and shook it. They had a good old-fashioned gentleman's agreement. He only hoped this didn't come back to bite him in the ass.

"It all began almost six months ago when a mysterious, beautiful, and infuriating woman drove into town...." Tom began.

Chapter Twenty-One

Target practice with Charlie had been fun. He'd given her a few pointers on adjusting her grip and stance, which helped her aim to improve. He was a good teacher, never harsh, yet patient enough to quietly wait until she mastered a new skill on her own. He would have been an amazing teacher had he chosen that route. The sun was setting as they pulled up to the ranch house. The sky was painted in all the shades of red, purple, orange, and pink that one could imagine. Kate was so lost in the beauty of the sky that she almost missed the strange truck parked in front of the house. She felt around for one of the handguns she'd been practicing with.

"No need to pull a gun, girl. That's just my jackass of a neighbor Doug Jenkins. As much as I'd love for you to shoot him, I promised Tom I'd try to refrain while you're here."

Kate visibly relaxed. "So, this is the infamous Doug, the bane of your existence."

"Sure enough. That's the old bastard."

"He's taller than I thought he'd be." Kate mused as Charlie parked next to Doug's truck.

"He's as mean as he is tall. C'mon out and say hi. Your hiding here will make him more suspicious, and he'll start asking questions."

Kate opened the truck door and hopped out while Charlie made his way over to Doug.

"What are you doing here, Doug?" Charlie practically growled. Kate had only ever known Charlie to be kind, if a little mischievous. It was a surprise to hear the anger in his voice now.

"Aren't you going to introduce me to your guest?" Doug's voice was smooth as liquid silk. It reminded Kate of a spider; she would have instantly disliked him even if she didn't know who he was.

"This is my great niece, Kate, not that it is any of your business. Tell me what you want, and then get off my land."

"Kate, what a popular name. Just a day ago, a gentleman came into Uncle Joe's Café looking for someone named Kate. Quite the coincidence you have a niece with the same name."

"Yeah, well, that's life, full of the unexplained. Speaking of unexplained, will you tell me what you want, or will I have to throw you out of here by your ear?"

"I just came by to tell you to keep your damn livestock out of my fields. It looks like your entire herd of longhorns held a dance in my sorghum field last night. You had best get yourself a lawyer because I'm suing you for the lost crop."

"I am a lawyer, Doug. And my entire herd is grazing on the opposite side of my ranch from your sorghum fields. Whatever got into your field, it wasn't my cattle."

"Be prepared to prove that to Judge Cooper" Doug turned to Kate and tipped his hat "Nice meeting you, Kate." With that, he climbed into his truck and sped down the dirt drive, spewing a trail of dust behind him.

Doug headed straight for town after leaving Charlie's. There was something familiar about that girl at his ranch; he'd eat his hat if she was Charlie's great niece. He didn't go into Cutler's Gap often, preferring to drive to Abilene or San Angelo for supplies when he needed them. But something was up with that girl, and he had every intention of finding out what it was. Maybe she would be what he needed to finally get Charlie out of his life once and for all. That man had been a thorn in his side for nigh on sixty years. He intended to live his last years, however many they may be, free of Charlie Benet.

"That is a crazy story. Do you have her somewhere safe now?" Mike had seen a lot of messed up stuff in his career, but he had only seen one crime scene with the kind of cruelty that Carina Wythcliff had endured. That had been the woman in the desert. He and Tom had to find this bastard and stop him before he killed anyone else.

"Yeah, I do. Hey, we've been in here talking half the day. Why don't we grab a bite to eat at Uncle Joe's?"

"That sounds great. I haven't eaten since I left the airport last night. I'm glad Carina's safe for now." Mike hadn't met the woman, and he was already feeling protective of her. No person should ever go through what she had been put through.

"Oh man, I'm sorry. I got so caught up with this case I didn't even think about getting food." Tom gave Mike a chagrinned half smile. "Oh, and Carina goes by Kate now. She says that Carina Wythcliff died that night two years ago."

"Hey, no worries. I could have said something, but I was just as caught up as you. You know we need to find this guy before he finds Carina...err, Kate, right? He won't let her go alive if he gets her again."

"Believe me, I know. I'm hoping he puts up a fight when we find him. I don't like the thought of him continuing to breathe the same oxygen as the rest of humanity."

"On that, we are in complete agreement, brother."

Griffin watched the Sheriff and a tall man as they left the police station and walked toward the café. He hadn't seen the other man before, but he walked like a cop. Griffin didn't like the idea that suddenly, there were not one but two cops in this little town, and one of them had already seen him. He would have to find out who this new guy was and what he was doing in Cutler's Gap. It could just be a coincidence that he showed up two days after Griffin had, but Griffin didn't believe in that kind of coincidence. Time to get cleaned up and head back into civilization. He needed intel.

It was a slow night at Joe's when Tom and Mike walked through the door.

"What is it with these stores and their damn bells?" Mike grumbled when the top of his head brushed the bottom of the bell above the door, causing it to jingle even louder.

"It never bothered me. I kind of like knowing when people are coming and going." Tom mused

"I bet you've never hit your head on one?"

"Can't say that I have. I guess the world wasn't built with giants in mind." Tom teased lightly.

"You're just a barrel of laughs, aren't you." But Mike was laughing when he said it.

Tom sat at his normal table with Mike across from him.

"Hey Anne Marie, Lucy, not working tonight?" Tom asked good-naturedly.

"I'm picking up a few of her shifts over the next few weeks. This little guy will be making his grand entrance soon. I'm trying to save as much money as possible before he arrives." Anne Marie rubbed her swollen abdomen. She was a pretty woman, with a sweet smile, tight curly brown hair that she wore pulled back with a colorful scarf and hanging loose down her back, caramel skin, and doe brown eyes. She hadn't expected to find herself a mom for the first time at 34 years old, much less a single mom. But she's always been one to take life in stride. So, she hadn't panicked when her ex-husband left her after six years of marriage, and she realized her period was late. She's gone to the pharmacy, bought a pregnancy test, and got a second job waiting tables here the same day. It was no use crying over spilled milk, and it was even less use crying over cheating bastards.

"I hadn't realized the little man was so close to making an appearance. Oh, this is my friend Mike. I told him all about Miss Doris' famous pies." Tom smiled

"Hi, Mike. Welcome to Cutler's Gap. Tom's right about the pies. They are amazing." she gave him a wink.

"Thanks, I'm enjoying my time away from the big city. I'll definitely save room for a piece of that pie!"

The bell above the door rang as Ms. Annetta came puffing in.

She walked up to the table and sat between Tom and Mike without ceremony.

"I saw you walking down Main Street and came on over. I had that visit you warned me about. Who's this?" Ms. Annetta asked suspiciously.

Tom smiled as Anne Marie came back with another menu for Ms. Annetta.

"Evening Anne Marie, don't you look about ready to pop! I bet you'll be glad when Little Man gets here." Ms. Annetta ordered a chicken salad sandwich and fries and looked back at Tom without giving Anne Marie a chance to get a word in edgewise.

Tom and Mike placed their orders while Ms. Annetta stared down Mike, waiting for someone to answer her question.

"Ms. Annetta, meet Mike Choctowsky. He is a police detective with Phoenix PD. He's here with questions about our mutual friend, who paid you a visit a few days ago." Tom clarified

"Ms. Annetta, it's a pleasure to meet you. Tom told me a lot about you this afternoon." Mike smiled at the large purple-haired woman before him as she lit a cigarette, uncaring that a No Smoking sign was hanging above her head on the post behind her.

"I'll just bet he did. So besides clucking around like a couple of hens, what have you two done today to help my Kate?"

"Mike has more information on our mystery man. He has been a big help. How did your visit go?" Tom asked in a hushed tone.

"I didn't tell him nothing, but I don't think he believed me. He gave me the creeps. He reminds me of one of those exotic spiders, all colorful, pretty, and deadly."

"You and I have very different definitions of pretty," Tom joked

"This ain't the time for joking, Tom. I'm worried about Kate. Now tell me how we are gonna kill this bug before he gets to her."

"Mike and I are working on a plan...." Tom stopped talking as the bell above the door rang again.

"That really doesn't bother you?" Mike asked

"Not when it gives me a heads up that someone like Doug Jenkins is coming in."

"He's been here twice in a few days. That's a record, and I don't like it." Ms. Annetta grumbled.

"Howdy, Sheriff" Doug made his way over to their table.

"Great, just great," Tom thought. Doug and Charlie's nonsense was the last thing he needed to deal with today.

"Howdy, Doug," Tom tried to sound friendly. The truth was, he couldn't stand the man, but he was the Sheriff for all the people of Cutler's Gap, even the ones he didn't like. "What brings you to town this fine evening?"

"It is a week for company, it seems. First, that Gary guy comes to town, then I go to Charlie's, and he has a girl staying with him on at the ranch, and now I see you and Annetta have a guest too. If this kind of tourism continues, we'll have to put an addition on Annetta's motel." If Doug was looking for information, he'd come to the wrong table for it.

"True enough. Cutler's Gap seems to be a popular place. Is there anything I can do for you, Doug? My friend and I were just about to eat." Anne Marie appeared at the table with their food as if on cue.

"Well, Sheriff, I came here to complain about Charlie's longhorns tearing up my sorghum field, but when I saw Charlie had a young woman all the way out on that ranch, I was concerned. You know how bad it looks for a confirmed bachelor like Charlie to be entertaining women alone on his ranch, especially since her name is Kate, just like the sister that man was looking for the other day" Doug was the picture of neighborly concern. Tom would laugh at the ridiculousness of the insinuation if it weren't for the fact that Doug not only knew Kate's name and where she was but also that someone was looking for her. Damn it! This complicated things.

"Last I looked, Doug, it wasn't a crime for a man to have company at his home. The woman that man was looking for left town over a week ago. I should know. I was dating her. We had a fight, and she left. I can guarantee you they aren't the same woman." That fight he and Kate had had in the street was the perfect cover story. Doug could ask around town all he wanted because everyone was still talking about it.

"I still think it's unseemly, a man his age, having a young girl like her on the ranch. He's up to no good, I tell you."

"Thanks for letting me know, Doug. I'll see what Charlie is up to and look into the cows tearing up your field."

"Thanks, Sheriff." Doug turned towards Mike. "I'm sorry, I didn't catch your name."

"That's because I hadn't given it." Mike answered abruptly, "Mike, I'm a friend of Tom's from the old days."

"Welcome to Cutler's Gap. You'll have to try a piece of Miss Doris' pie." Doug smiled

"So, I've been told." Mike chuckled. "Nice meeting you." That was a lie. He had an instant dislike for the old man in front of him.

"Yes, well, enjoy your meal, folks." With that, Doug made his way to a table on the other side of the diner.

"Thank God, he's gone. I can't stand that man." Ms. Annetta was never one to sugarcoat anything. "And I don't like him knowing where Kate is."

"That makes two of us," Tom agreed wholeheartedly.

"Let's finish up here and head back to the station. I want to call Charlie and bring him up to speed."

"You're welcome to crash at my place tonight" Tom looked over at Mike as he said it.

"Nonsense, he'll be staying at the motel. The man has come all the way from Arizona. The least we can do is offer him a comfortable bed instead of your lumpy sofa" Ms. Annetta left no room for argument.

"My sofa is not lumpy. It's just finally broken in." Tom said defensively.

"It most certainly is lumpy. It was ready to be retired before you left Colorado, and that was five years ago." Ms. Annetta insisted

"Don't you know that insulting a bachelor's sofa is like insulting his mother? There are just some lines that shouldn't be crossed. Back me up here" Tom looked at Mike for support.

"It's true. You don't insult a man's sofa or his TV. It's also true that I will be sleeping in a bed at Ms. Annetta's motel." Mike laughed. "Thank you for the offer, ma'am." Mike gave her a grateful smile.

"No need to thank me. It's fifty dollars a night." Ms. Annetta may have a heart the size of Texas under that gruff exterior, but she was also a businesswoman.

Mike burst out laughing. God, this town was amazing. The people here were crazy; you couldn't have created a better set and characters if it were a movie.

Chapter Twenty-Two

The satellite phone rang. Shit, why had he bothered to bring it, Griffin thought. Only one person would be calling, and he had no desire to talk with him.

"Griffin here." He might as well answer. Grant Wythcliff would just keep calling.

"Do you have her?"

"I'm about a week behind her. She left town right after her prints were run. Seems she was dating the sheriff, and they had a fight. Or at least that's the official story."

"I am getting tired of your excuses. I'm out of patience. If she isn't back in New York within 72 hours, I'm coming to Texas. If I have to do that, you know what will happen, don't you? Your name, address, safe houses, aliases, and bank accounts will be given to some very nasty people who want you dead. Find her and get her home!"

"I wouldn't be issuing too many threats, Senator. Remember, I have my own insurance policy where you are concerned."

"That only works if you're alive to use it."

"I'll get you your sister. But after this, we're done. I want the file, the money you owe me, and for you to lose my number."

"Done. Bring me, my sister." Grant slammed the phone down, breaking yet another burner cell. Once Griffin brought back Carina, his usefulness would be at an end. It was time for Griffin to retire permanently.

"You're telling me that the man after her killed and cut up a woman, buried her in the desert, and then blew up a building?" Charlie asked incredulously

"Among other things." Tom paced the station floor and cradled his cell between his ear and shoulder.

"And this man is in the area?"

"Yup. We need to figure out how to get him before he finds Kate. Oh, that just got a lot more likely, since Doug came into town asking questions about the girl named Kate out at your ranch."

"Yeah, I was going to tell you about that. He showed up at the ranch while Kate and I were out doing target practice. He saw me pull up to the house with Kate. There was no way to hide her from him. Should have known that old pole cat would show up."

"It's alright, Charlie. You're doing all you can. Do you want me and Mike to come out there to help guard her?"

"Nah, you're better off there, figuring out where he is. If you come out here, you may lead him to us. There is no guarantee he ain't watching y'all."

"I'm sending a guy out tomorrow to install cameras around the perimeter of your property. Don't worry about the bill. I already covered it with some savings I had."

"That ain't necessary. I got the money to cover it. I ain't indigent, you know." Charlie huffed.

"I know, but since Kate won't let me protect her physically, at least let me do this. I need to help her, Charlie. I love her."

"I know you do, son. Now if you stop acting a fool long enough, she may have a chance to love you too. Go ahead and send the guy here. I will never forgive myself if something happens to our girl."

Griffin checked into the first hotel he came to in Abilene. It was one of those that catered to families with a free breakfast buffet served every morning. The sound of kids laughing and splashing in the pool grated on his nerves. After the last few hellish days camping out in the scrubland of bum fuck Texas, he just wanted a hot shower, a bug-free bed, and about a gallon of Benadryl. He ignored the look the receptionist gave him when he checked in. He knew he looked like hell warmed over, but he didn't have the energy to care.

He stood under the hot water of the shower for 45 minutes. He'd stopped at the pharmacy before checking into the hotel. He took a few big gulps of Benadryl straight from the bottle, covered himself in a calamine lotion, turned the A/C down to sub-artic, and climbed into the bed. He didn't give a fuck that it was only 6pm and the sun was still out. He needed a decent night's sleep.

He slept until ten the next morning, took another shower to wash away what was left of the calamine lotion, and got dressed in decent clothes. He was surprised at how fast the Benadryl had reduced the redness and swelling of the ant bites. He looked almost normal again.

Breakfast was over by the time he made it down to the reception area, not that he would have eaten it anyway. He would not eat anything touched or drooled on by all the kids running around. He'd never understood why people found children cute or endearing. They were parasites that drained all the resources around them and infested any bystanders with their diseases.

He found a coffee shop in downtown Abilene with internet access. He began the painstaking process of figuring out who the tall stranger was with the Cutler's Gap sheriff. He'd managed to get a blurry shot of his face using his camera and telephoto lens. He'd had a hacker create a specialty facial recognition program for him. He had hacked into major law enforcement and media databases. It had cost him several hundred thousand dollars in bitcoins, but the software had more than paid for itself over the years. While the program ran, Griffin looked at his maps and tried to figure out where Carina Wythcliff would head next. A part of him thought she hadn't really left the shit-hole town she'd been living in all these months. She seemed to have started a life for herself there, and that purple-haired motel lady had been lying to him about not knowing anything. But everyone had seen that big fight in the street with the Sheriff. It would be her MO to run away from conflict. Then again, that fight could have been staged. But why would the Sheriff run her prints if it was staged? The whole thing made no sense, and Griffin hated it when things didn't add up. After forty-five minutes, his computer dinged, and his program had a result.

"Shit!" Griffin said it aloud before he stopped himself. This was not good at all. What was a Phoenix PD detective doing in Cutler's Gap, Texas? He'd been careful and hadn't left any evidence. He'd even blown his storage unit to hell. Griffin was beginning to feel trapped for the first time since he was ten years old. The walls were closing in on him. Things were spiraling out of control. That was not something that he would allow. He needed to take care of Carina and the Phoenix cop and get the hell out of this God-awful state. After this job, he would retire to an island in the Pacific because he was getting too old to keep pushing his luck. He had enough money to last him three lifetimes in various offshore accounts. Time for Conrad Griffin to disappear for good.

Doug Jenkins walked through the door of his favorite coffee shop in Abilene. Every three months, he came here for ranch supplies and some female companionship. He may be pushing 80, but he was as fit as men half his age, and by God, he still had needs. He'd started this arrangement nearly fifty years ago.

Ella had been a frigid bitch. She'd only put out when he didn't give her a choice; she would just lay there like a cold fish while he did whatever he was doing. There had been a thrill in that, at first, having the power to do whatever you wanted to another person and them having no choice but to take it. But after a while, it had grown old, pushing into her dried-out sex; watching her silent tears as he took her in every way he wanted had stopped turning him on.

He'd needed more, and he'd found it in Abilene. Sister Margret's Whorehouse catered to people with certain unusual interests like him. When Sister Margaret passed, her daughter took over running the place. She called herself Sister Susan, though Lord knows neither had ever been a nun except in some freak's bed.

He made his way to the counter and placed his order. That's when he noticed that Gary fellow sitting in the corner with his laptop open. Well, wasn't fate smiling on him today. Even if that girl at Charlie's wasn't his sister, it would cause a hassle for old Charlie, which would be worth it.

"Gary, right?"

Griffin looked up to see that old man he'd met in Cutler's Gap standing above him.

"Yeah, it's Doug, isn't it?" Time to play nice with the locals again.

"You have a good memory." Doug smiled. "Do you mind if I sit down for a spell; I'm an old man?" Griffin couldn't think of anything he wanted less than old man Doug sitting there chatting his ear off. Still, he needed to keep the locals friendly until he found Carina.

"Sure, have a seat." Griffin shut his computer and placed it back in its carrying case.

"I see you have a map out. Still looking for that sister of yours?"

"Yeah, trying to figure out where she may have headed after your town." Griffin didn't have to fake the sigh he gave. He was so over this job.

"I just might have a lead for you," Doug said nonchalantly. Griffin tried not to look too excited; finally, a potential break!

"Really? I would appreciate that. I just heard from Mom last night. Dad has taken a turn for the worst."

"I'm sorry to hear that. I don't know if it's anything, but a young lady named Kate is staying with my neighbor on his ranch. I'm not sure if it's her or not. Do you have that photo on you? I can tell for sure if I look at it."

Griffin took the worn, folded photo from his billfold and handed it to Doug.

"That's her, alright. Her hair is shorter now, and she ain't dressed in fancy city clothes, but that's her." Doug handed Griffin back the photo.

"Thank you. When was the last time you saw her?" Griffin tried to keep his excitement in check. She could have already flown the coop.

"Yesterday evening. I stopped over to discuss a livestock issue, and there she was, plain as day, sitting in the truck with Charlie."

"Who is this Charlie character? I thought she was dating the sheriff."

"Charlie is a bitter old man. If I were you, I'd get my sister away from him as soon as possible." Doug did his best to sound concerned.

"Thank you for telling me. I have a strange favor to ask. Could you keep this between us? I'm afraid if my sister knows I'm here, she'll take off again before I get to talk with her. There was some family drama before she left. "

"Sure thing. I understand how flighty women can be. I'll be here in Abilene for another few days, anyway."

"Thank you again for the information." Griffin hurriedly folded his map. He needed to get back to Cutler's Gap immediately. He wasn't giving her a chance to disappear again.

"Choctowsky here," Mike answered his cell on the third ring. He'd slept surprisingly well at Ms. Annetta's motel. It may look like a reject from 1982, but the room was clean, the shower was hot, and the bed was comfortable.

"Hey Mike, It's Danny."

"Hey Danny, how's it going?"

"It's going. I turned that video of Vanessa over to IA, so the shit is about to hit the fan for her. It's my guess they will be closing their investigation into you anytime now."

"Thanks for that, dude. You really helped me out with that video."

"Yeah, well, what some people call paranoia, I call covering my ass. Speaking of which, I didn't call you about the Vanessa thing. While running a custom security program that I built, I found that our system had been hacked."

"Woah, that's bad news. Can you tell what they were looking for?"

"That's the weird thing, man. They only looked at the Phoenix Butcher case files and your personnel file. Whoever they were has a real thing for you. They spent the most time going over your file. I called to give you a heads up."

"Thanks, man. Hey, can you tell when they got into the system?"

"Of course, it was this morning. I can't tell you much else because they routed it through a VPN. I'm chasing them down now, but they're good whoever they are."

"If you find out anything else, call me. Thanks again, man. If you keep saving my ass like this, I will have to name a couple of kids after you."

Danny laughed. "Dude, you have to get laid to make kids. At this rate, I'll be lucky if you name a goldfish after me."

"Wow, you are one cruel bastard." Mike laughed good-naturedly

"Yeah, well, the truth hurts, man. But seriously, stay safe. I don't know what you're up to, but someone doesn't like it."

"I will. Thanks for having my back Danny." Mike motioned for Tom as he hung up the call.

"What's up?" Tom didn't know what the call was about, but if the look on Mike's face was any indication, it wasn't good news.

"That was my buddy, Danny. He does the computer shit for all of Phoenix PD. We have other tech guys, but he's some kind of genius, which he never lets us forget." Mike gave a half chuckle, but his face was still grim. "Someone hacked into Phoenix PD this morning. They only looked at the Butcher case and my personnel file. I have a bad feeling about this. Why would someone hack into such a high-security system just to check me out? I'm nobody special, just an average Joe detective. The only thing that makes sense is if it's Griffin, and he knows I'm here, which means he's still in town or close enough by to know what's going on."

"I'm with you; I don't like this one bit. I'm heading out to Charlie's ranch. I won't leave them alone if this guy is prowling around."

"I'll come with you."

"Technically, you have no jurisdiction here, Mike. If something goes down, your ass will be on the line."

"I know, but I'm still coming. There's no way I will sit this out while you have no backup." Mike was adamant

"I appreciate that." Tom walked over to his desk and began to dig in one of the bottom drawers. "Hey, sign this." He tossed Mike a pen as he handed him a piece of paper.

"What's this?" Mike asked without glancing at the sheet.

"I'm hiring you; ass covered, problem solved."

"Awesome. How much am I getting paid?" laughing, Mike scribbled his name on the signature line.

"This is Texas, son. We pay in barbeque and margaritas." Tom drawled in a thick Texan accent.

"So, I'm getting a raise then." Mike could give as good as he got.

Tom walked the four steps to the gun safe against the back wall. He spun the old dial, entering a combination as ancient as the safe.

"Here's a badge" He tossed the leather-encased shield to Mike, who caught it mid-air. "Dig around in there, grab whatever firearms you prefer. I believe we have two or three bulletproof vests somewhere around here. To be honest, I have no idea where." Tom squinted as he looked around the station.

"I can see how easy it would be to lose something like that in a palatial station like this. How do you even find your way to the front door every night?" Mike liked Tom; he liked that he could easily banter with him. He liked that underneath that light exterior was an experienced and hardened cop. Tom was young, but he'd done some digging on him while on the plane to Texas. Okay, he hadn't done the digging; Danny had.

Yet another thing he owed Danny for. He would have to buy the guy a diamond ring or something if he kept doing him favors like this, Mike thought with a silent chuckle. By the time the plane had landed, Mike had an email with an attached file that told him everything he would ever want to know about Sheriff Thomas Eugene Fletcher. Who named their kid Eugene anyway? He even knew his shoe size and the fact he wore braces throughout middle school. He also learned that Tom was the youngest cop to ever make homicide detective in Denver PD history. That his close rate on cases was equally impressive. In one of his reviews, Tom's Captain had called him "obsessed with finding the truth." It was said as a compliment. Tom had stayed in Denver PD until five years ago when he'd abruptly resigned and taken a job in this Podunk town in west Texas. There had been no scandal that Danny had been able to find, and Danny would have found it had there been one. He'd simply walked away from a promising career at the ripe old age of 31. If they survived this case, Mike would have to remember to ask him why.

"It's not like I've had a lot of use for bulletproof vests here in Cutler's Gap. I know it's policy to wear them all the time now that cops are getting gunned down all over the country during traffic stops or even off duty. But Cutler's Gap isn't like the rest of the country. When you pass that Welcome to Cutler's Gap sign on the edge of town, it's like you are driving a DeLorean and being transported back in time by fifty or sixty years. My biggest troublemakers, until recently, are two eighty-year-old men who regularly torture each other with wayward livestock.

"Doug and Charlie?" Mike quizzed

"Yeah, something about Doug's wife and a baby. It's a long story."

"It would have to be if they've been at it for sixty years," Mike said matter-of-factly.

"Here they are" Tom pulled the vests out of the bottom of a cluttered closet and swiped his hand across them a few times to dust them off. "I'm not looking forward to putting one of these on again," Tom sighed.

"If this Griffin character is who we think he is, it's better to be safe than sorry." Mike had grabbed a Rock River AR-15 rifle, two Glock 22s, and a Sig 9m just to be safe. He then grabbed a duffle bag Tom had tossed out of the closet he was digging around in and started loading it with ammo."

'Planning on going to war?" Tom asked dryly.

"With this guy, I'm assuming we're already at war. He already tried to blow me to hell once. I'm not taking any chances."

"Fair enough." Tom fastened his regular sidearm to his belt and grabbed his Remington 870 Wingmaster, a Colt AR-15, and two more handguns for good measure. "While in Rome, do as the Romans, as they say," He threw a few more cases of ammo into the duffle, grabbed his trusted fishing knife, and put it in a sheath on his belt.

"A fishing knife, really?" Mike was skeptical

"Don't knock it. This baby has gotten me out of some tough spots."

"With what, a tangled fishing lure?" Mike shot back.

Tom ignored him. "Let's hit the road." They loaded everything into his truck and sped out of town towards Charlie's ranch. Tom had a knot in the pit of his stomach that hadn't loosened since Mike told him someone was nosing around Phoenix PD's database. He didn't know what was happening but knew he needed to get to Kate ASAP.

Chapter Twenty-Three

Kate hummed while she peeled potatoes and watched the setting sun from the kitchen window. She was cooking Charlie a rosemary and red wine marinated roast with roasted root vegetables and garlic herb mashed potatoes. She even made homemade shortcakes for the strawberries soaking in sugar with a splash of brandy. She had really enjoyed cooking for Charlie the past week or so. She'd almost forgotten how much she loved to cook, the lessons their French chef had given her seemingly from another lifetime. She'd gone all out tonight because Charlie had been quieter than usual over the past few days. He seemed to be worried about something. Kate knew that he's lived alone for more than half a century. She hoped her being at the ranch wasn't bothering him. Tonight, she would feed him a good meal, clean up and then make herself scarce. She needed to get some more work done on Brenda's books anyway. She would work on that in her bedroom until she fell asleep.

"Something smells delicious," Charlie called from the front porch as he stomped the dirt and whatever else off his boots. One thing about ranch life was that it was a dirty business. Kate felt like she swept the ranch house's tile and wood floors at least three times a day and mopped it half as much. She now understood why there was no carpet to be found anywhere in the house. It wouldn't last a day under these conditions, she laughed to herself. Look at her being all domestic. Before Cutler's Gap, she couldn't remember when she had used a mop, much less cleaned a bathroom. What a different life she lived now. In all honestly, she loved this life. Her old life now looked too bright and flashy, almost like it was covered in cheap-looking rhinestones. All flash but no substance.

"I made roast and strawberry shortcake," Kate called back. "Figured we were due for a treat tonight."

"I haven't had real strawberry shortcake in years." Charlie had entered the kitchen and was washing his hands in the sink. "My momma used to make it in the summer after we'd gone strawberry picking, if we had the sugar." Charlie didn't talk much about his childhood, but from the little bits and pieces he'd told her, Kate gathered that he'd grown up with a wonderful mother, but they'd been dirt poor. Basically, Charlie's early life had been the exact opposite of what hers had been. Maybe that's why they had clicked so quickly. They were two opposite sides of the same coin.

Charlie looked out the big window he'd built over the kitchen sink. God, he loved this land. Maybe he'd bought it initially to spite Doug and look out for Ella. But after sixty years, this land was in his blood. Hell, it was more than that. It was his very bones. He really loved sharing it with Kate. She fits here like a puzzle piece he hadn't known he was missing. When Tom had called and told him someone had been asking about Kate in town, he'd made some arrangements just in case things went sideways. He had left his entire estate to Kate instead of in trust to the town. He would not let Doug have it after all these years of fighting to keep it away from him. Now it would go to Kate. He didn't know if she would even want it, but if she didn't, it would revert to the original trust. However, he hoped she would keep it, maybe even raise a family with Tom, if she ever forgave him.

"Kate, after supper, I hoped we could talk." Charlie continued to look pensively out the big window over the sink.

Here it comes, Kate thought, he's going to ask me to leave. The thought cut surprisingly deep. She hadn't realized how much she'd come to rely on Charlie's quiet companionship.

"Sure, Charlie." She worked to keep the tremor out of her voice and wiped the tear from her eye with the back of her hand before it could fall.

"What are you crying over, girl?" Charlie asked brusquely. Female tears had always been his weakness. He didn't know what to do when they started all that emotional stuff.

"I'm not crying. It was just those onions I cut. Those things were potent. Where'd you buy those things at, a pepper spray factory?" Kate tried to joke, but the laughter didn't reach her eyes.

Charlie looked around the kitchen, and there wasn't an onion or onion peel in sight. He decided he'd let it go for the time being. He didn't understand women.

They ate dinner in relative silence, each lost in their own thoughts. Kate noticed that Charlie ate three helpings of everything, even the shortcake. How such a skinny old man could pack away that much food was beyond her. It must be all the hard ranch work, she thought.

"Katie girl, I'm not lying when I say that was the best roast I have ever had. And the strawberry shortcake, whoo-eee! That was almost as good as my momma's, and ain't no one ever even come close to that before! I had no idea you were such a great cook before you came out to stay here. Had I known that, I would have asked you to come out here as soon as I met you." Charlie laughed his deep laugh. There were few things in this world that Kate loved as much as hearing Charlie's laugh. When he really laughed, it was like the deep rumble of distant thunder, and his whole face lit up, making him look twenty years younger. His laughter was infectious, and soon Kate was laughing along, unsure of what she was laughing at.

Charlie couldn't bring himself to sour the mood by bringing up the stranger asking about her in town. It was rare to see Kate really laugh. Their serious discussion could wait until tomorrow, for tonight, he'd let the girl have one last night of peaceful sleep.

"You said you wanted to talk to me after dinner." Kate gripped her hands under the table; she focused on the feeling of her fingernails digging into her palms. It was a trick she'd learned when she was young, always hiding her true thoughts and feelings so they wouldn't be used against her. She would focus on the pain of her fingernails, and all her other feelings would fade into the background.

"Yeah, I wanted to tell you how much I've enjoyed having you out here the last week and a half. I didn't know how it would work, me being a grumpy old rancher and you being young and not used to the ranch life. You have just taken to it like a duck to water. You've been a real help to me." This was not where Kate had seen this conversation going. She'd gotten so used to expecting the worst that she never gave herself a chance to hope for anything good. She forced herself to unclench her hands and glanced down, at least she hadn't drawn blood this time, and smiled a huge smile.

"Thank you, Charlie. I've loved living out here. I love the quiet, and I'm even learning to love the animals. I still don't love the smell of them, though." Kate wrinkled her nose and laughed.

"Before you know it, you won't even notice the smell of manure. In fact, you'll miss it when you're in town." Charlie chuckled. "It may become your new favorite perfume, "Ode de Ranch Hand" Charlie was laughing for real again.

"I don't know that I'd go that far," Kate chuckled.

"Anyway, I wanted you to know whenever this mess you're in is cleared up, you're welcome to stay on. You don't have to do the ranch work or cook if you don't want to. I'm just enjoying having someone else in the house." Charlie turned red and looked down. Well, I'll be, Kate thought. I never thought I'd see the day Charlie Benet blushed.

"Charlie, are you blushing?" Kate teased

"Nah, why you'd say something crazy like that?" he grumbled, obviously uncomfortable.

"I don't know what will happen over the next few weeks, but if I have a choice, I'd love to stay here for a while. I'd still have to go into town a few days a week to do Ms. Annetta's and Brenda's books, but I love it here, Charlie. I really do." Kate took a deep breath. That feeling of being home had settled firmly in her chest, maybe for the first time. This was a life worth fighting to keep.

Charlie leaned back in his chair to stretch, and Kate was lost in her thoughts when the sound of glass shattering pierced the air, and a bullet hit the wall right behind Charlie.

It took Kate a second to realize what was happening. In that time, Charlie had dived out of his chair and pulled her down to the floor.

"Stay down, Kate! "Charlie yelled as another bullet slammed into the dining room wall. Charlie started to pull himself across the floor towards the living room.

"Are you hit, Charlie?" Kate panicked at the thought.

"Nah, bastard missed me because I was stretching. Now I will try to get to the gun safe in the living room. I want you to crawl to my office and lock yourself in. There are no windows in there!"

"Are you crazy, Charlie? You go to the office, and I'll go to the gun safe!!" Kate started to inch toward the living room.

"You don't even know the combination. Now do what I said" Charlie grabbed hold of her foot and tried to pull her back.

"Look, old man, I'm a third of your age, and this is my fault. If anyone is going to risk going out to that living room, it's me!"

"I'm not letting you go out there! My house, my rules!" Charlie yelled over the next round of bullets that were crashing through the house,

"Look, if we keep arguing, no one will get the guns, and we will both end up dead. So, let's both get in there, get the guns, and get to safety!" Kate started belly crawling again. This time Charlie didn't argue. They needed those guns, and they needed them now.

It was a short crawl to the living room, but Charlie was struggling by the time they made it to the gun safe. Charlie was bigger than life. Sometimes you could forget that he was eighty. Belly scooting across the floor while being shot at was not easy on an eighty-year-old body. But he made it, despite the difficulty. Charlie hadn't bothered locking the safe after they'd gone target-shooting. In fact, the door was still slightly ajar. "Thank God for small miracles," Kate thought. She could open the safe without standing up and revealing herself to anyone outside. She had a good idea who it was. She grabbed all the guns she could get her hands on from where she lay and handed them back to Charlie. She also grabbed the ammo boxes in a drawer inside the safe. Charlie pushed the ammo and guns to the hallway, and they made their way around the corner. Out of breath, they sat up and started loading the guns. Kate paused as she heard her name being called by a voice she'd hoped to never again hear; the demon was back.

"Carina, come out, come out wherever you are." He called to her in a sing-songy voice, like a kid asking her to come out to play.

"Don't you even think about it," Charlie growled at her

"How about this? You get your ass off my property, and I won't shoot you." Charlie yelled back before Kate could respond.

"Besides, there ain't no one by the name of Carina here. Just my granddaughter." Kate gave Charlie an incredulous look. "What? it was worth a shot." Charlie whispered.

Heavy steps sounded on the front porch. "Nice try, old man, but Carina Wythcliff is there with you. Hell, I saw her through the scope of my rifle sitting at the dinner table with you. Now she either comes out to me right now, or I'm coming in and getting her. If I have to do that, I won't play nice. Ask Carina what happened the last time we played. You remember that, don't you, princess? We had such a good time, didn't we?"

Carina started to stand up, and Charlie jerked her back down to the floor.

"Kate, there is no way I'll let you go outside to that psychopath. If you do, he will kill you and come after me anyway. So, there is no point in trying to be a hero here. Even if you could trust that he wouldn't hurt me, there is still no way I'd let you go out there. He came to the wrong place if he thought we would roll over and play dead while he took you. Here we protect family, and like it or not, Kate, you are my family. Now sit your ass down and finish loading those guns. We're going to need them before this is all said and done."

"Charlie, I can't have another person I love die because of me. I barely survived Eric's death. There is no way I'm going to let him hurt you. He's not here to kill me. He's here to take me back."

"Kate, what are you talking about? Take you back where? That man just shot my dining room to hell. He's here to kill you." Charlie sounded like he wanted to shake her.

"He's not going to kill me." Kate said sadly, "He's just the errand boy. He was trying to kill you, not me. Let me go, Charlie, please. Believe me, when I say it will be better for everyone if I do."

"Stop talking foolishness. You are not going anywhere as long as I'm here to stop you."

"I was afraid you'd say that." Kate gave Charlie a sad smile. She picked up the Glock she'd just finished loading and brought it down as hard as she could on Charlie's temple. She leaned over and kissed his weathered cheek.

"I love you, Charlie Jenkins. Hopefully, one day you will forgive me for this." She whispered to his unconscious body. Then she stood, hid the Glock in the

waistband of her jeans, at the small of her back, made
sure her t-shirt was pulled down and called to the man
outside.

Chapter Twenty-Four

"Do I have your word that you will leave the old man alone and won't kill him?"

"You do." The voice of her nightmares called.

"Okay, I'll come out."

"Come out with your hands above your head, princess. It's not that I don't trust you, but...." He let the rest of his sentence trail off.

Kate took a last look around the house that had so quickly become her home. She would not cry. She wouldn't give the bastard outside the satisfaction. Then she made her way to the front door.

She pushed out onto the darkened porch, and there he stood, the soft glow of the porch light reflecting off his golden hair, giving him a halo. How could such a monster have such a beautiful face? Kate wondered not for the first time.

"Ah, Ah, hands up, princess." Kate reached her hands up. "Higher, princess." Kate raised them completely above her head and slowly walked towards him.

"Okay, princess, that's far enough." Kate stopped and started to lower her hands.

"Ah, ah, keep your hands up. Now I want you to slowly use your left hand to take off your shirt. I'd frisk you, but I really don't want to put down my gun. And it's really hard to hide a weapon when you aren't wearing any clothes." His voice was dispassionate.

Kate started to shake, despite her vow to not let him see her weakness. Last time she'd pled, bargained, and begged but hadn't made a difference in the end. This time she wasn't that naïve. But the idea of being naked in front of him again made her stomach roll and her knees shake. She could not control her physical reaction; her body betrayed her will. She started to follow his order to remove her shirt when her stomach completely revolted. She vomited everything she'd eaten just moments before all over the front porch.

Griffin stepped back involuntarily. The smell of the vomit turned his stomach. He looked down, and vomit had spewed onto his shoe. The girl would pay for that. Her weakness disgusted him, and the vomit made him want to bathe in bleach. Why were humans such disgusting creatures? He thought. Griffin sidestepped the vomit and returned to the girl, who was still double over, dry heaving. Sticking out of her waistband was a gun. He grabbed it and shoved it in his waistband, then punched her in the side of the head.

"Stop that, you cow." Kate's vision went blurry from the severity of the blow, but at least her stomach stopped trying to exit her body. Next, she realized he'd taken the gun, and she couldn't stop the tears from coming. Her one chance was gone. Now she was truly at his mercy.

"You thought you'd be able to use this on me?" Griffin laughed as he motioned toward the gun. "You honestly thought a little, spoiled, rich princess like you would get the better of me?" He couldn't believe her audacity. He smacked her with an open hand across the face. "It looks like you didn't learn your lesson the last time. You made me chase you over half the country, make me come to nowhere Texas, and then you think you can get a weapon past me." Griffin continued to rain blows down upon her head and shoulders as he ranted. He roughly grabbed her arms and zip-tied them together.

"You know who will pay for that, don't you?"

Kate began to sob. "You told me you wouldn't hurt him if I came out." She hated the sound of her voice, pleading with this monster again.

"I did indeed. Then you broke our deal by bringing a weapon to our party."

"I never promised not to bring a weapon."

"It was implied, princess. What happens to the old man is on your head."

"I wouldn't count on it." Charlie leaned against the door jam, a large lump on his temple, a rifle in his hand. Before Griffin could react, Charlie shot.

The shot missed the bastard's heart and lodged in his shoulder. The blow Kate had given him on the head had him seeing double; that wasn't good when trying to aim.

Before Charlie could get another shot off, Griffin jumped off the porch and hit the ground. He raised his gun a shot at the old man in the doorway.

Kate screamed as the shot sent Charlie flying backward. She ran to him, uncaring of the monster at her back.

"No, Charlie!!!" Kate screamed as she bent over him. He'd been hit in the stomach, from what she could tell. She pulled her shirt over her head and tried to stop the bleeding. "Don't you die on me, old man! You hear me! Don't you dare die, Charlie!"

Kate heard a noise at her back as Griffin returned to the porch. Without a second thought, Kate grabbed the gun beside Charlie, swung around, and shot the man coming up behind her. She hadn't even had time to aim. She just reacted. The shot hit Griffin full in the chest, and fell backward, dead, though she didn't check. Kate started to stand up. She needed to get Charlie to the hospital when she heard the noise of a truck pulling up to the house, the tires screeching to a halt.

She saw Tom and another man running towards the porch. Tom raced straight to Kate while the other man approached the dead man.

"Kate! Are you okay?" Tom looked her over, noting the blood and the marks on her face.

"I'm fine," Kate managed through the tears, the words sounding mushy to her own ears. "But Charlie," she started crying harder.

Tom saw the old man lying on the entryway floor of the house. He'd obviously been shot, and blood was soaking through Kate's shirt on top of the wound.

"Mike, we've got a man down."

"I'll call an ambulance," Mike started for his cell phone.

"No time. It'll take them almost an hour to get here and then another hour and a half to the hospital. Tell them we need a Care Flight chopper." Kate kept pressure on the wound as Mike made the call. Tom gently tried to pry her hands from Charlie, but Kate refused to move.

"Kate, honey, I know you're hurt and in shock. Let me help Charlie, okay. I promise I won't let go. Can you do that, honey?" Tom wanted to scoop her up and never let her go, but there was no time. He had to get this bleeding stopped until the paramedics arrived.

After Mike hung up, he made his way to Griffin, his head and torso hanging off the side of the porch in the dust, blood dripping off the edge and forming a pool under his head. Mike bent down and was shocked to find that he had a slight pulse. He shook his head. How come bad guys seemed to have all the luck?

"Hey Tom, I need your knife?"

Tom was busy applying pressure to Charlie's wound. He'd just barely managed to pry Kate away from him.

"It's on my belt, man, but I can't bring it to you." Kate pushed his hands aside and replaced them with her own. She nodded for him to go help Mike.

Tom raced over to Mike's side.

"Here." He handed him the knife, handle out. "Don't tell me that bastard is still breathing."

"Yup, but I doubt he will be for long." Mike used the knife to cut away Griffin's shirt. The rifle shot had done a lot of damage. Kate must have shot him at point-blank range. Tom had already returned to Kate and Charlie, leaving Mike to try to stop the bleeding.

"It's not over" Mike almost missed the thread-like whisper.

"What did you say?"

"She hasn't won. He's still coming." Mike had to lean down almost to Griffin's face to hear the whisper.

"Who is coming?" Mike had seen death enough times to know Griffin was almost gone.

"You'll find..." the whisper was cut off by a gurgling sound. Mike felt for a pulse but found none. He began to do chest compressions but knew it was pointless. You didn't survive a chest wound like that.

The Care Flight helicopter landed moments later. The paramedics stabilized Charlie as best they could and loaded him into the chopper. A paramedic ran over to Griffin, confirmed he was gone, and hopped back on the chopper. They had no time for the dead while there were living to save.

Tom picked up Kate and carried her to his truck. He gently placed her in the back seat of his quad cab.

"Want me to drive?" Mike asked

"Yes, but I know these roads. I'll get us to the hospital quicker. Here you call the State Police and put it on speakerphone. They will need to go to Charlie's and deal with the body."

Mike nodded and rounded the truck to the passenger seat.

Mike looked at the woman sitting on the edge of the bench seat in the back of the truck. He didn't know what he expected of Carina Wythcliff, but it wasn't the small woman in a lacy bra and dirty jeans. She had short dark hair, haunted blue eyes, and looked like she'd just gone nine rounds with Ali in the ring.

"Hey, you got an extra shirt somewhere in here?" Mike looked pointedly in the rearview mirror towards Carina or Kate or whatever she called herself now.

"Oh yeah, there should be one in my gym bag on the floor back there."

"Hey Katie, honey," Tom's voice was gentle as if he was afraid she would shatter into a thousand pieces if he spoke too loudly. "There is a gym bag on the floor with a t-shirt in it if you want to put it on."

"Katie, I know you don't feel it yet, but you are in shock and shivering. Your body is running on adrenalin right now, but it will crash. I need you to put on that shirt, grab the water bottle, and drink it." Kate still stared at him blankly.

"Mike, can you help her? She's in shock."

"Absolutely. No problem, man. You drive. I'll make sure Kate is okay."

"Kate, this is my friend Mike. He's a cop in Arizona. Don't be afraid. He's going to lean over the seat and find you that shirt and water." Mike grunted as he tried to dig around the back seat. After a few moments, his hands found the gym bag and dragged it to the front seat. He dug around until he found the shirt and water.

"Ma'am, here, put this on." Mike's voice was gentle while he kept his focus on her face. What kind of monster did this to a woman? The bastard deserved what he got, he thought to himself.

Kate took the shirt from his hands and put it on, her entire body shaking violently, causing her to get tangled in the cloth before pulling her head through the collar. The shirt was huge on her, but it smelled like Tom. She held the fabric to her nose and inhaled. Tom smelled like the woods and waterfalls and comfort. She tried to take a few gulps of the water, spilling more than she swallowed. Giving up, she laid her head back against the seat and stared at the ceiling, holding the tears at bay by her last thread of sanity.

Tom glanced at the speedometer, backlit on the dash of his truck, as he raced towards Abilene. He was going at least 90 miles an hour down the pitch-black country roads; he prayed that the coyotes and armadillos were smart enough to stay away from the road tonight. At this speed, he was outdriving his headlights.

The drive to Abilene was quiet except for Kate's chattering teeth and the sound of the truck. They made the nearly two-hour drive in just over an hour.

Chapter Twenty-Five

Tom's tires screeched as he pulled up to the doors of the ER department. Kate had collapsed into a pile on the back seat; the tears she'd held back during the drive wracked her body. Tom tenderly picked her up and carried her into the hospital. Once she was safe in Tom's arms, the world around her went blurry, and she passed out.

Kate regained consciousness and saw that she lay in a hospital bed in a small ER room. She had an IV in her arm. Someone just out of her line of sight was talking. She tried to move her head to see who it was, only to realize it had been immobilized. She started to hyperventilate. This couldn't be happening again.

"Let me go! Let me out of here!!" She screamed and kicked her legs, her hands clawing frantically at the thing around her neck.

"Kate, calm down. You're okay, honey. C'mon Kate, calm down." Kate began to register Tom's voice and his worried face above her when she felt the burn of something being injected into her IV. Tom's voice became distant, his face blurry as she heard a far-off voice say, "We gave your fiancé a sedative, sir."

Kate awoke in a different hospital room. It took her a minute to remember how she got there. She tried to look around the room and was relieved to be able to move her head with no problem. To her right, Tom sat in a hospital chair, quietly dozing; the sun was streaming in through a large window. She had an IV in one arm and a blood pressure cuff on her other. She didn't want to wake Tom, but she had to know where Charlie was.

Tom stirred out of sleep, the sound of a quiet sob breaking through his exhaustion. He had been up most of the night watching over Kate and getting updates on Charlie.

Mike had stayed with him until the nurse said only one of them could stay in the room with Kate. Then Mike stayed in the waiting room, updating him on

Charlie and delivering cups of hospital coffee. He only left for the hotel once they knew Charlie was out of surgery and on his way to ICU.

Tom was on his feet and next to Kate's bed almost before his eyes opened.

"Hey honey, how are you feeling?" He gently brushed the hair away from her forehead while gently holding her hand.

"How's Charlie?" Kate was almost afraid of the answer, but she had to know. When she noted the worried expression on Tom's face, she added, "Tell me the truth, Tom; the whole truth. I will never forgive you if you don't. He's dead, isn't he?" Tears were pouring down her face.

"No, no, he isn't dead." Tom quickly reassured Kate. Seeing her there with tears pouring down her battered face was tearing his heart out. He should have been there sooner. Hell, he should have stayed there. If that bastard wasn't already dead, he'd kill him himself. Kate's eyes were full of doubt. "I swear, he isn't dead.

He's alive. I promise, Kate." He gave her a tender smile and crossed his heart with his hand.

"Tell me how he is. Tell me everything," Kate demanded.

Tom had to smile at her tone. At least they could be sure that her sassiness wasn't hurt. "He's in the ICU. I'm not going to lie, it was touch and go there for a while in surgery, and he isn't out of the woods yet. But the doctor was cautiously optimistic this morning when they moved him to ICU after surgery."

If he thought Kate had been crying before now, she was bawling. The sobs wracked her body. He gently laid down next to her and gathered her into his arms. He held her that way for the hour that she cried. He still held her when the nurse came to get Kate's vitals. They had fallen asleep, and she had to nudge him awake to reach Kate.

"I'm sorry to wake you, Sheriff, but I need to get her vitals." Tom disentangled himself from Kate and moved back to the chair

"It's okay." He stretched before he sat down. As much as he loved holding Kate, that hospital bed was cramped.

The nurse noticed him studying Kate. "It looks worse than it is. She's going to be fine. They should release her tomorrow or the day after at the latest." She reassured him. He hoped they kept Kate as long as they could because once they released her, there was no way in hell they would get her to go home and rest until Charlie was released. His woman was as stubborn as they came.

He would have to return to Charlie's ranch and figure out what happened. He'd called the state police to deal with Conrad Griffin's body, and they were processing the crime scene. He knew he would have to answer a lot of questions about how he had handled the whole case. But right now, all he cared about was that Kate and Charlie were alive. Nothing else really mattered.

Kate was released the next day, just as the nurse had predicted. She had minor fractures of her cheekbone and jaw, and her right shoulder had been dislocated. They popped her shoulder back into place and gave her a prescription for pain meds. Then told her the fractures should heal on their own. She was given strict instructions to rest and recover.

As he had predicted, Kate immediately went to the ICU floor. She told them she was Charlie's granddaughter and refused to leave his side. At least he knew she couldn't get into much trouble at the hospital. Ms. Annetta, Brenda, and Lucy had promised to take turns staying with Kate in Abilene while he dealt with the fallout of the whole mess. He still didn't know what had gone down at the ranch. He'd been trying to give Kate time to regroup before he asked her about it. Now he didn't have a choice. The state police would be coming to question her this afternoon. He had to know what happened before they got there to protect her if he needed to.

Mike packed the small bag he'd brought from Arizona. His flight back was in the morning. The entire trip had been surreal. He'd gone there to get answers and stop a killer. The killer had been stopped, but he had more questions now than when he arrived in Texas. Griffin had been the one to blow the storage unit. They had found an app on his phone that he had used to monitor multiple storage units nationwide. The local bomb squads had found and disarmed bombs in every unit. At least the owners of the storage facility in Phoenix could collect their insurance money now that they had been cleared of fraud.

The investigation had stalled, though. Besides his military records and the storage units, Conrad Griffin was a ghost. The FBI had been called in because of the jurisdiction issues that came with a case that spanned from coast to coast.

The leading theory was that he was a hired assassin. The FBI profilers had some interesting theories as to what made Griffin tick. As far as Mike was concerned, he didn't give a rat's ass why Griffin was screwed up. Everyone had shit happen in their lives, but most people didn't become hired killers. They didn't spread bombs across the country like some kind of fucked up Johnny Appleseed meets Rambo.

What he did care about was what Griffin had whispered to him before dying. Who was still after Kate, and why? Tom didn't know, and he refused to push Kate for answers until she had a chance to recover a little. Mike had that uneasy feeling in his gut that he got right before the shit was about to hit the fan. That feeling had never been wrong in all his years on the force. Whatever was happening, it wasn't over, and he had a very bad feeling about whoever Griffin warned was coming for Kate.

Mike picked up his cell and called Tom. "Hey, I'll be flying back to Phoenix in the morning. I have to go finish clearing up something there."

"I understand, man. I can't thank you enough for following your gut out here and helping me out. If it weren't for you, Kate and Charlie would both be dead."

"Thank you for listening to my crazy-ass gut feeling."

"Your crazy-ass gut feeling saved the day. If you are ever looking for a job, you'll always have a place here."

"Thanks for the offer. I appreciate it. Hey man, don't lose my number. If you ever need backup, I'm just a call away."

"Thanks, but you may not want to say that. I might take you up on it."

"I mean it, Tom. If something else goes down. Call me. My gut is saying crazy things again. I don't think this is over yet."

"I hope to God that you're wrong. I want to return to the days when my biggest concern was feuding geriatrics." Tom gave a strained laugh

"I hope that's the case. It's been good working with you. Take care of that woman of yours."

"Will do," Mike almost groaned at how sappy Tom sounded. He hung up the call and plugged in his phone. He half smiled as he packed the Texas badge Tom had told him to keep, as he was an honorary Cutler's Gap PD member forever. Maybe he would retire to Texas instead of Montana, he thought briefly.

He shook his head and laughed aloud. No way in hell! Texas was too damn hot.

"Kate, can you take a walk with me? Ms. Annetta will stay with Charlie, won't you?" Ms. Annetta had been the first to arrive. She'd arrived in Abilene the morning after they had brought Charlie in.

"Sure thing. You stretch your legs for a minute with your handsome young man." Ms. Annetta shoed them out of the room

"He's not my young man," Kate called over her shoulder as they walked out.

"Shhh, you know you are supposed to be resting your jaw while it heals. You shouldn't use it to spread such lies." Tom teased as they started walking down the hallway. Kate snorted but didn't argue when he grabbed her hand and laced his fingers with hers. They walked to the cafeteria and grabbed something cold to drink. Then Tom led her to a quiet courtyard garden.

They sat side by side on a carved bench. He pulled her close by her waist, carefully avoiding her injured shoulder. He half turned to face her and tipped her face up. He gently kissed her forehead, one of the only places on her face not bruised.

"Katie, I don't want to upset you, but I have to ask you about what happened the other night at the ranch. I put it off as long as possible, but the state police are coming today to talk to you."

"It's okay, Tom. I know you have to do your job. I'm the one that killed him, not Charlie."

"Oh baby, I'm so sorry."

"I'm not. It was either kill him or let him kill Charlie. I would choose Charlie every time." There wasn't a hint of regret in Kate's voice.

"You made the right call. Now start from the beginning; tell me everything you can remember."

"Charlie and I had just finished dinner. He was quiet and thinking about something for a few days, so I made him roast and strawberry shortcake for dinner to cheer him up." Kate began to tell her story, her words sometimes sounding mushy or slurred because of her fractured jaw. She had to take breaks to rest but didn't stop until she had told the entire story from beginning to end.

"I'm so sorry I wasn't there to protect you." Tom had tears in his eyes by the end.

"You were there when I needed you. Charlie would have died if you hadn't shown up when you did." Kate gently touched his cheek.

"I know you don't want to hear this, Katie, but I love you. You don't have to love me and don't owe me anything. But if you ever need me, I'm here."

Kate tried to smile, but her swollen mouth and jaw made it look more like a grimace. "I don't know how I feel, Tom. I'm not mad at you anymore, but so much has happened to me over the past few months. I need to figure out my life before I can be in the kind of relationship you want."

"I understand, and I'll give you space. Just know I'm not going anywhere, Katie. You're it for me. I hope that one day I can be it for you." He gave her one last kiss on the forehead before slowly walking back to Charlie's room.

Three months later, Kate stood on the front porch of Charlie's ranch. It had been a rough few months. Charlie's health was touch-and-go more than once. It seemed his prognosis changed daily for a while. The ups and downs had been hard to deal with emotionally, but he had pulled through. He was too stubborn to die like that. He reminded her more than once.

Today he was finally released to come home. Tom had repaired all the damage to the house. He had done an amazing job. You couldn't even tell where the bullets had hit the walls. She wanted to do a deep cleaning while Tom drove Charlie home. This was her first time back at the ranch since that night. Tom hadn't wanted to leave her alone, but she needed time to process all the emotions with no one else around. She expected to have a panic attack being back. Instead, she felt at home. She smiled and sat on one of the rockers with her sweet tea, the "Welcome Home" banner she had hung from the porch roof gently blowing in the breeze. The warm sun shining, the sounds of the birds, and the breeze blowing through the scrub lulled her into a peaceful sleep. She awoke to the ominous sound of the wind chimes clanging, sounding eerily like the bells from St Margarete's hospital. A shiver ran down her spine. She could feel someone watching her. She slowly looked to her right.

"Hello, little sister. Did you miss me?